A HOUSE DIVIDED

Special thanks to Eve Jay, Annelie Wagner, and
Charlie Olsen for their continual help and support

Script by Haiko Hörnig
Art by Marius Pawlitza

First American edition published in 2020 by Graphic Universe™

Copyright © 2016 by Haiko Hörnig and Marius Pawlitza

Graphic Universe™ is a trademark of Lerner Publishing Group, Inc.

Graphic Universe™
An imprint of Lerner Publishing Group, Inc.
241 First Avenue North
Minneapolis, MN 55401 USA

For reading levels and more information, look up this title at
www.lernerbooks.com.

Main body text set in CC Dave Gibbons Lower.
Typeface provided by Comicraft.

Library of Congress Cataloging-in-Publication Data

Names: Hörnig, Haiko, 1984– author. | Pawlitza, Marius, 1984– illustrator.
Title: The accursed inheritance of Henrietta Achilles / Haiko Hörnig, Marius Pawlitza.
Other titles: Ein gefährliches Erbe. English
Description: First American edition. | Minneapolis, MN : Graphic Universe, 2020. | Series: A house
    divided ; Book 1 | Audience: Ages 12–18 | Audience: Grades 10–12 | Summary: "After years as an
    orphan, Henrietta Achilles is summoned to the town of Malrenard. She learns she's the only living
    relative of a notorious wizard—and she's just inherited his house and everything in it." —Provided
    by publisher.
Identifiers: LCCN 2019029606 (print) | LCCN 2019029607 (ebook) | ISBN 9781541572430 (library binding)
    | ISBN 9781541586925 (paperback) | ISBN 9781541582330 (ebook)
Subjects: LCSH: Graphic novels. | CYAC: Graphic novels. | Inheritance and succession—Fiction. |
    Blessing and cursing—Fiction. | Magic—Fiction.
Classification: LCC PZ7.7.H665 Ac 2020 (print) | LCC PZ7.7.H665 (ebook) | DDC 741.5/973—dc23

LC record available at https://lccn.loc.gov/2019029606
LC ebook record available at https://lccn.loc.gov/2019029607

Manufactured in the United States of America
1-46520-47549-8/28/2019

1

A HOUSE DIVIDED

THE ACCURSED INHERITANCE OF HENRIETTA ACHILLES

HAIKO HÖRNIG • MARIUS PAWLITZA

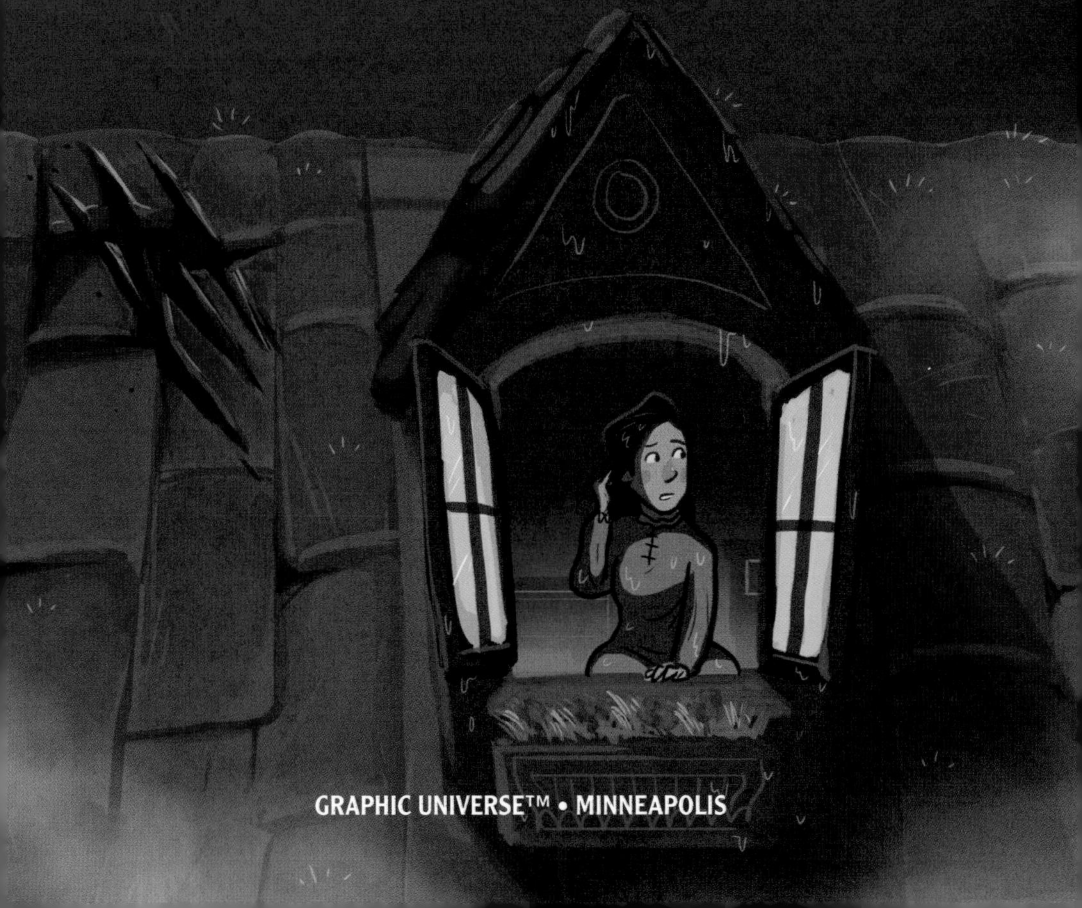

GRAPHIC UNIVERSE™ • MINNEAPOLIS

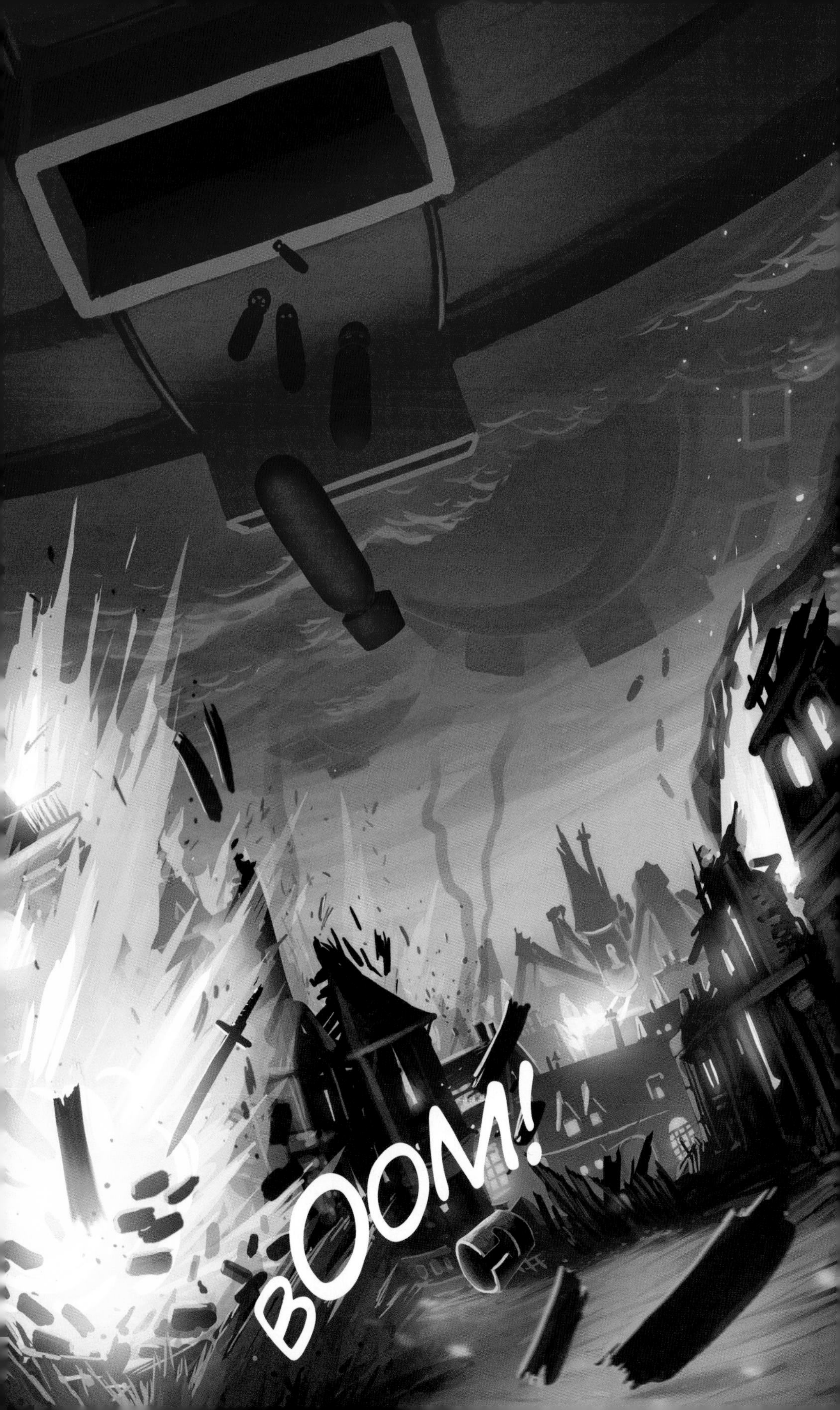
BOOM!

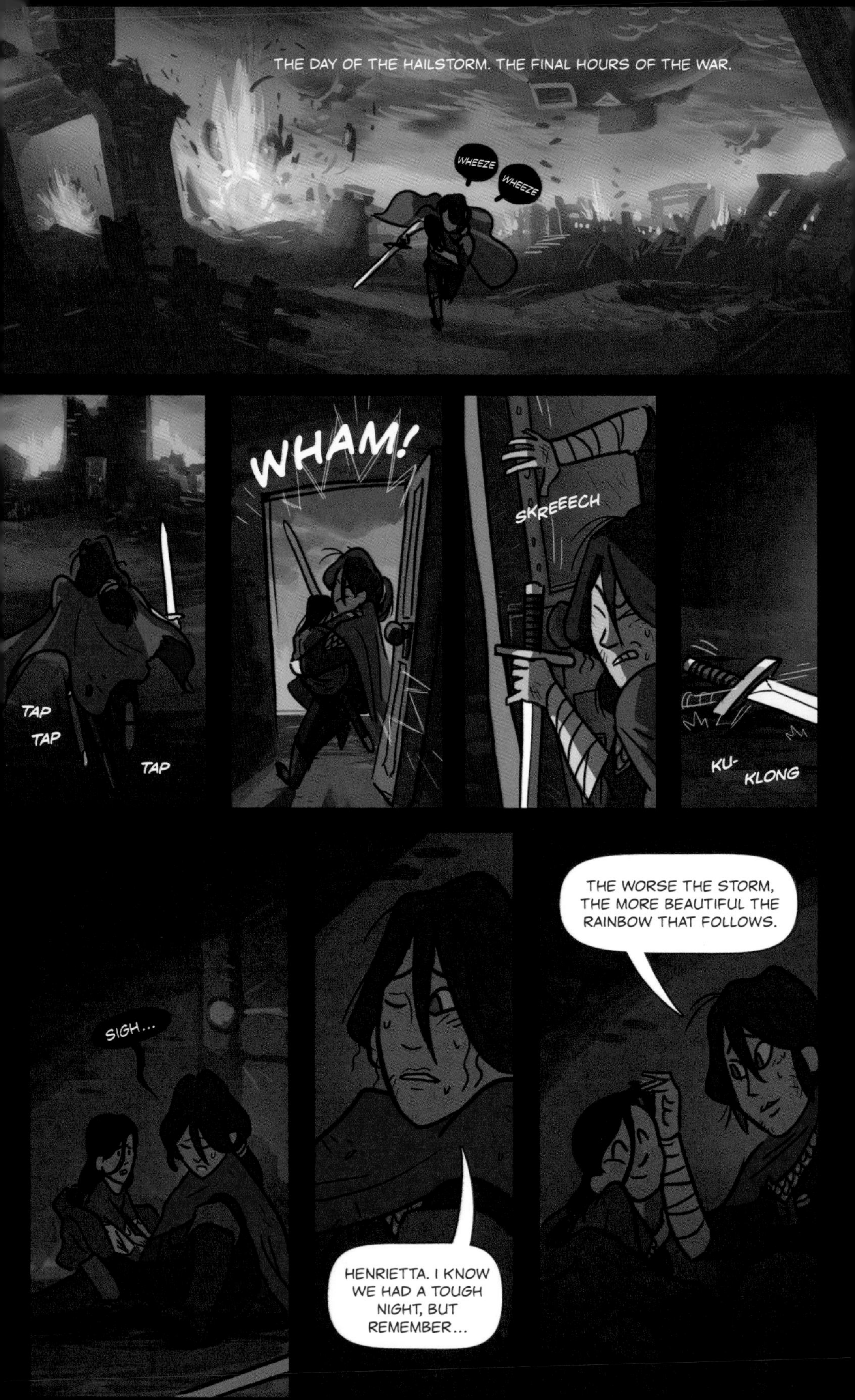
THE DAY OF THE HAILSTORM. THE FINAL HOURS OF THE WAR.
WHEEZE
WHEEZE
TAP
TAP
TAP
WHAM!
SKREEECH
KU-
KLONG
SIGH...
HENRIETTA. I KNOW WE HAD A TOUGH NIGHT, BUT REMEMBER...
THE WORSE THE STORM, THE MORE BEAUTIFUL THE RAINBOW THAT FOLLOWS.

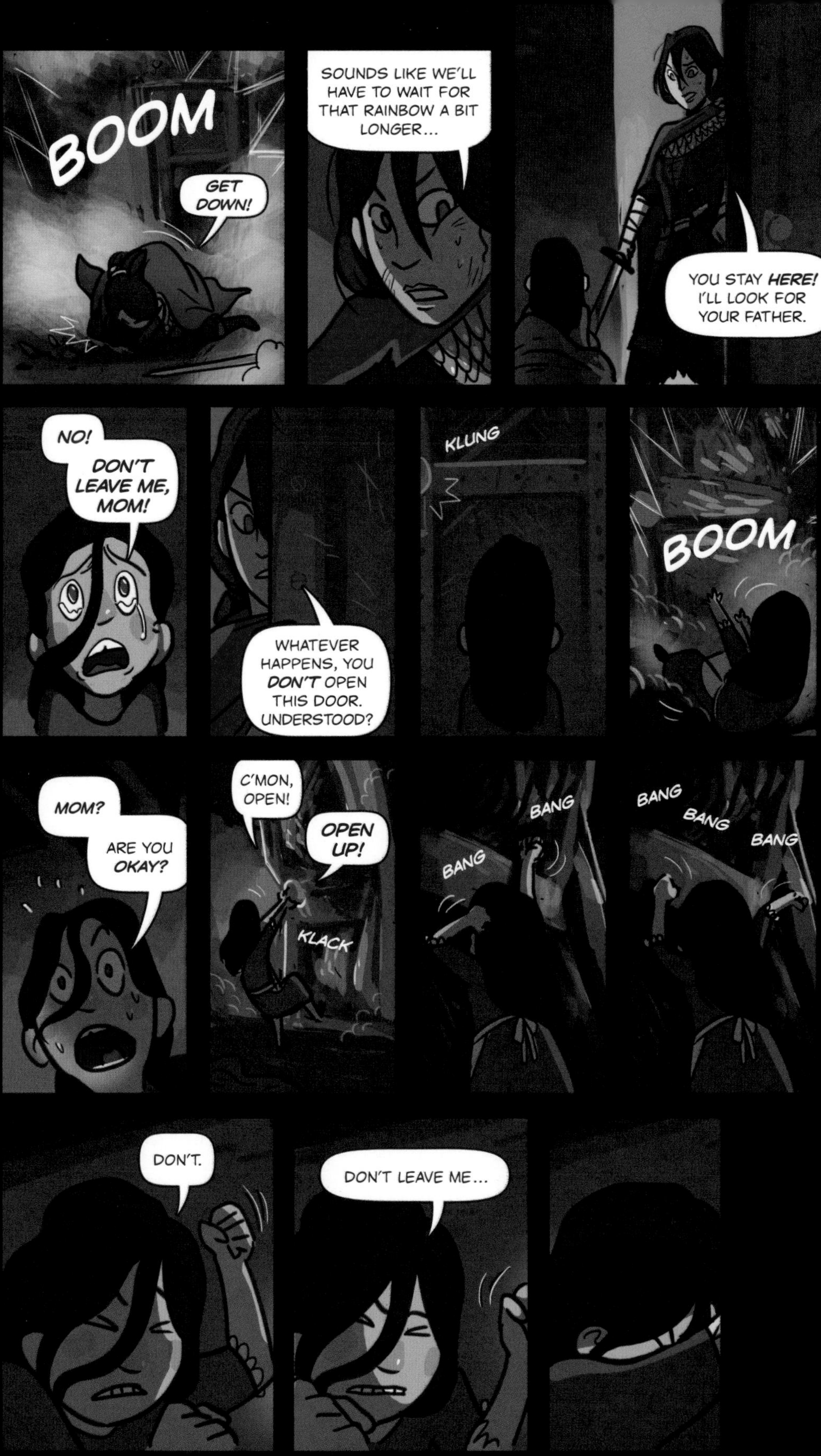
BOOM
GET DOWN!
SOUNDS LIKE WE'LL HAVE TO WAIT FOR THAT RAINBOW A BIT LONGER...
YOU STAY *HERE!* I'LL LOOK FOR YOUR FATHER.
NO!
DON'T LEAVE ME, MOM!
WHATEVER HAPPENS, YOU *DON'T* OPEN THIS DOOR. UNDERSTOOD?
KLUNG
BOOM
MOM?
ARE YOU *OKAY?*
C'MON, OPEN!
OPEN UP!
KLACK
BANG
BANG
BANG
BANG
BANG
DON'T.
DON'T LEAVE ME...

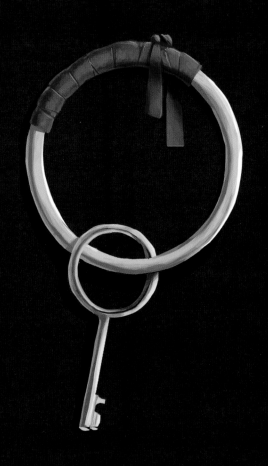

NINE YEARS LATER.

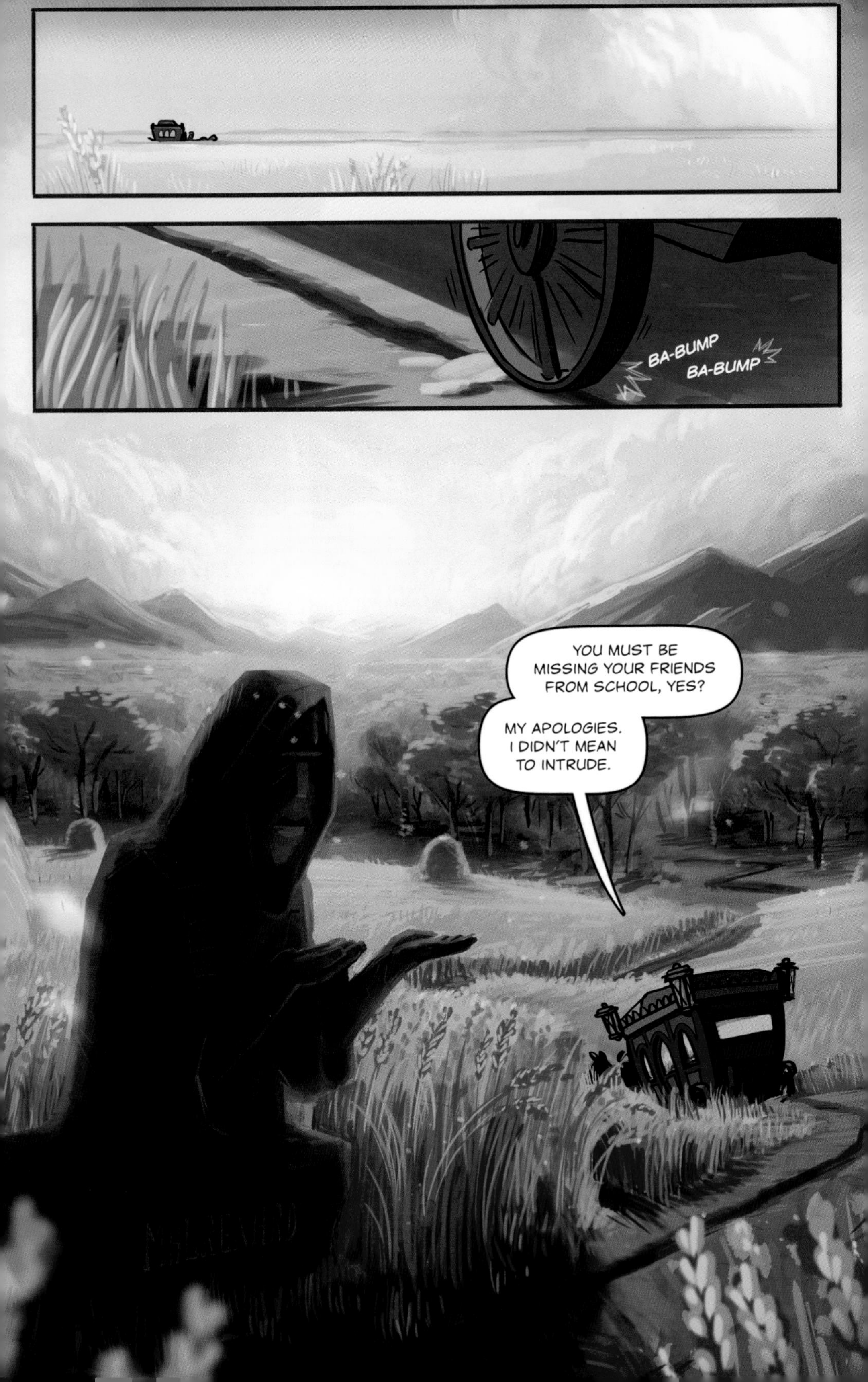
BA-BUMP
BA-BUMP
YOU MUST BE MISSING YOUR FRIENDS FROM SCHOOL, YES?
MY APOLOGIES. I DIDN'T MEAN TO INTRUDE.

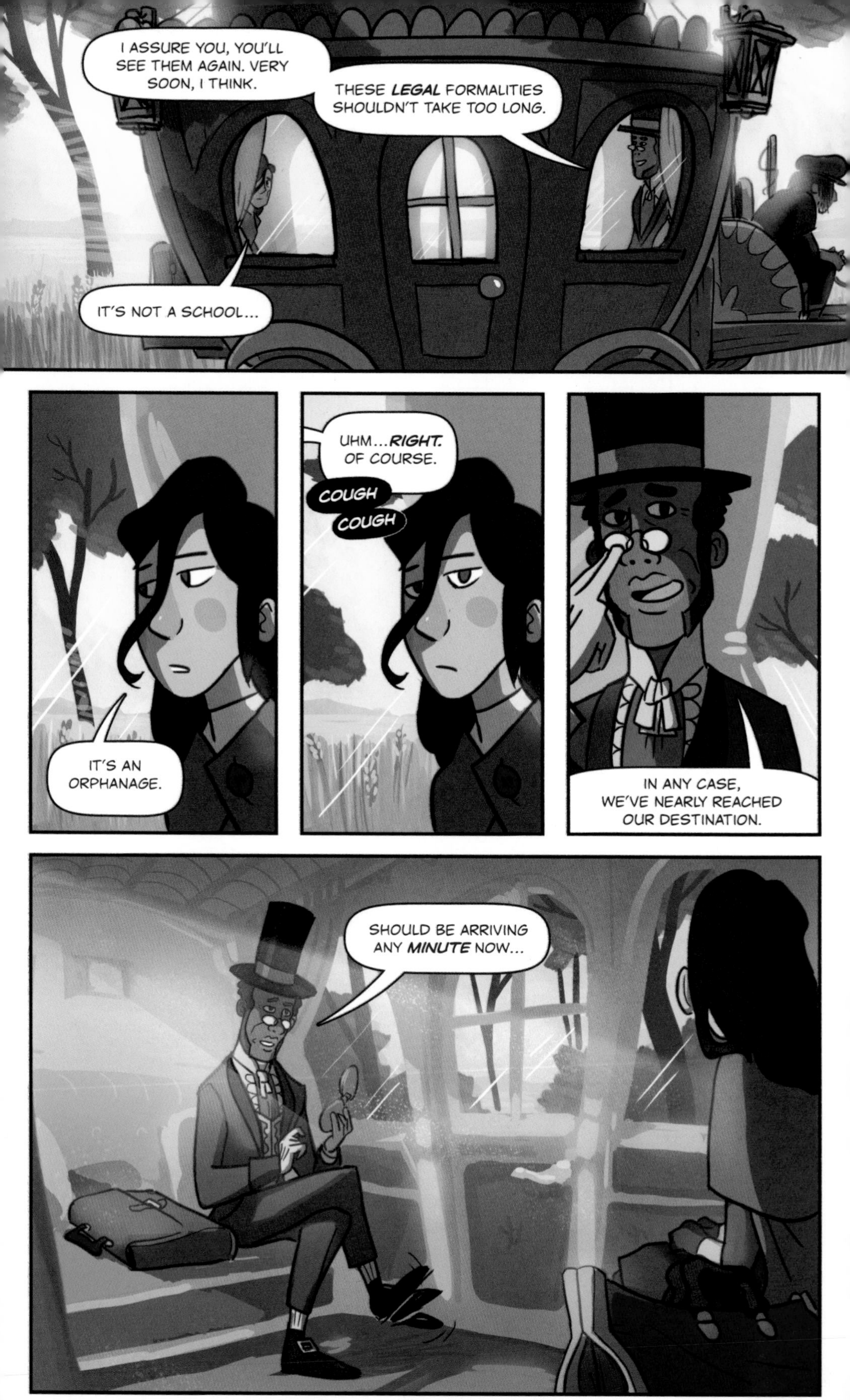
I ASSURE YOU, YOU'LL SEE THEM AGAIN. VERY SOON, I THINK.
THESE **LEGAL** FORMALITIES SHOULDN'T TAKE TOO LONG.
IT'S NOT A SCHOOL...
IT'S AN ORPHANAGE.
UHM... **RIGHT.** OF COURSE.
COUGH
COUGH
IN ANY CASE, WE'VE NEARLY REACHED OUR DESTINATION.
SHOULD BE ARRIVING ANY **MINUTE** NOW...

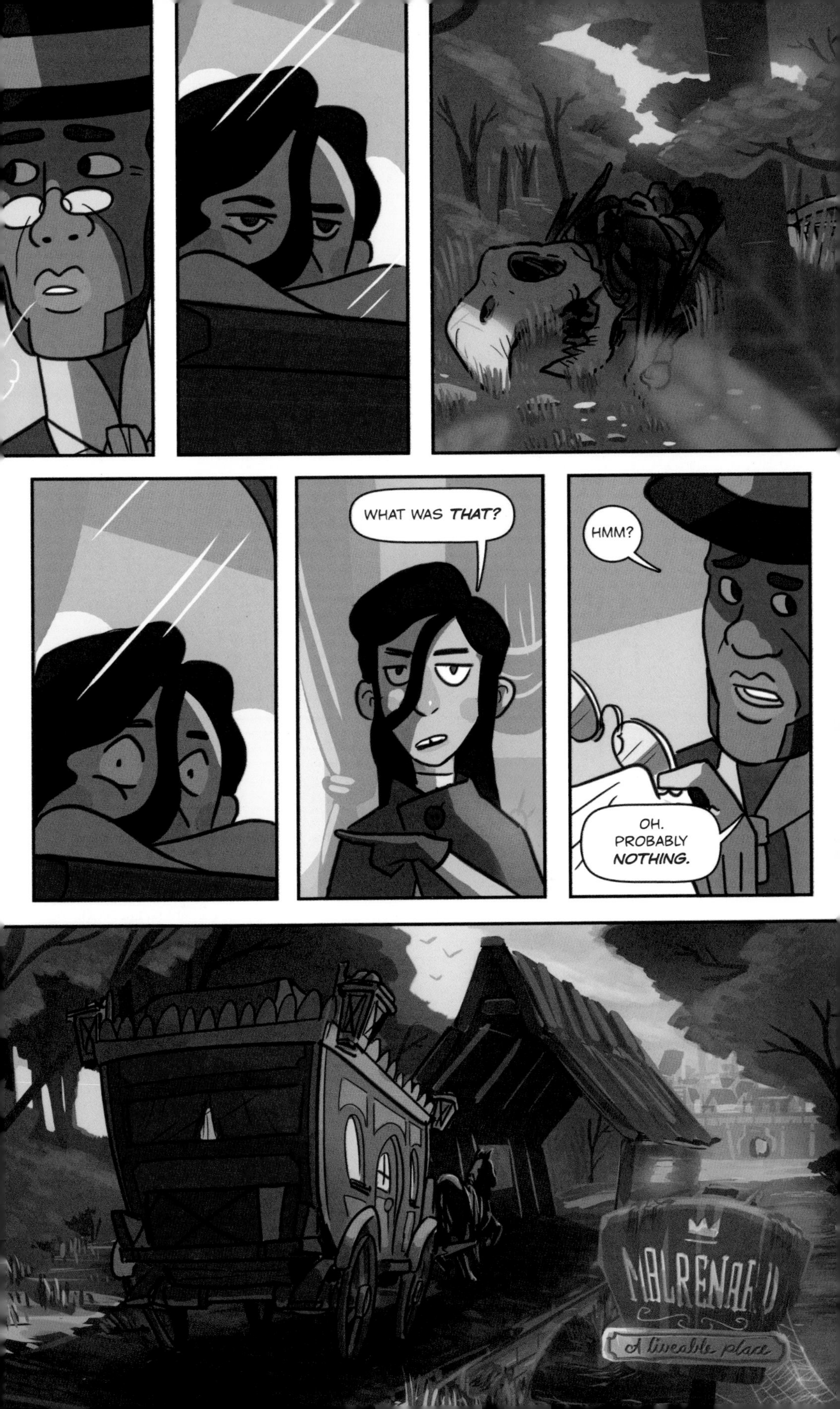
WHAT WAS *THAT?*
HMM?
OH. PROBABLY *NOTHING.*
A liveable place

HUH?

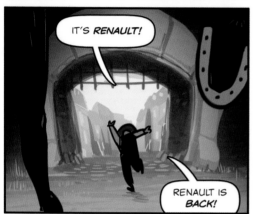

IT'S *RENAULT!*

RENAULT IS *BACK!*

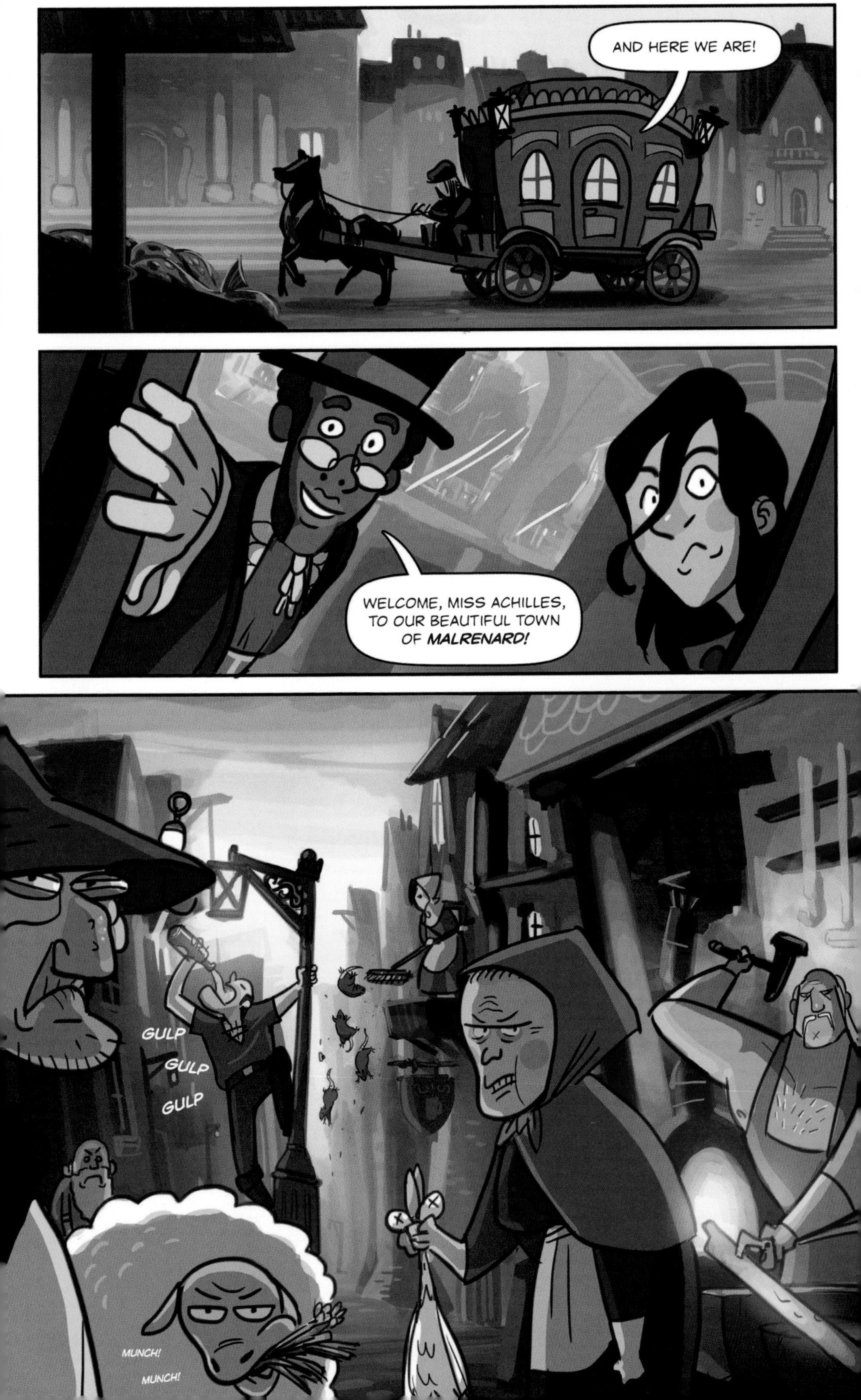

AND HERE WE ARE!
WELCOME, MISS ACHILLES, TO OUR BEAUTIFUL TOWN OF **MALRENARD!**
GULP
GULP
GULP
MUNCH!
MUNCH!

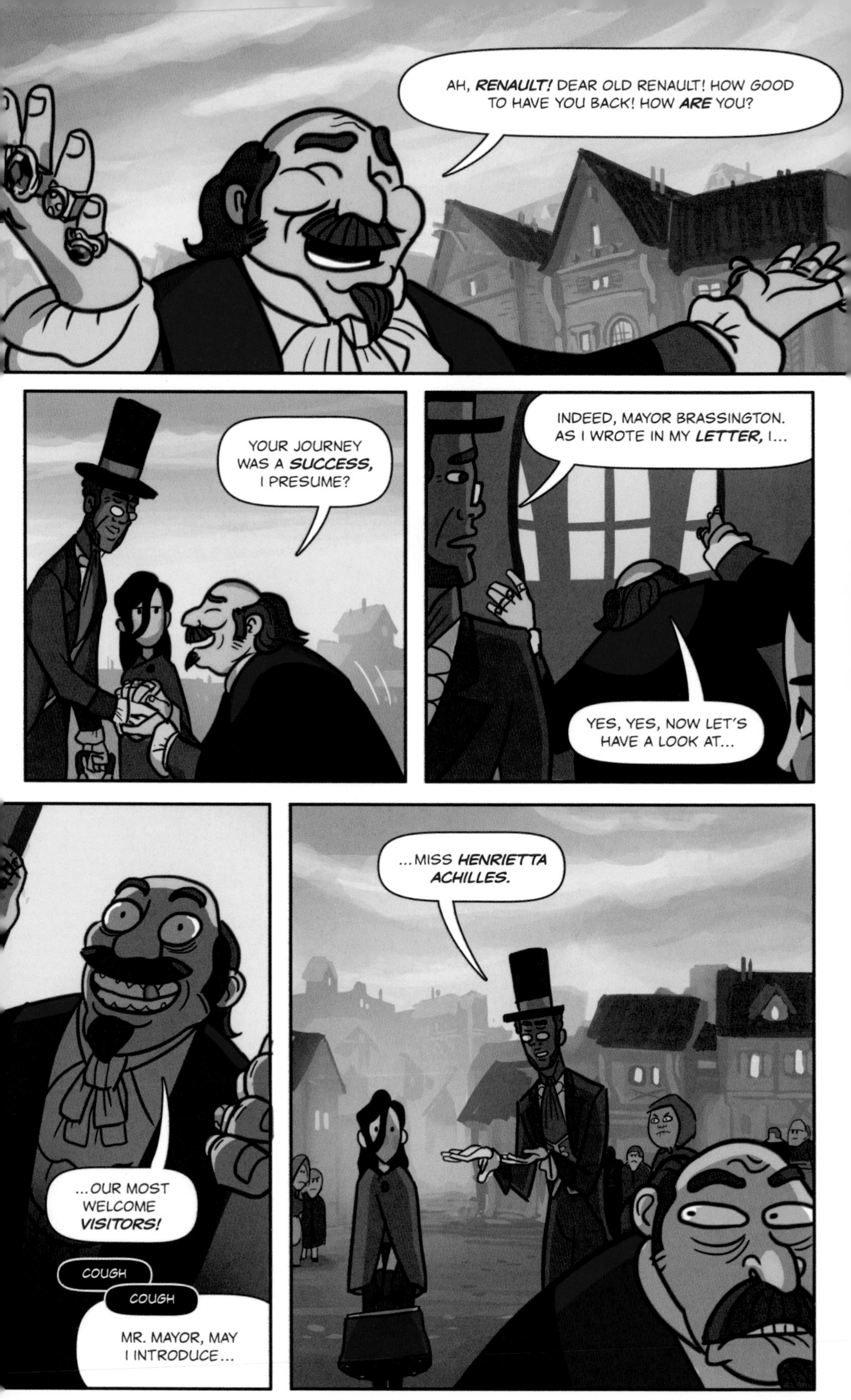
AH, RENAULT! DEAR OLD RENAULT! HOW GOOD TO HAVE YOU BACK! HOW ARE YOU?
YOUR JOURNEY WAS A SUCCESS, I PRESUME?
INDEED, MAYOR BRASSINGTON. AS I WROTE IN MY LETTER, I...
YES, YES, NOW LET'S HAVE A LOOK AT...
...OUR MOST WELCOME VISITORS!
COUGH
COUGH
MR. MAYOR, MAY I INTRODUCE...
...MISS HENRIETTA ACHILLES.

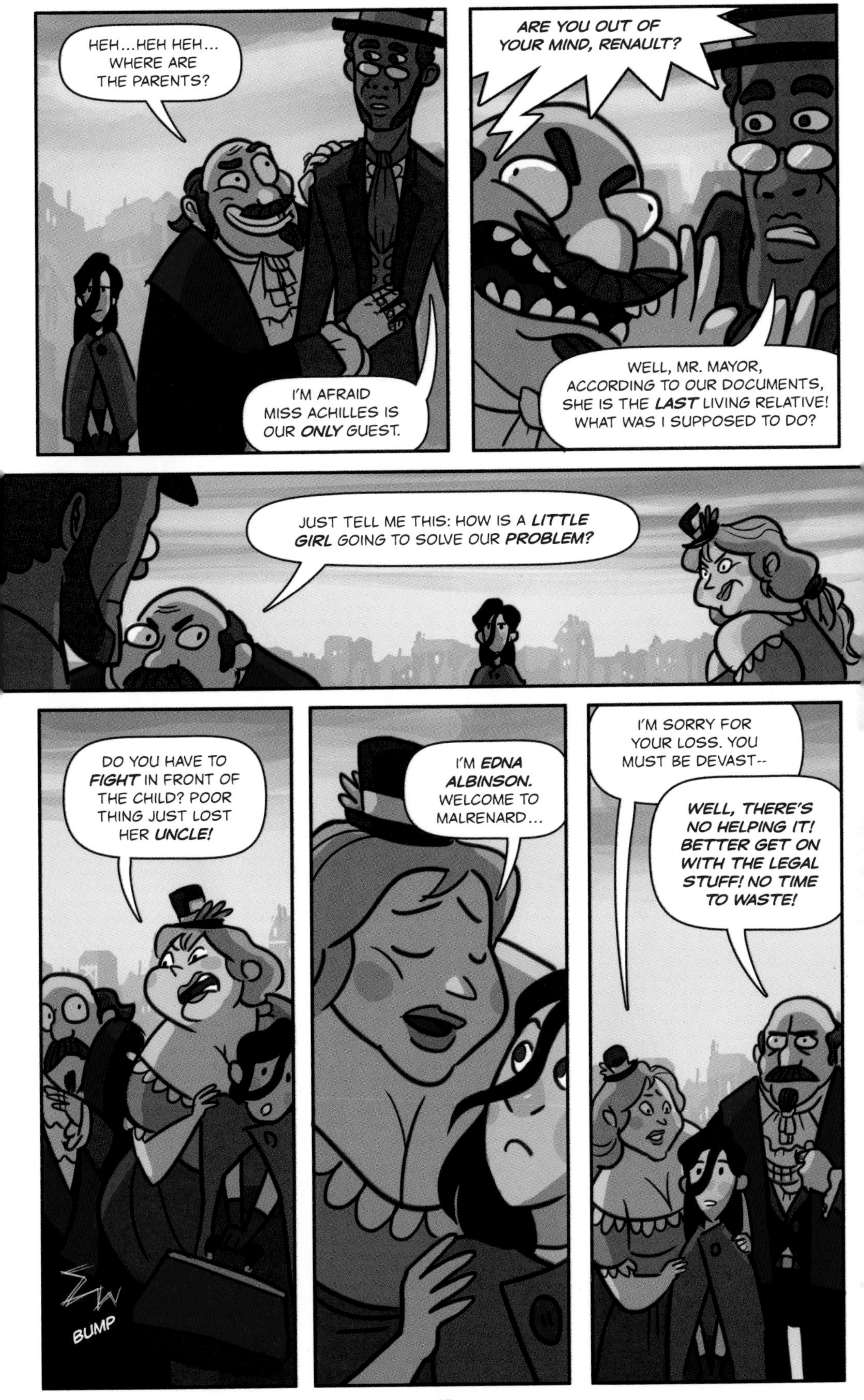
HEH...HEH HEH... WHERE ARE THE PARENTS?
I'M AFRAID MISS ACHILLES IS OUR ONLY GUEST.
ARE YOU OUT OF YOUR MIND, RENAULT?
WELL, MR. MAYOR, ACCORDING TO OUR DOCUMENTS, SHE IS THE LAST LIVING RELATIVE! WHAT WAS I SUPPOSED TO DO?
JUST TELL ME THIS: HOW IS A LITTLE GIRL GOING TO SOLVE OUR PROBLEM?
DO YOU HAVE TO FIGHT IN FRONT OF THE CHILD? POOR THING JUST LOST HER UNCLE!
BUMP
I'M EDNA ALBINSON. WELCOME TO MALRENARD...
I'M SORRY FOR YOUR LOSS. YOU MUST BE DEVAST--
WELL, THERE'S NO HELPING IT! BETTER GET ON WITH THE LEGAL STUFF! NO TIME TO WASTE!

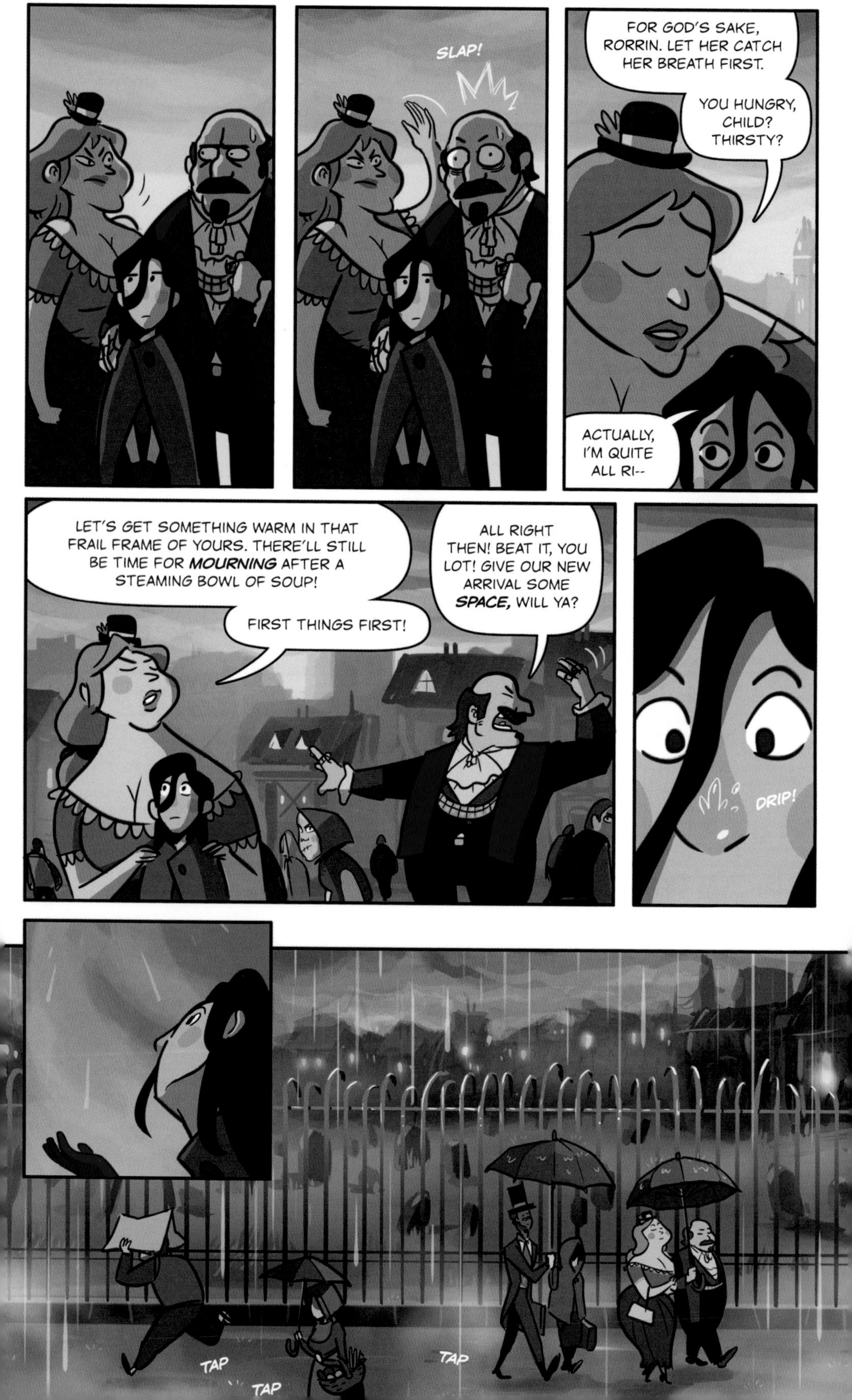
SLAP!
FOR GOD'S SAKE, RORRIN. LET HER CATCH HER BREATH FIRST.
YOU HUNGRY, CHILD? THIRSTY?
ACTUALLY, I'M QUITE ALL RI--
LET'S GET SOMETHING WARM IN THAT FRAIL FRAME OF YOURS. THERE'LL STILL BE TIME FOR MOURNING AFTER A STEAMING BOWL OF SOUP!
FIRST THINGS FIRST!
ALL RIGHT THEN! BEAT IT, YOU LOT! GIVE OUR NEW ARRIVAL SOME SPACE, WILL YA?
DRIP!
TAP
TAP
TAP

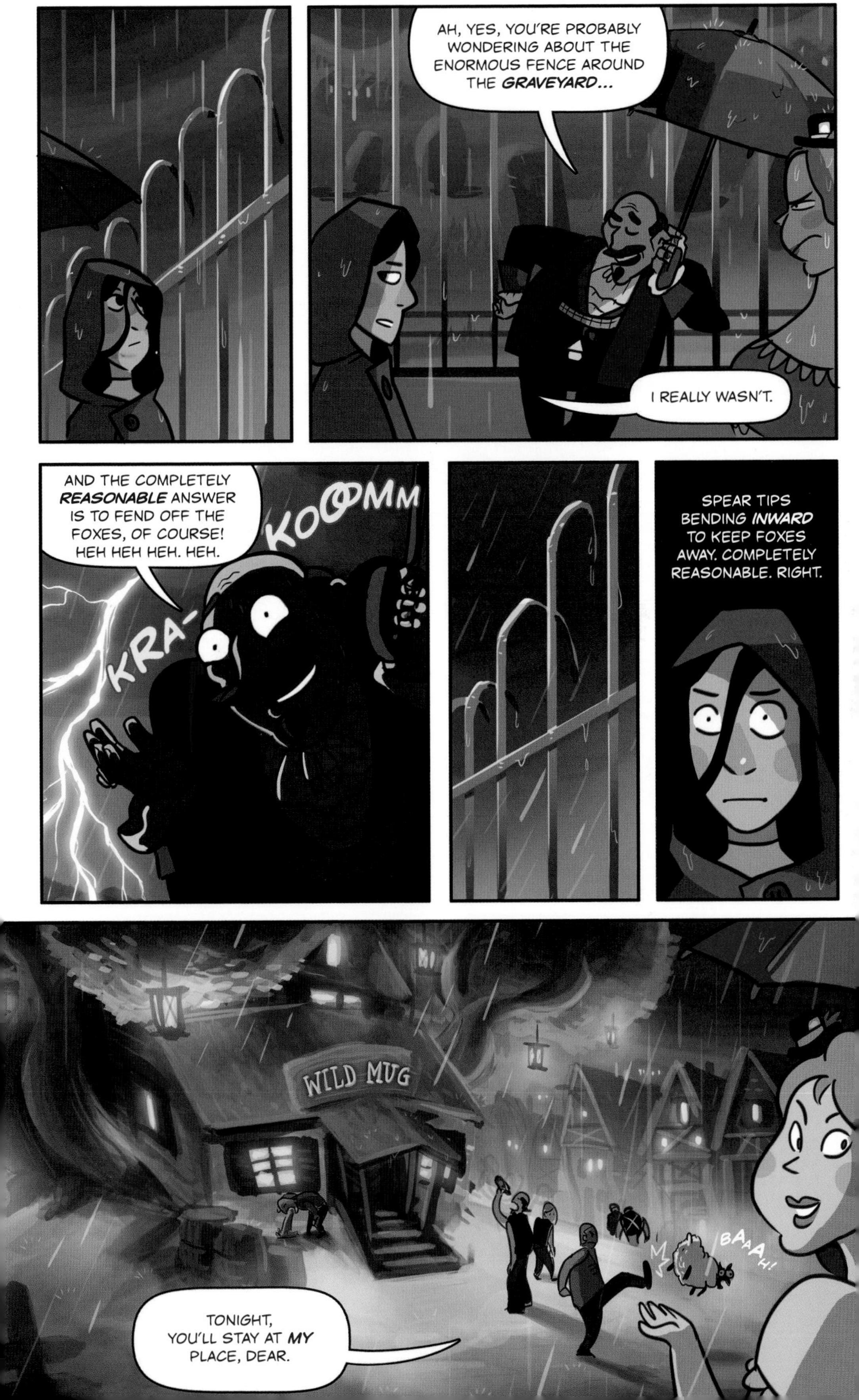
AH, YES, YOU'RE PROBABLY WONDERING ABOUT THE ENORMOUS FENCE AROUND THE *GRAVEYARD...*
I REALLY WASN'T.
AND THE COMPLETELY *REASONABLE* ANSWER IS TO FEND OFF THE FOXES, OF COURSE! HEH HEH HEH. HEH.
KRA-
KOOMM
SPEAR TIPS BENDING *INWARD* TO KEEP FOXES AWAY. COMPLETELY REASONABLE. RIGHT.
WILD MUG
BAAAH!
TONIGHT, YOU'LL STAY AT *MY* PLACE, DEAR.

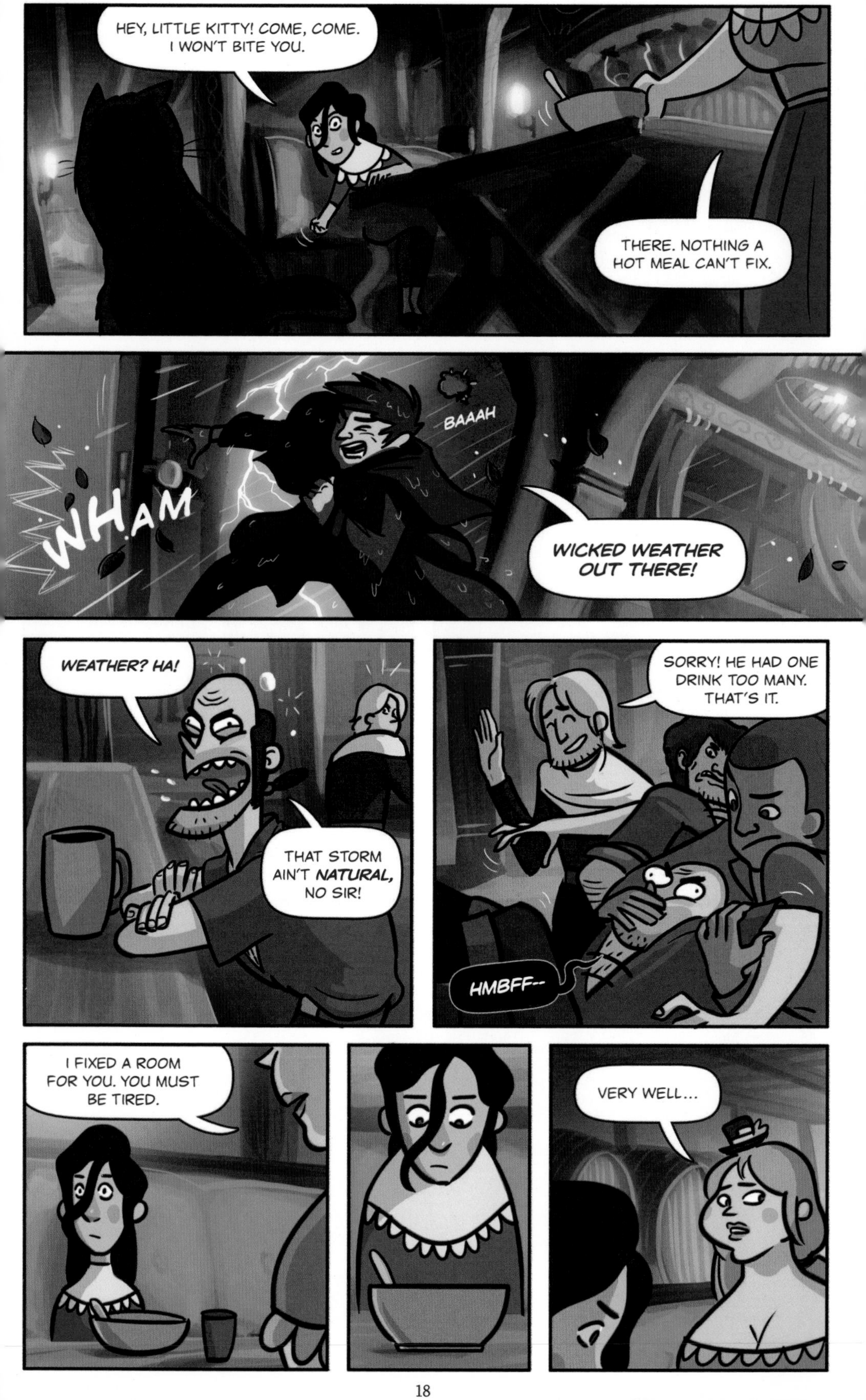
HEY, LITTLE KITTY! COME, COME. I WON'T BITE YOU.
THERE. NOTHING A HOT MEAL CAN'T FIX.
BAAAH
WHAM
WICKED WEATHER OUT THERE!
WEATHER? HA!
THAT STORM AIN'T ***NATURAL,*** NO SIR!
SORRY! HE HAD ONE DRINK TOO MANY. THAT'S IT.
HMBFF--
I FIXED A ROOM FOR YOU. YOU MUST BE TIRED.
VERY WELL...

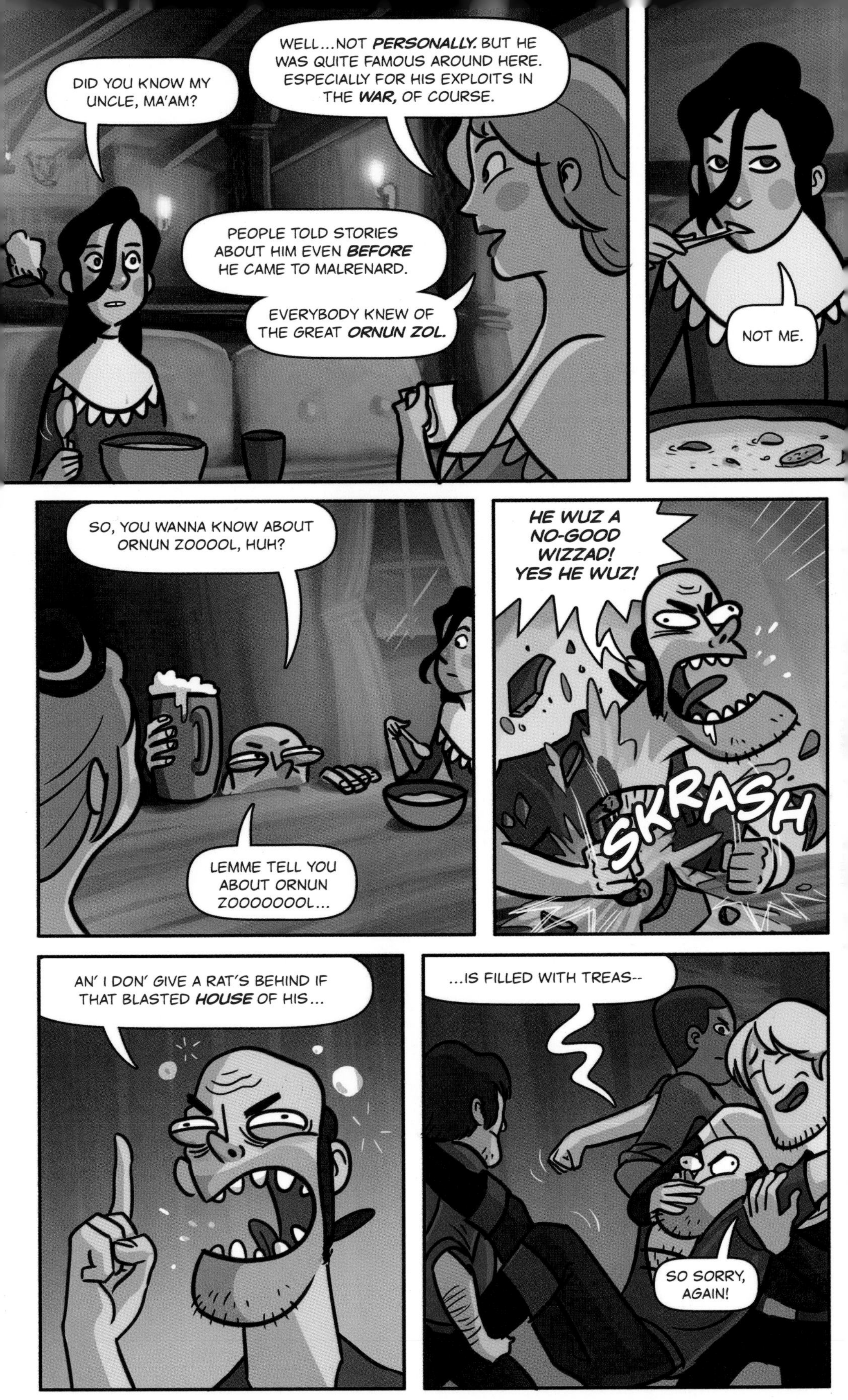
DID YOU KNOW MY UNCLE, MA'AM?
WELL...NOT PERSONALLY. BUT HE WAS QUITE FAMOUS AROUND HERE. ESPECIALLY FOR HIS EXPLOITS IN THE WAR, OF COURSE.
PEOPLE TOLD STORIES ABOUT HIM EVEN BEFORE HE CAME TO MALRENARD.
EVERYBODY KNEW OF THE GREAT ORNUN ZOL.
NOT ME.
SO, YOU WANNA KNOW ABOUT ORNUN ZOOOOL, HUH?
LEMME TELL YOU ABOUT ORNUN ZOOOOOOOL...
HE WUZ A NO-GOOD WIZZAD! YES HE WUZ!
SKRASH
AN' I DON' GIVE A RAT'S BEHIND IF THAT BLASTED HOUSE OF HIS...
...IS FILLED WITH TREAS--
SO SORRY, AGAIN!

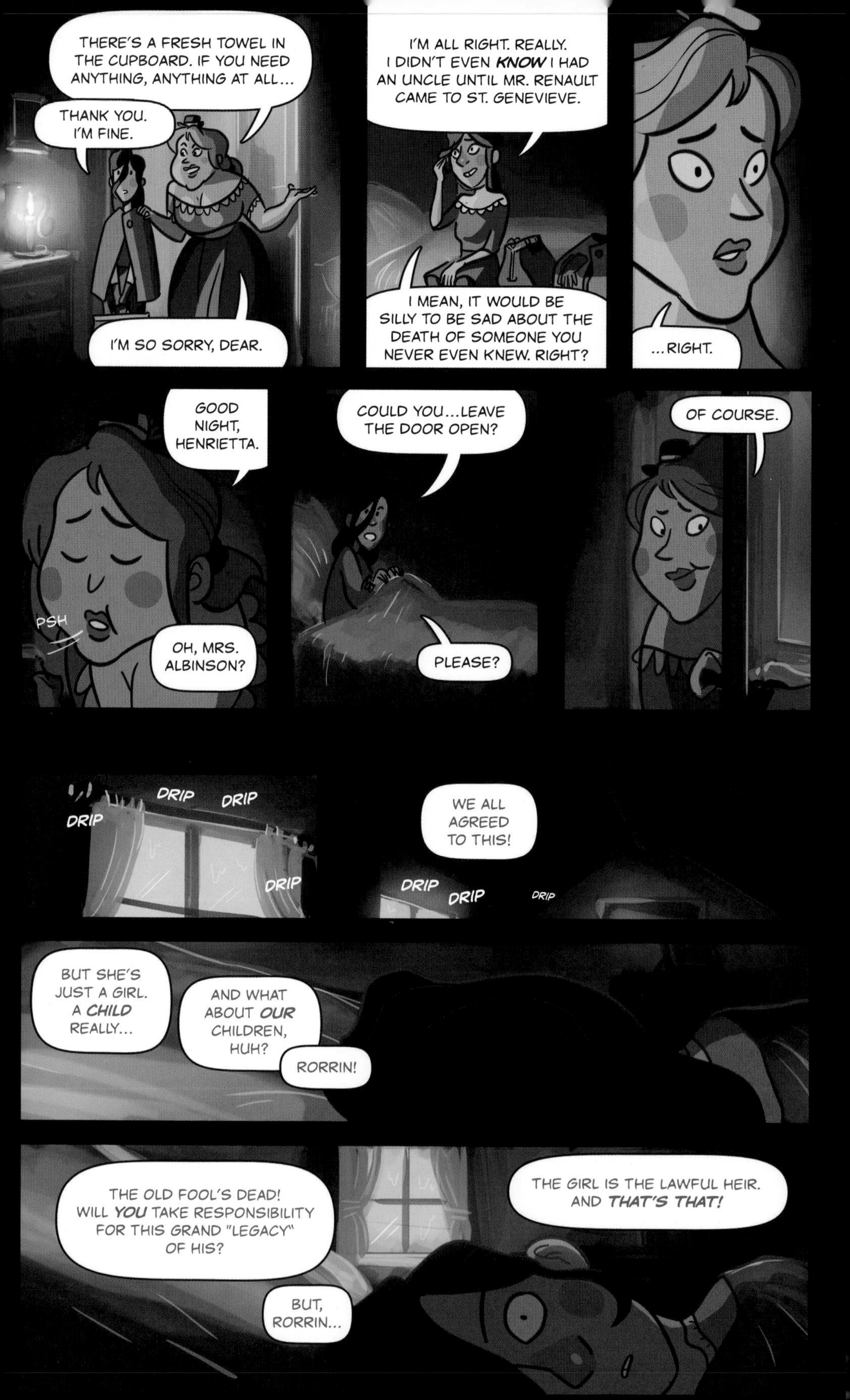

THERE'S A FRESH TOWEL IN THE CUPBOARD. IF YOU NEED ANYTHING, ANYTHING AT ALL...
THANK YOU. I'M FINE.
I'M SO SORRY, DEAR.
I'M ALL RIGHT. REALLY. I DIDN'T EVEN KNOW I HAD AN UNCLE UNTIL MR. RENAULT CAME TO ST. GENEVIEVE.
I MEAN, IT WOULD BE SILLY TO BE SAD ABOUT THE DEATH OF SOMEONE YOU NEVER EVEN KNEW. RIGHT?
...RIGHT.
GOOD NIGHT, HENRIETTA.
PSH
OH, MRS. ALBINSON?
COULD YOU...LEAVE THE DOOR OPEN?
PLEASE?
OF COURSE.
DRIP DRIP DRIP
DRIP
WE ALL AGREED TO THIS!
DRIP DRIP DRIP
BUT SHE'S JUST A GIRL. A CHILD REALLY...
AND WHAT ABOUT OUR CHILDREN, HUH?
RORRIN!
THE OLD FOOL'S DEAD! WILL YOU TAKE RESPONSIBILITY FOR THIS GRAND "LEGACY" OF HIS?
BUT, RORRIN...
THE GIRL IS THE LAWFUL HEIR. AND THAT'S THAT!

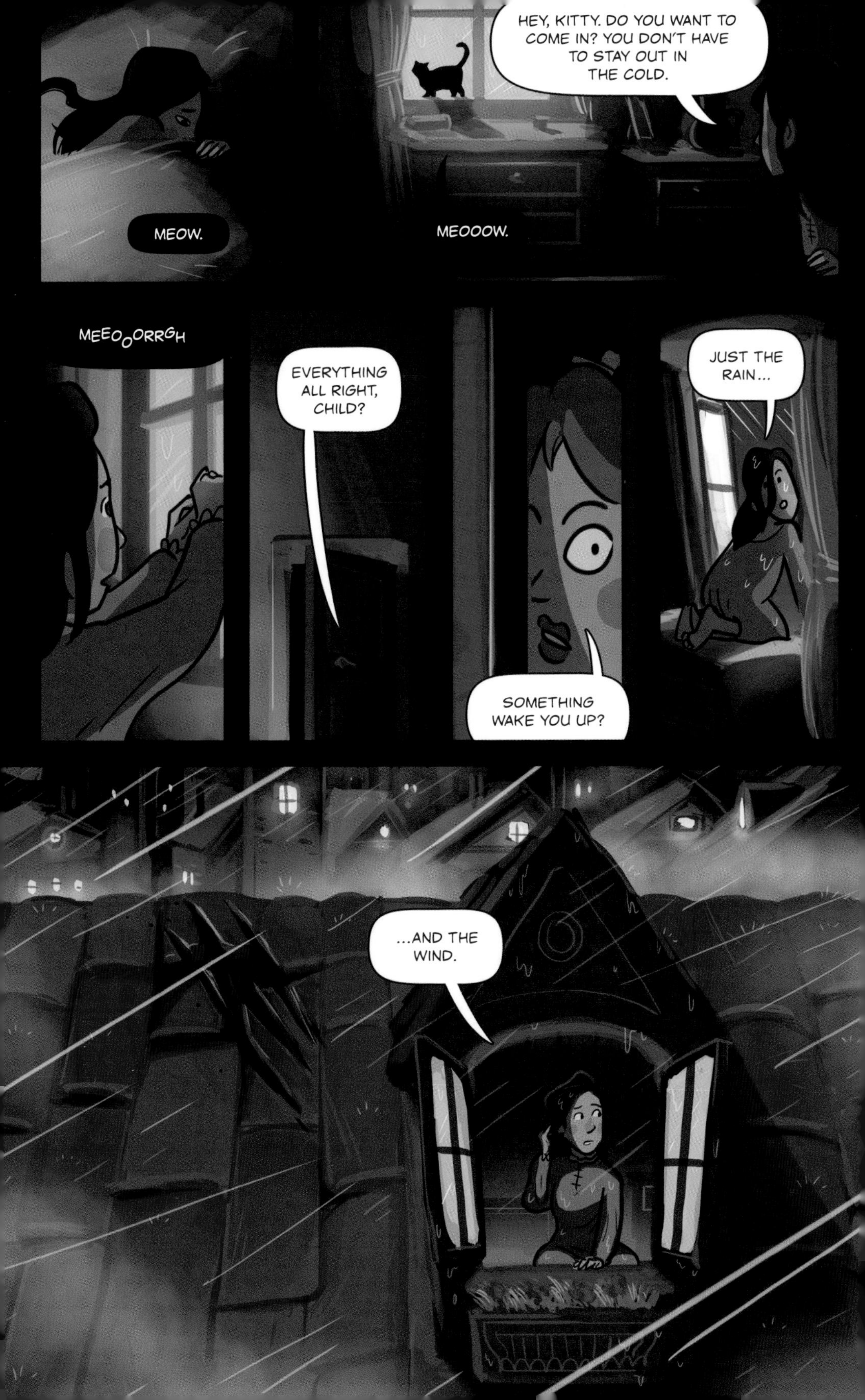
MEOW.
HEY, KITTY. DO YOU WANT TO COME IN? YOU DON'T HAVE TO STAY OUT IN THE COLD.
MEOOOW.
MEEOOORRGH
EVERYTHING ALL RIGHT, CHILD?
SOMETHING WAKE YOU UP?
JUST THE RAIN...
...AND THE WIND.

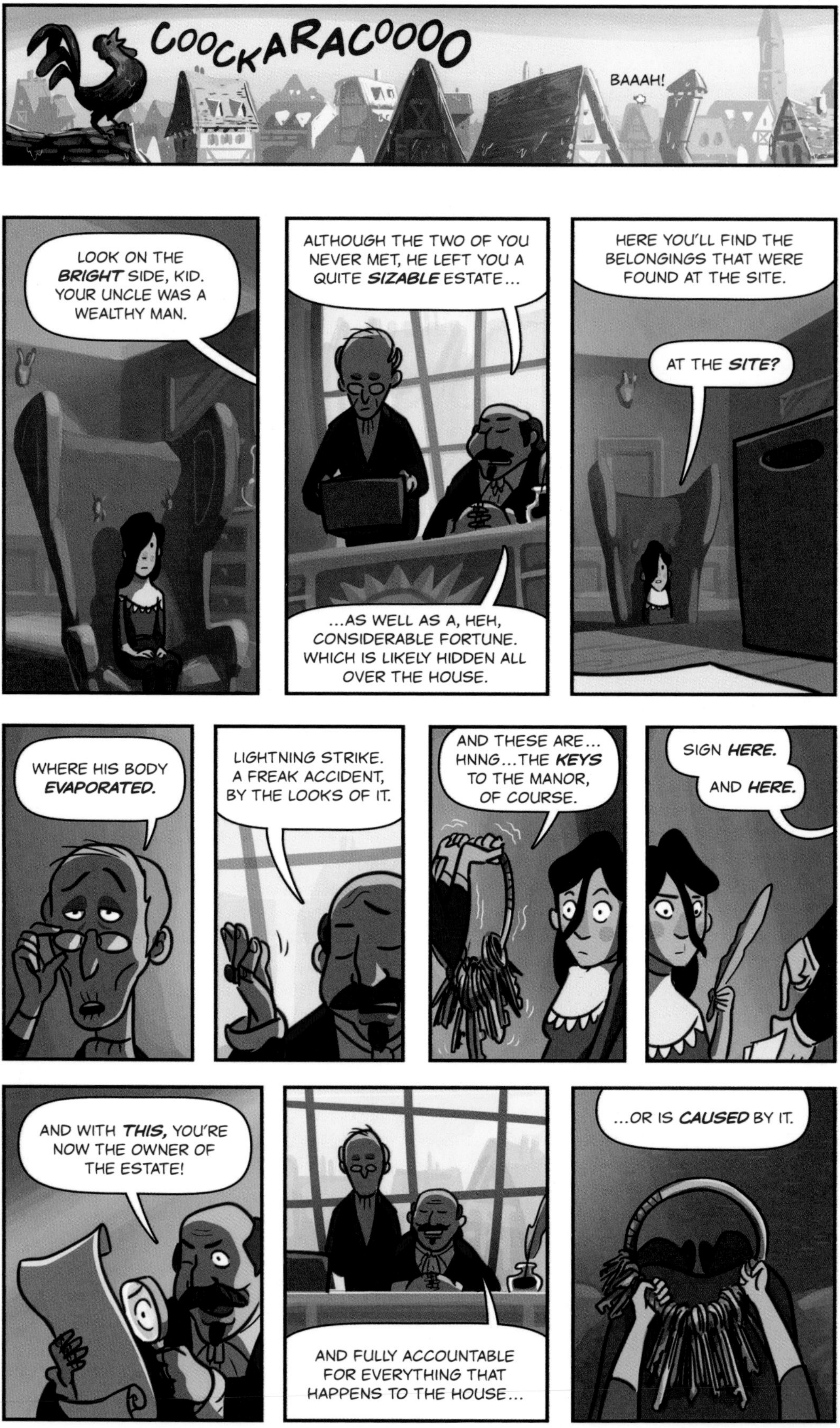
COOCKARACOOOO
BAAAH!
LOOK ON THE BRIGHT SIDE, KID. YOUR UNCLE WAS A WEALTHY MAN.
ALTHOUGH THE TWO OF YOU NEVER MET, HE LEFT YOU A QUITE SIZABLE ESTATE...
...AS WELL AS A, HEH, CONSIDERABLE FORTUNE. WHICH IS LIKELY HIDDEN ALL OVER THE HOUSE.
HERE YOU'LL FIND THE BELONGINGS THAT WERE FOUND AT THE SITE.
AT THE SITE?
WHERE HIS BODY EVAPORATED.
LIGHTNING STRIKE. A FREAK ACCIDENT, BY THE LOOKS OF IT.
AND THESE ARE... HNNG...THE KEYS TO THE MANOR, OF COURSE.
SIGN HERE.
AND HERE.
AND WITH THIS, YOU'RE NOW THE OWNER OF THE ESTATE!
AND FULLY ACCOUNTABLE FOR EVERYTHING THAT HAPPENS TO THE HOUSE...
...OR IS CAUSED BY IT.

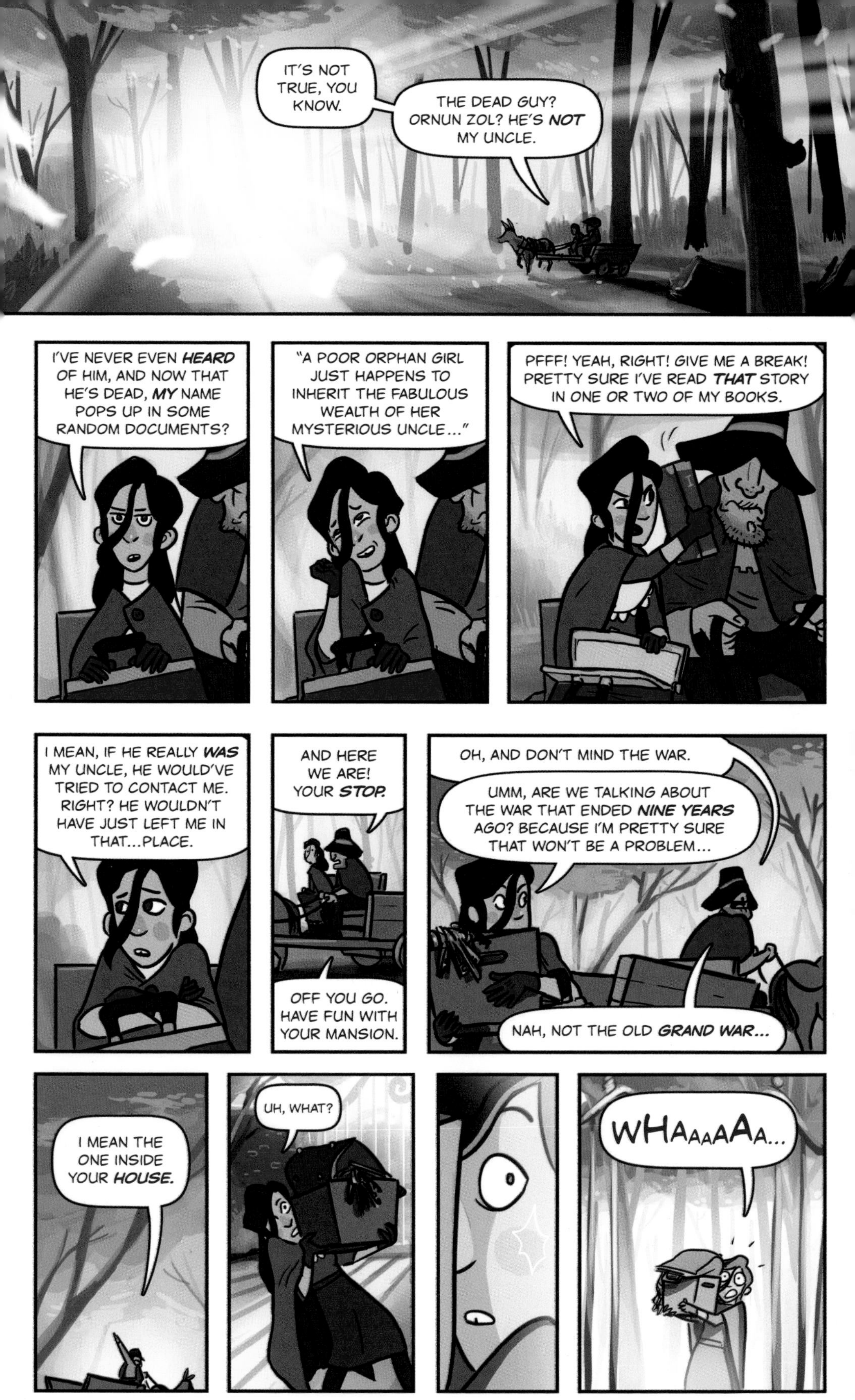
IT'S NOT TRUE, YOU KNOW.
THE DEAD GUY? ORNUN ZOL? HE'S NOT MY UNCLE.
I'VE NEVER EVEN HEARD OF HIM, AND NOW THAT HE'S DEAD, MY NAME POPS UP IN SOME RANDOM DOCUMENTS?
"A POOR ORPHAN GIRL JUST HAPPENS TO INHERIT THE FABULOUS WEALTH OF HER MYSTERIOUS UNCLE..."
PFFF! YEAH, RIGHT! GIVE ME A BREAK! PRETTY SURE I'VE READ THAT STORY IN ONE OR TWO OF MY BOOKS.
I MEAN, IF HE REALLY WAS MY UNCLE, HE WOULD'VE TRIED TO CONTACT ME. RIGHT? HE WOULDN'T HAVE JUST LEFT ME IN THAT...PLACE.
AND HERE WE ARE! YOUR STOP.
OFF YOU GO. HAVE FUN WITH YOUR MANSION.
OH, AND DON'T MIND THE WAR.
UMM, ARE WE TALKING ABOUT THE WAR THAT ENDED NINE YEARS AGO? BECAUSE I'M PRETTY SURE THAT WON'T BE A PROBLEM...
NAH, NOT THE OLD GRAND WAR...
I MEAN THE ONE INSIDE YOUR HOUSE.
UH, WHAT?
WHAAAAAA...

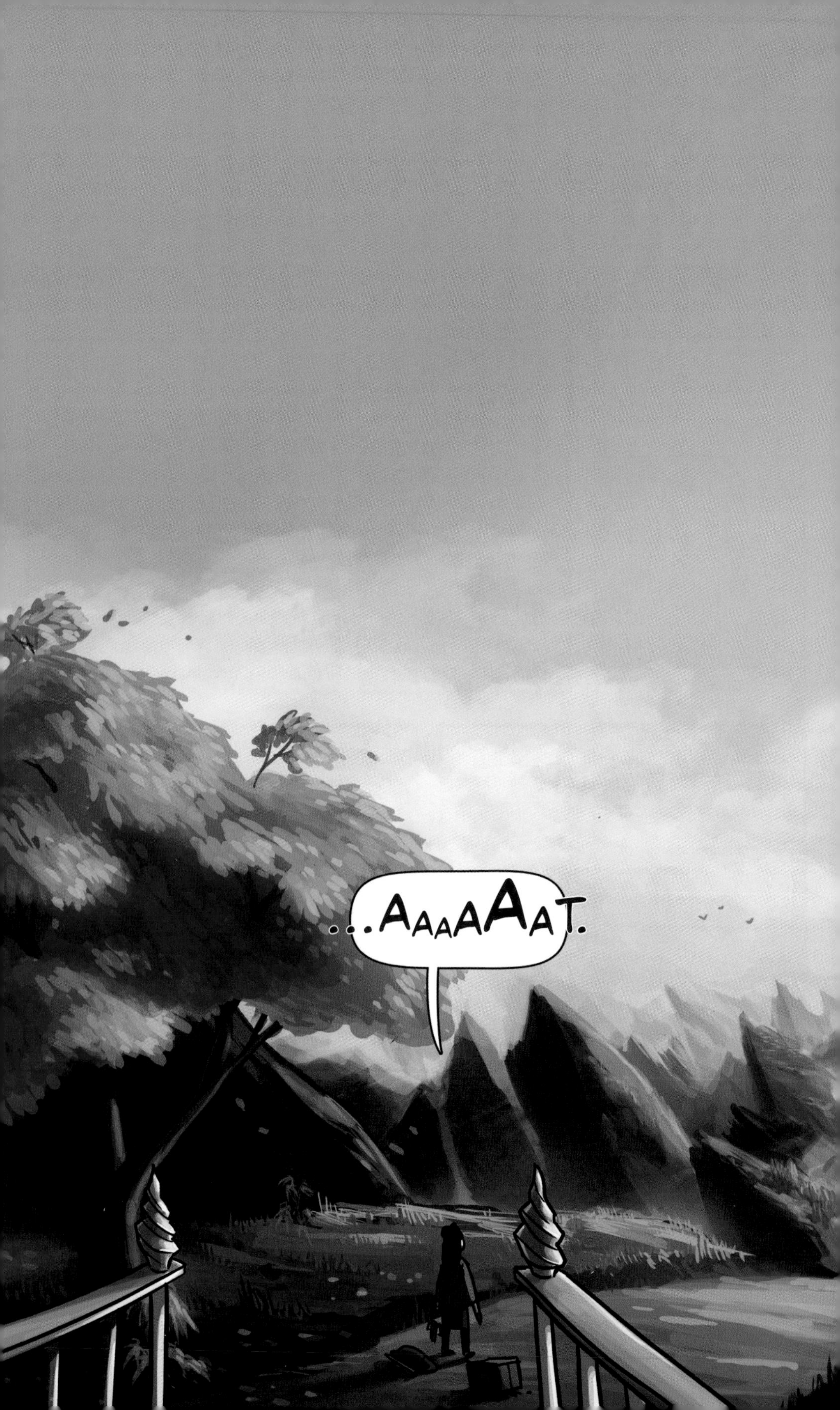
...AAAAAAT.

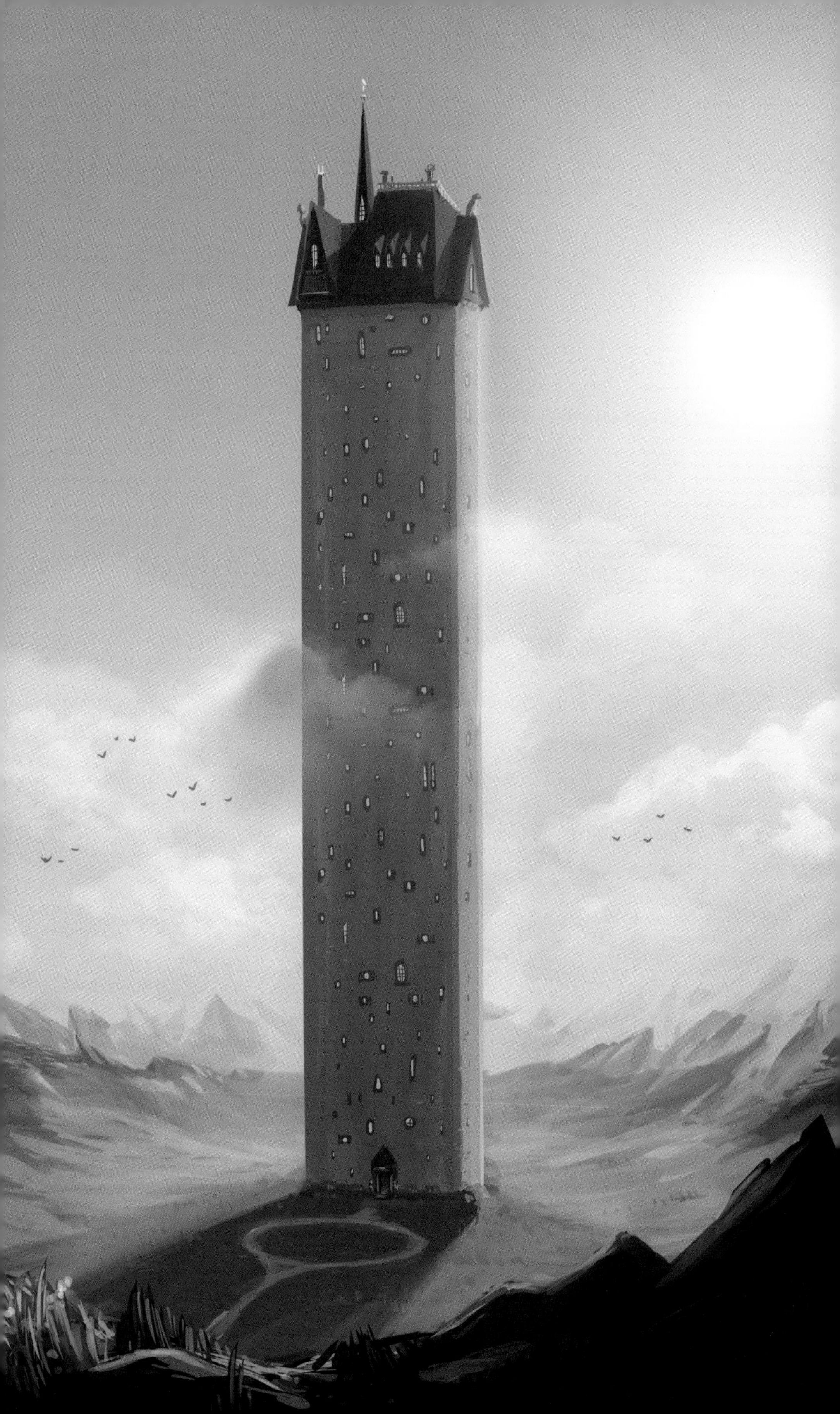

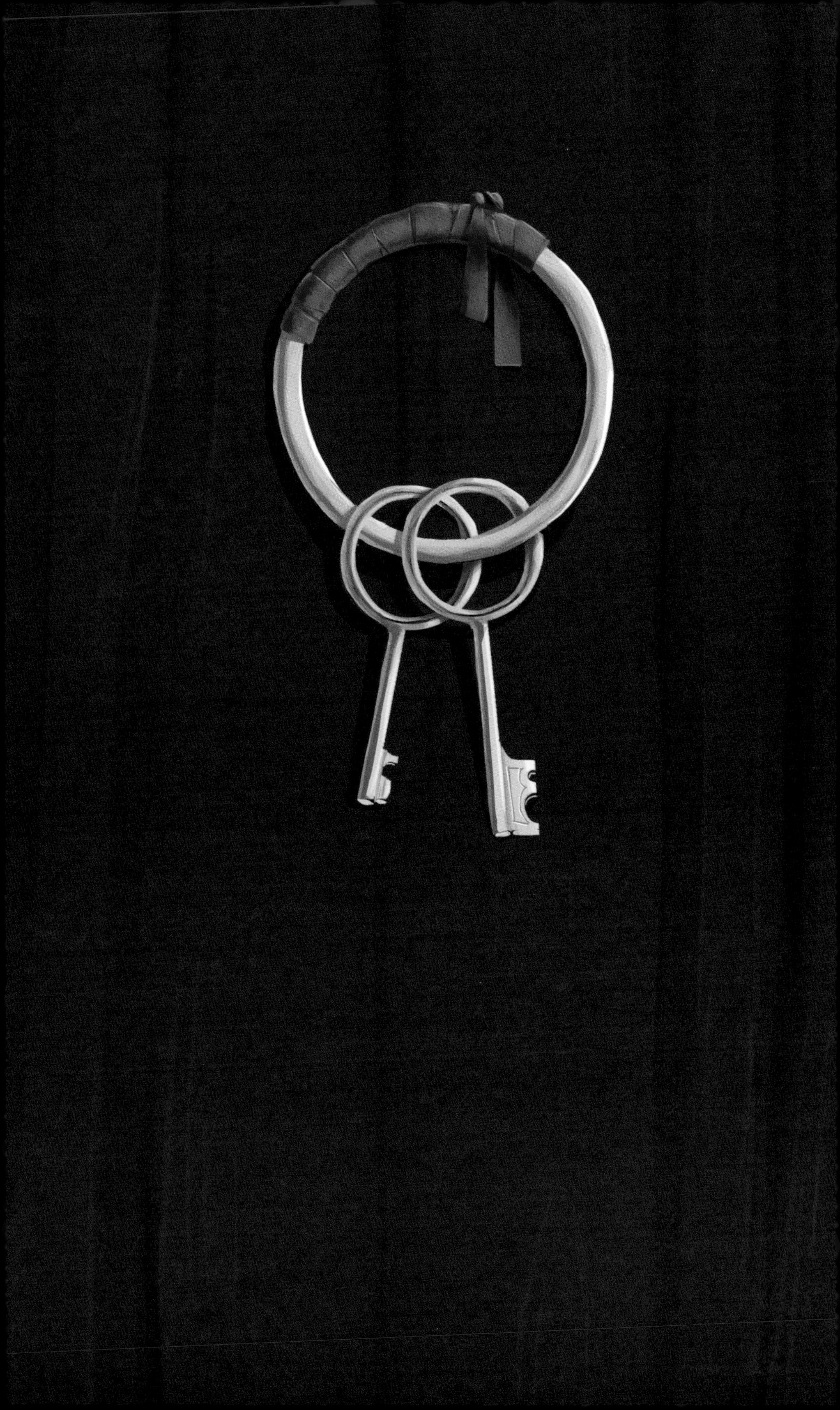

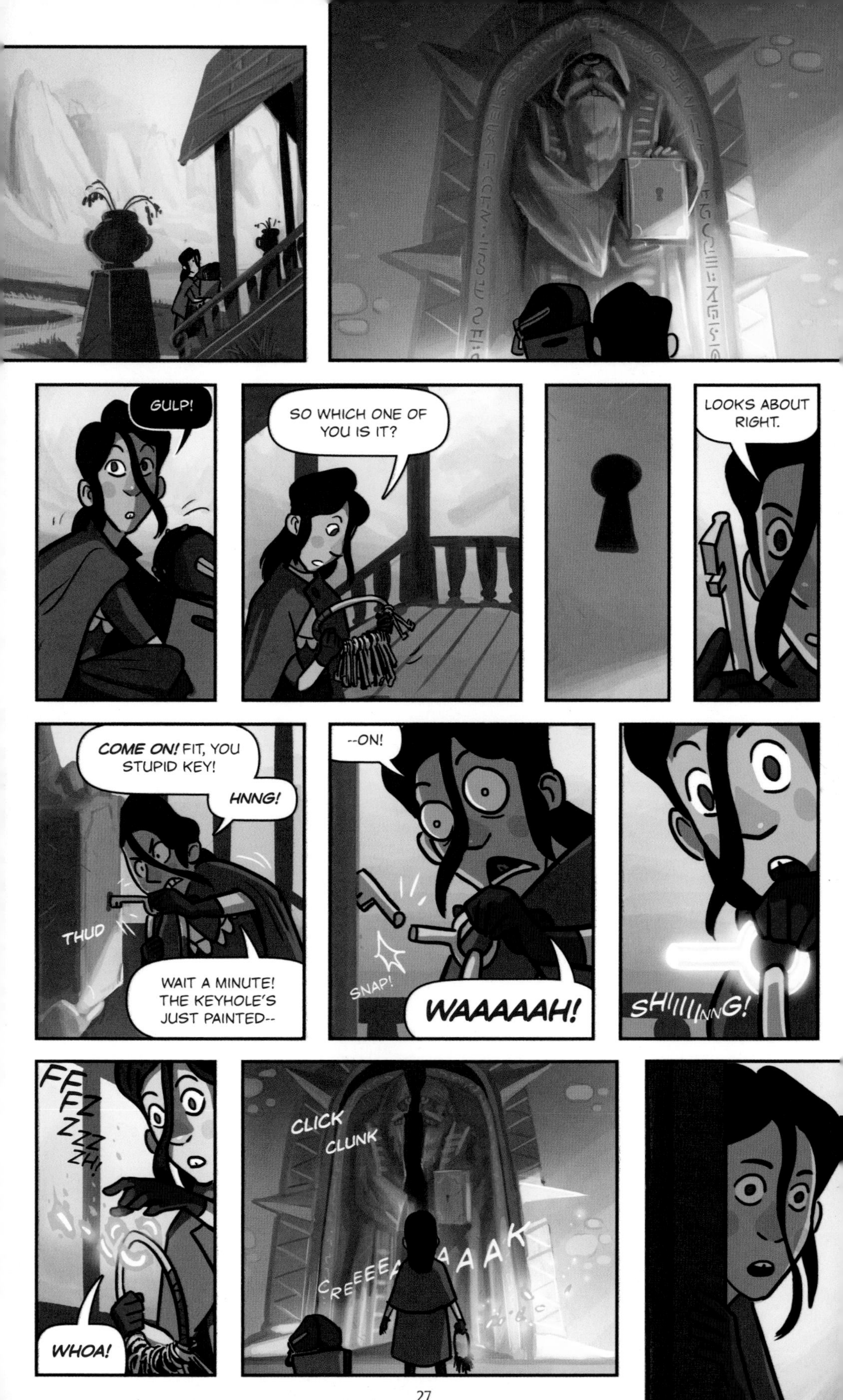
GULP!
SO WHICH ONE OF YOU IS IT?
LOOKS ABOUT RIGHT.
COME ON! FIT, YOU STUPID KEY!
HNNG!
THUD
WAIT A MINUTE! THE KEYHOLE'S JUST PAINTED--
--ON!
SNAP!
WAAAAAH!
SHIIIIINNG!
FFFZZZZZH!
WHOA!
CLICK
CLUNK
CREEEEAAAAK

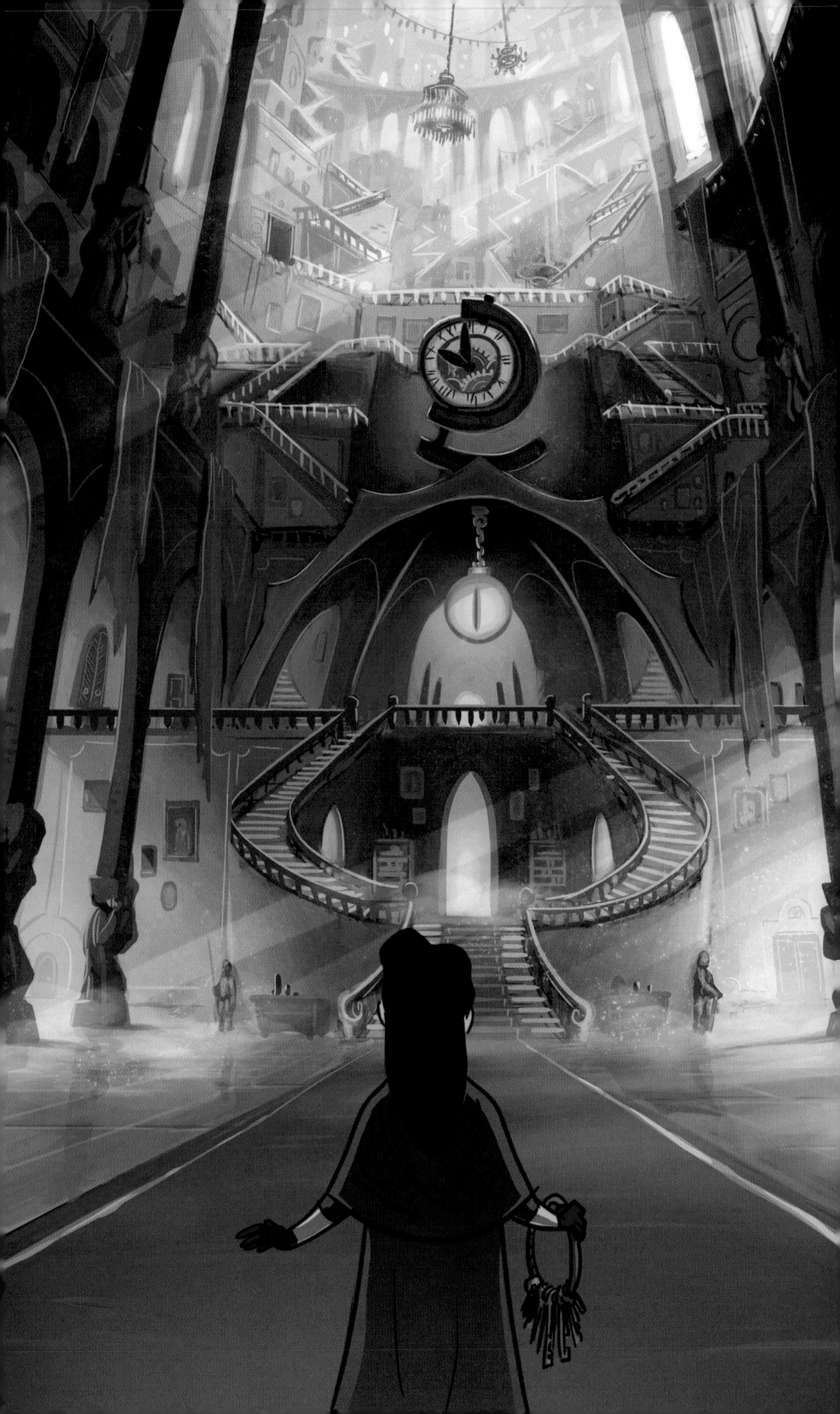

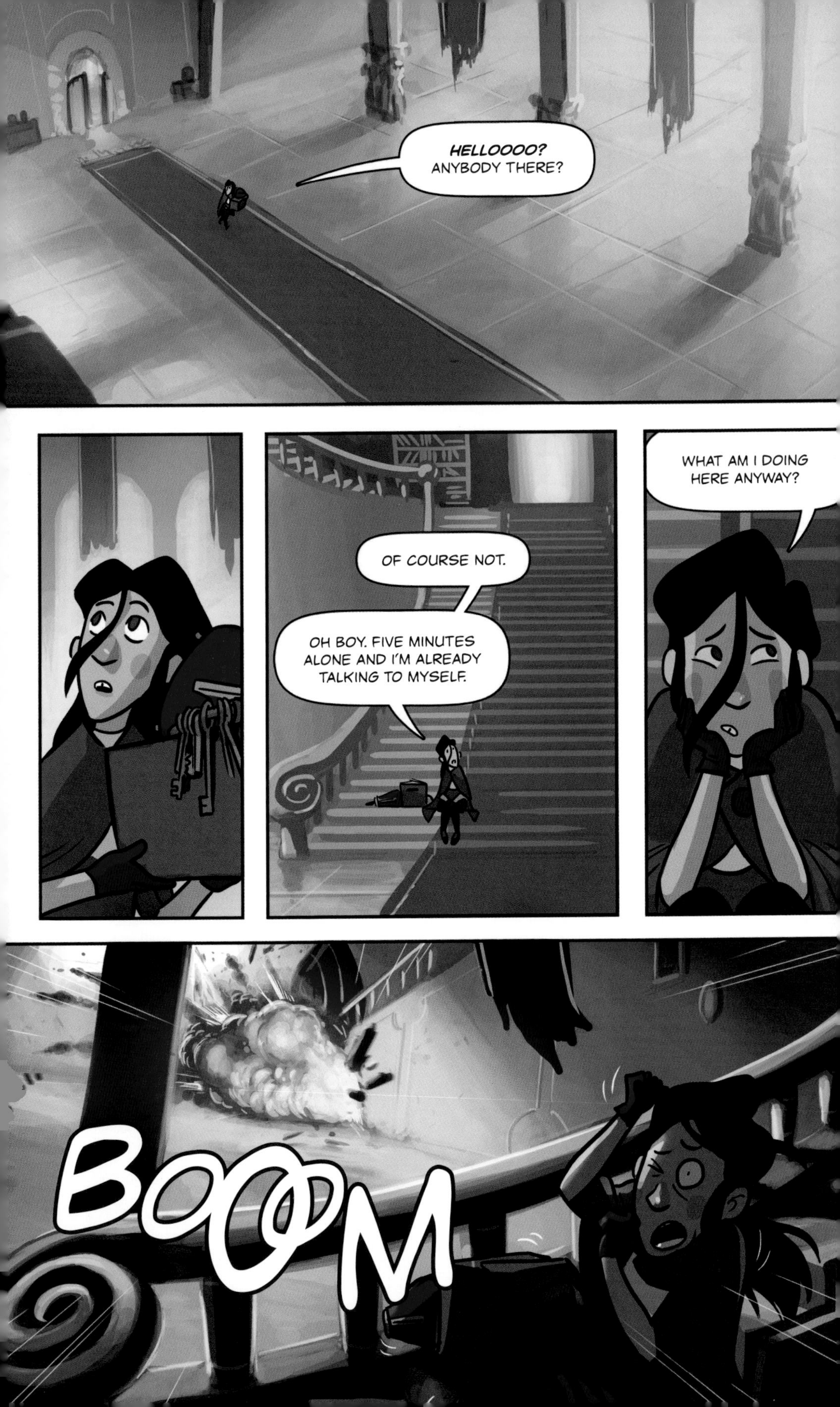

HELLOOOO? ANYBODY THERE?
OF COURSE NOT.
OH BOY. FIVE MINUTES ALONE AND I'M ALREADY TALKING TO MYSELF.
WHAT AM I DOING HERE ANYWAY?
BOOOM

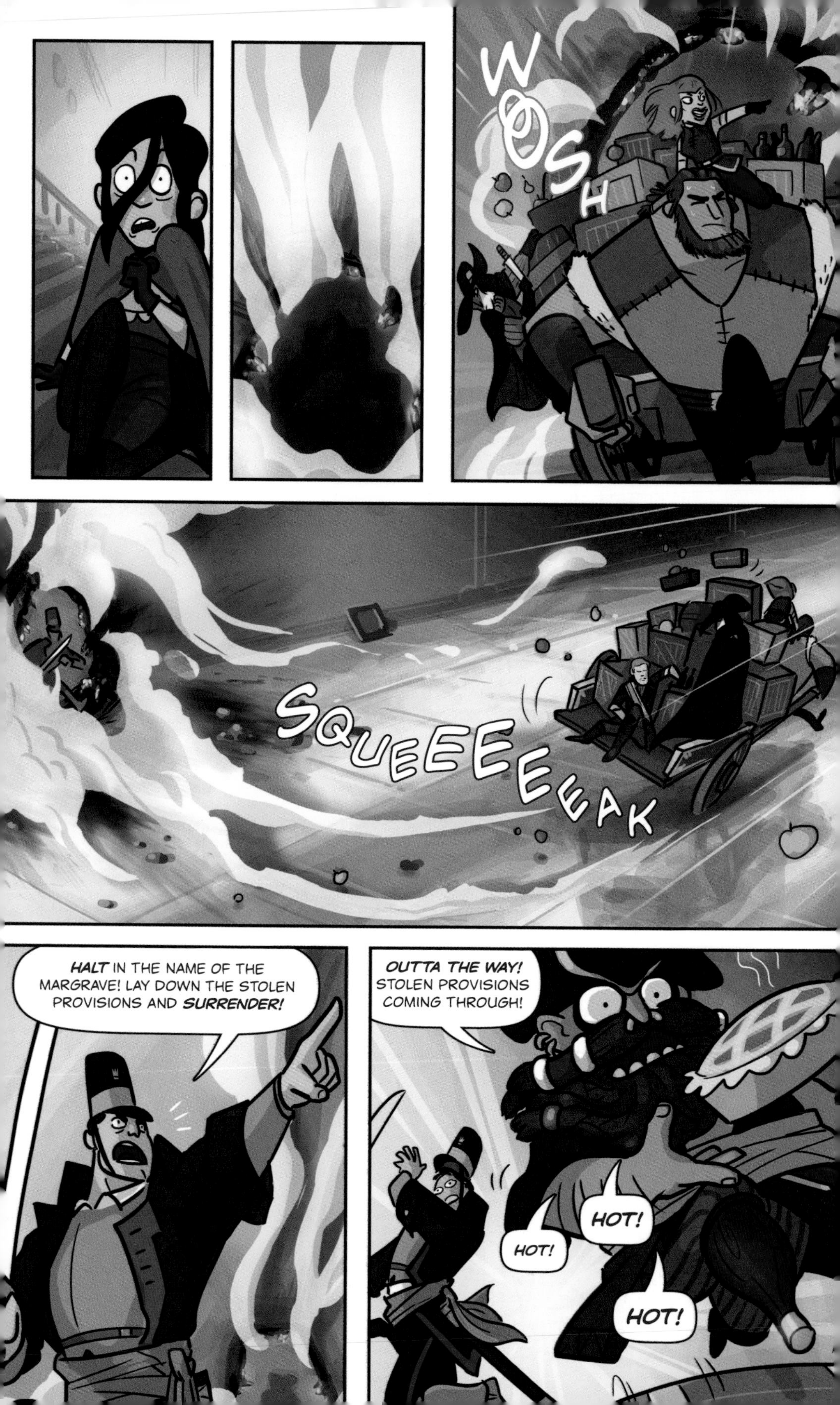
WOOSH
SQUEEEEEAK
HALT IN THE NAME OF THE MARGRAVE! LAY DOWN THE STOLEN PROVISIONS AND SURRENDER!
OUTTA THE WAY! STOLEN PROVISIONS COMING THROUGH!
HOT!
HOT!
HOT!

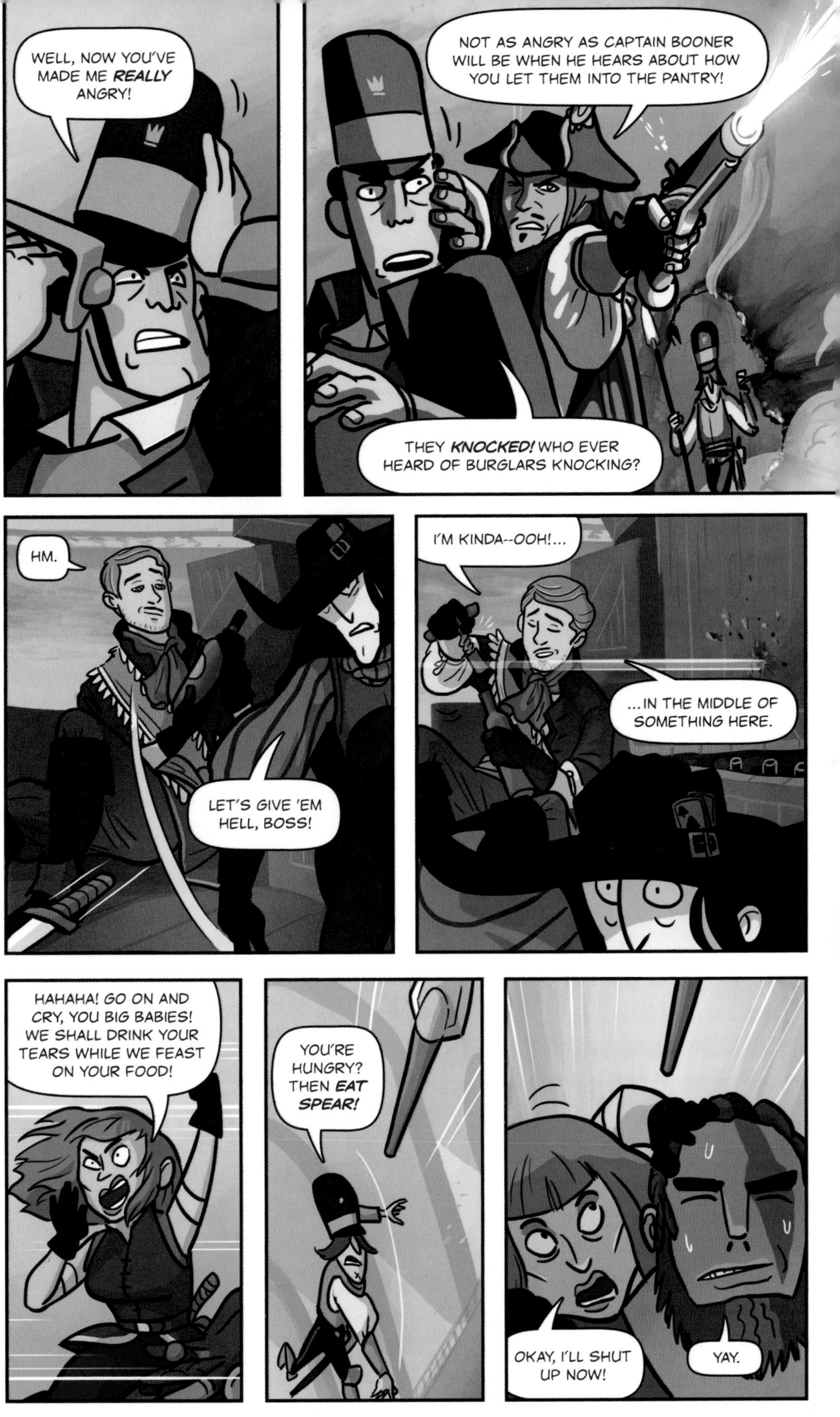
WELL, NOW YOU'VE MADE ME **REALLY** ANGRY!
NOT AS ANGRY AS CAPTAIN BOONER WILL BE WHEN HE HEARS ABOUT HOW YOU LET THEM INTO THE PANTRY!
THEY **KNOCKED!** WHO EVER HEARD OF BURGLARS KNOCKING?
HM.
LET'S GIVE 'EM HELL, BOSS!
I'M KINDA--OOH!...
...IN THE MIDDLE OF SOMETHING HERE.
HAHAHA! GO ON AND CRY, YOU BIG BABIES! WE SHALL DRINK YOUR TEARS WHILE WE FEAST ON YOUR FOOD!
YOU'RE HUNGRY? THEN **EAT SPEAR!**
OKAY, I'LL SHUT UP NOW!
YAY.

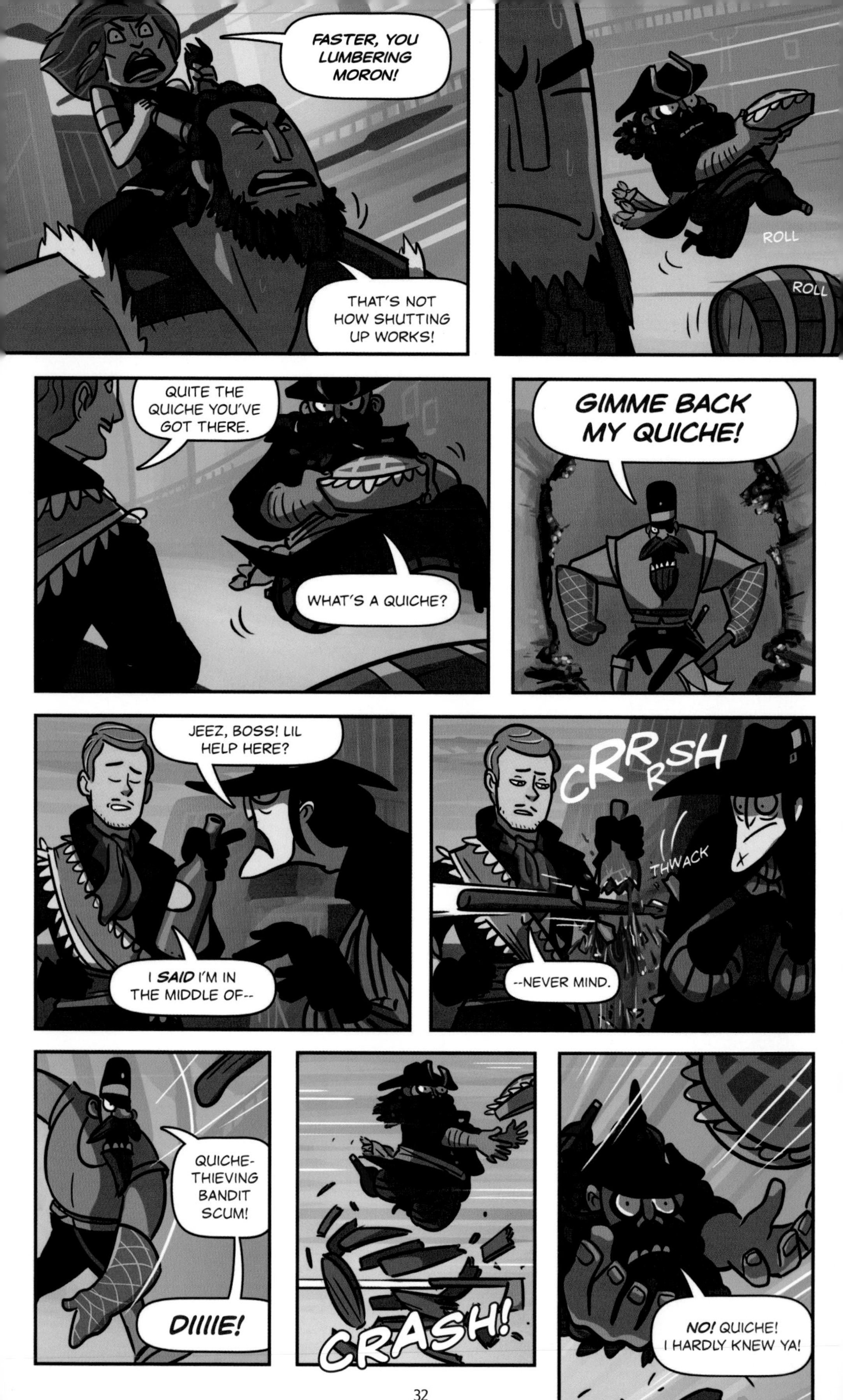

FASTER, YOU LUMBERING MORON!
THAT'S NOT HOW SHUTTING UP WORKS!
ROLL
ROLL
QUITE THE QUICHE YOU'VE GOT THERE.
WHAT'S A QUICHE?
GIMME BACK MY QUICHE!
JEEZ, BOSS! LIL HELP HERE?
I SAID I'M IN THE MIDDLE OF--
CRRRSH
THWACK
--NEVER MIND.
QUICHE-THIEVING BANDIT SCUM!
DIIIIE!
CRASH!
NO! QUICHE! I HARDLY KNEW YA!

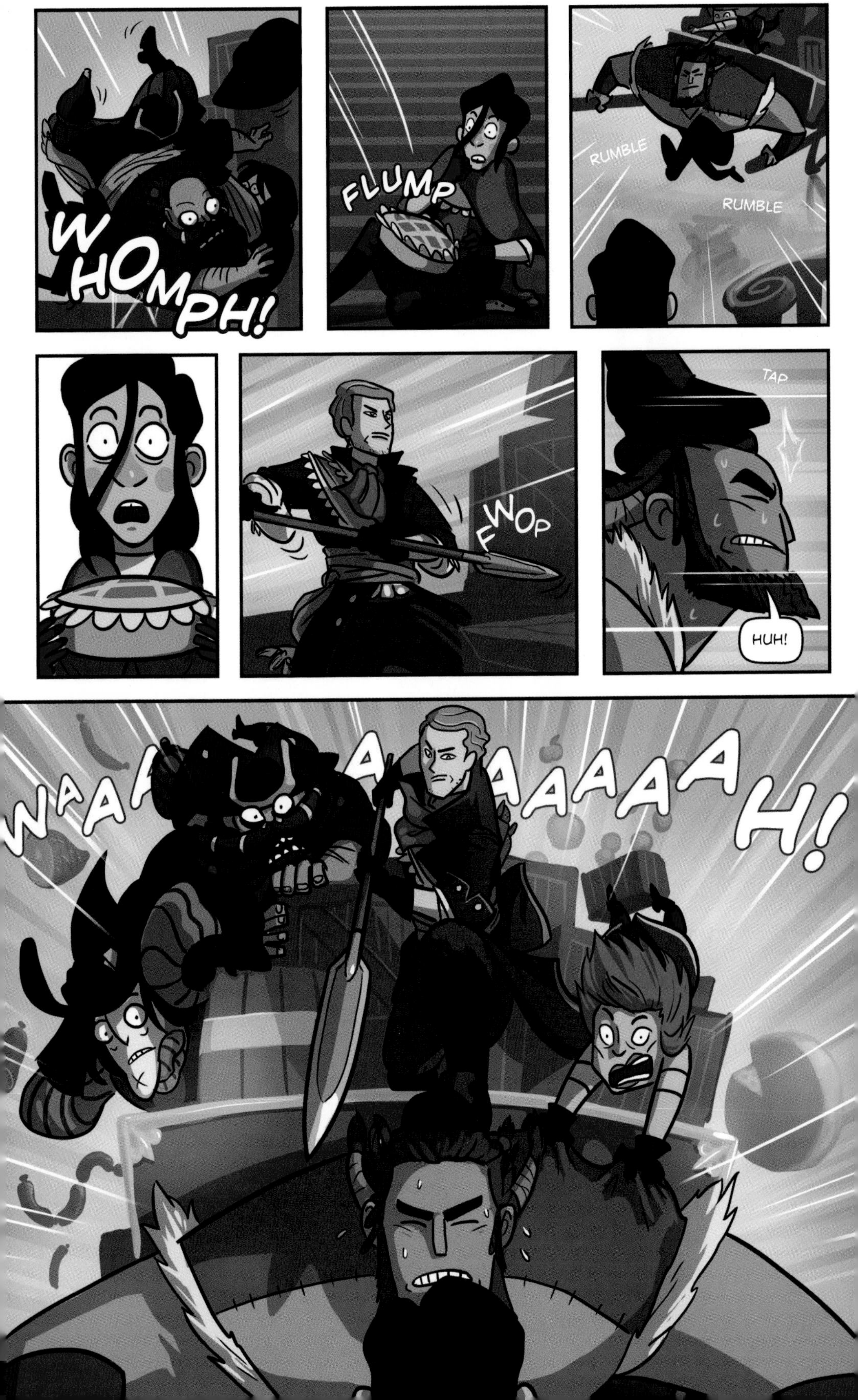
WHOMPH!
FLUMP
RUMBLE
RUMBLE
FWOP
TAP
HUH!
WAAAAAAAAAAH!

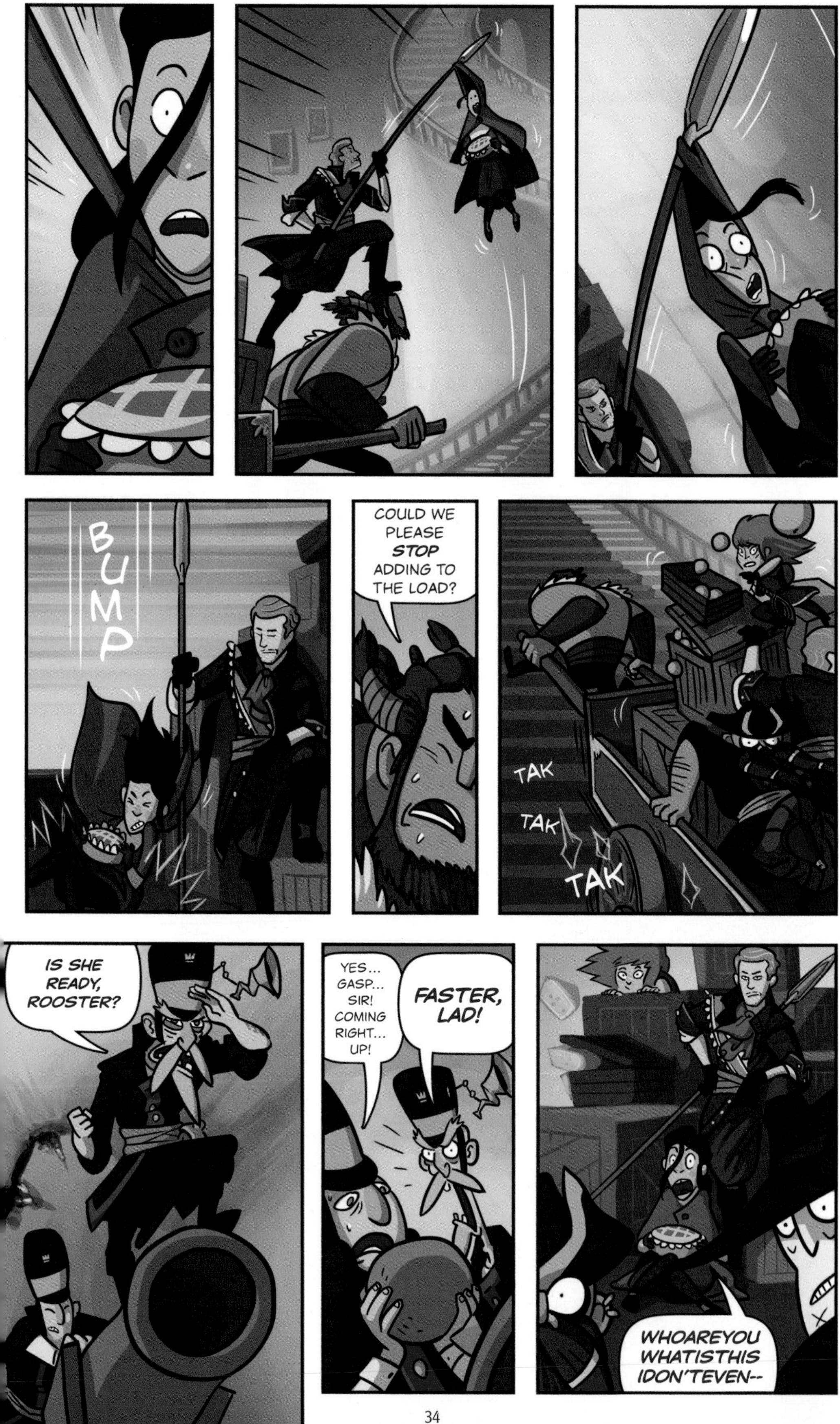
BUMP
COULD WE PLEASE STOP ADDING TO THE LOAD?
TAK
TAK
TAK
IS SHE READY, ROOSTER?
YES... GASP... SIR! COMING RIGHT... UP!
FASTER, LAD!
WHOAREYOU WHATISTHIS IDON'TEVEN--

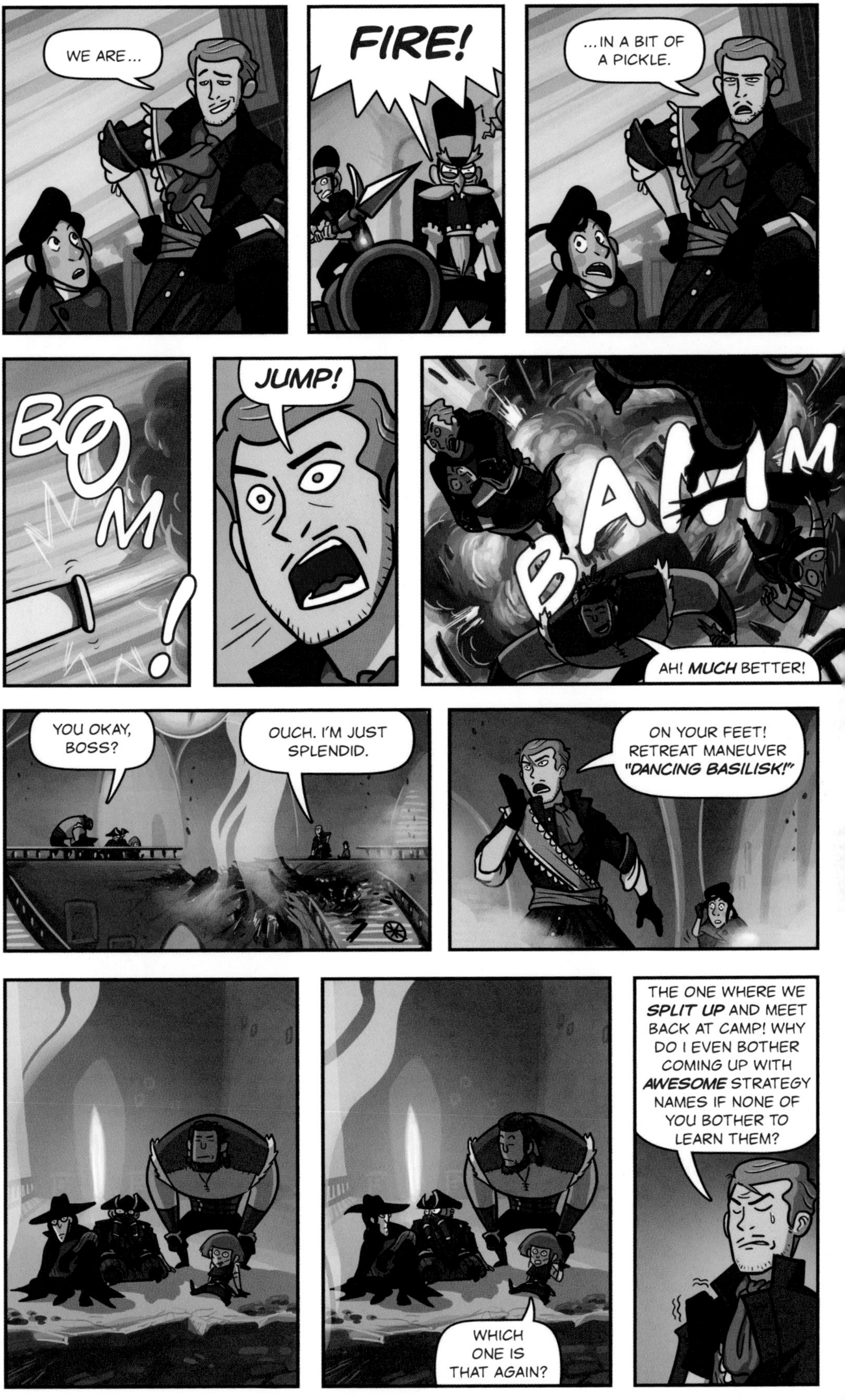
WE ARE...
FIRE!
...IN A BIT OF A PICKLE.
BOOM!
JUMP!
BAMM
AH! MUCH BETTER!
YOU OKAY, BOSS?
OUCH. I'M JUST SPLENDID.
ON YOUR FEET! RETREAT MANEUVER "DANCING BASILISK!"
WHICH ONE IS THAT AGAIN?
THE ONE WHERE WE SPLIT UP AND MEET BACK AT CAMP! WHY DO I EVEN BOTHER COMING UP WITH AWESOME STRATEGY NAMES IF NONE OF YOU BOTHER TO LEARN THEM?

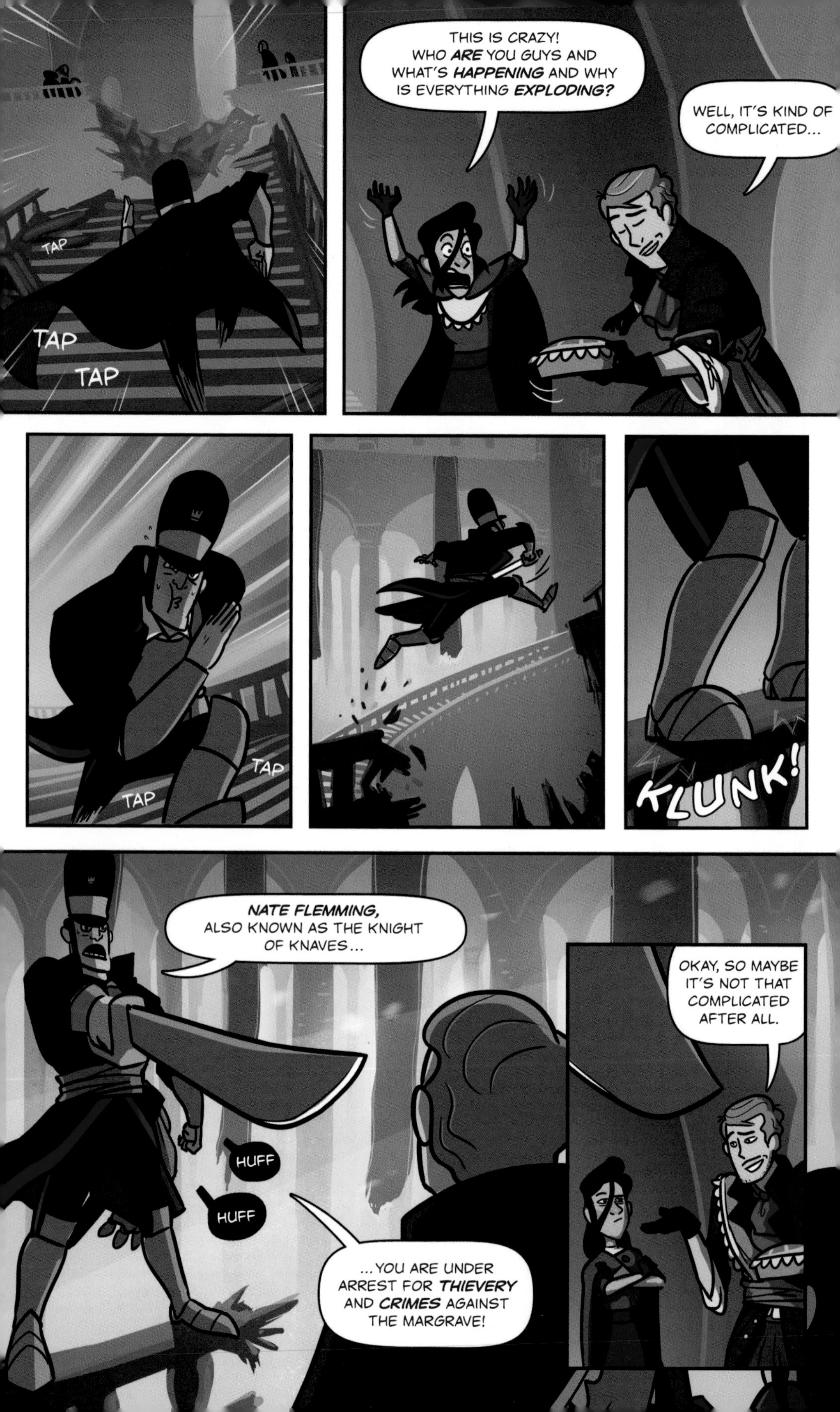

TAP
TAP
TAP
THIS IS CRAZY! WHO *ARE* YOU GUYS AND WHAT'S *HAPPENING* AND WHY IS EVERYTHING *EXPLODING?*
WELL, IT'S KIND OF COMPLICATED...
TAP
TAP
KLUNK!
NATE FLEMMING, ALSO KNOWN AS THE KNIGHT OF KNAVES...
HUFF
HUFF
...YOU ARE UNDER ARREST FOR *THIEVERY* AND *CRIMES* AGAINST THE MARGRAVE!
OKAY, SO MAYBE IT'S NOT THAT COMPLICATED AFTER ALL.

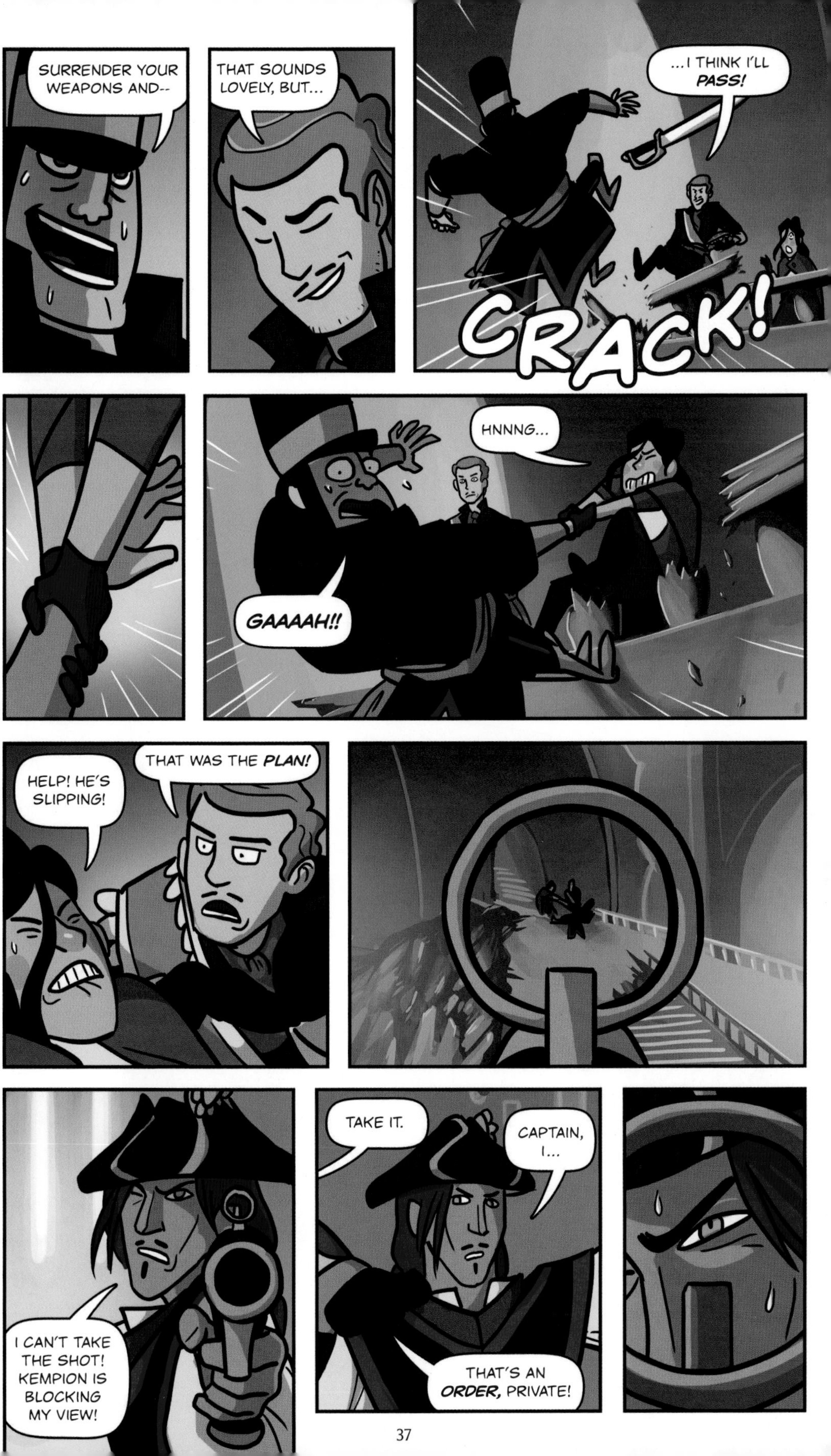
SURRENDER YOUR WEAPONS AND--
THAT SOUNDS LOVELY, BUT...
...I THINK I'LL PASS!
CRACK!
HNNNG...
GAAAAH!!
HELP! HE'S SLIPPING!
THAT WAS THE PLAN!
I CAN'T TAKE THE SHOT! KEMPION IS BLOCKING MY VIEW!
TAKE IT.
CAPTAIN, I...
THAT'S AN ORDER, PRIVATE!

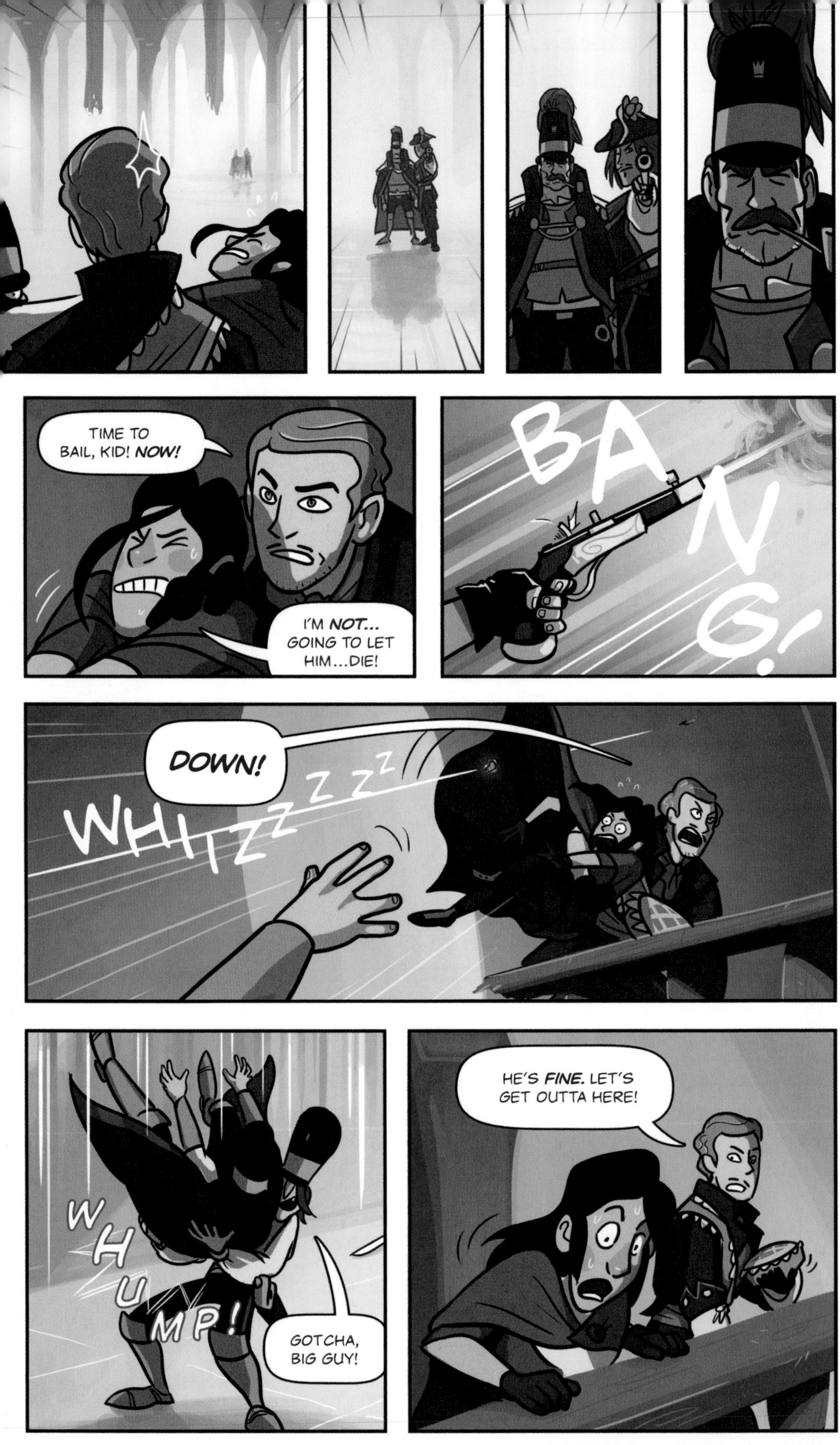
TIME TO BAIL, KID! **NOW!**
I'M **NOT...** GOING TO LET HIM...DIE!
BANG!
DOWN!
WHIZZZZZ
WHUMP!
GOTCHA, BIG GUY!
HE'S **FINE.** LET'S GET OUTTA HERE!

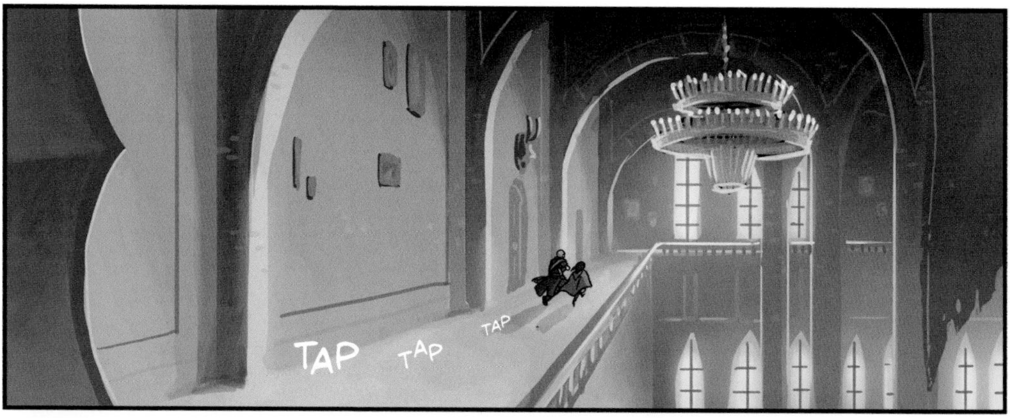
TAP TAP TAP

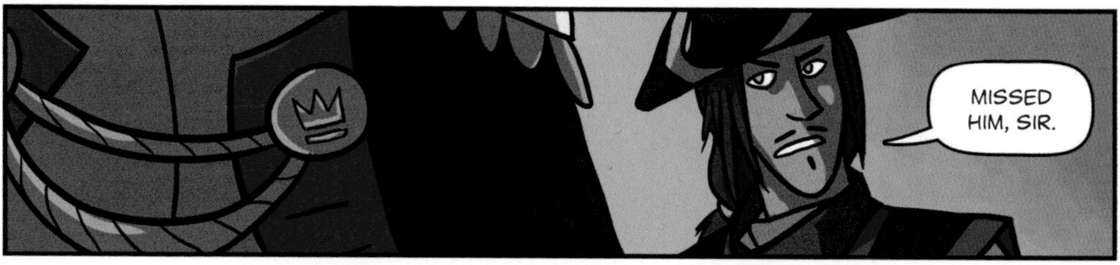
MISSED HIM, SIR.

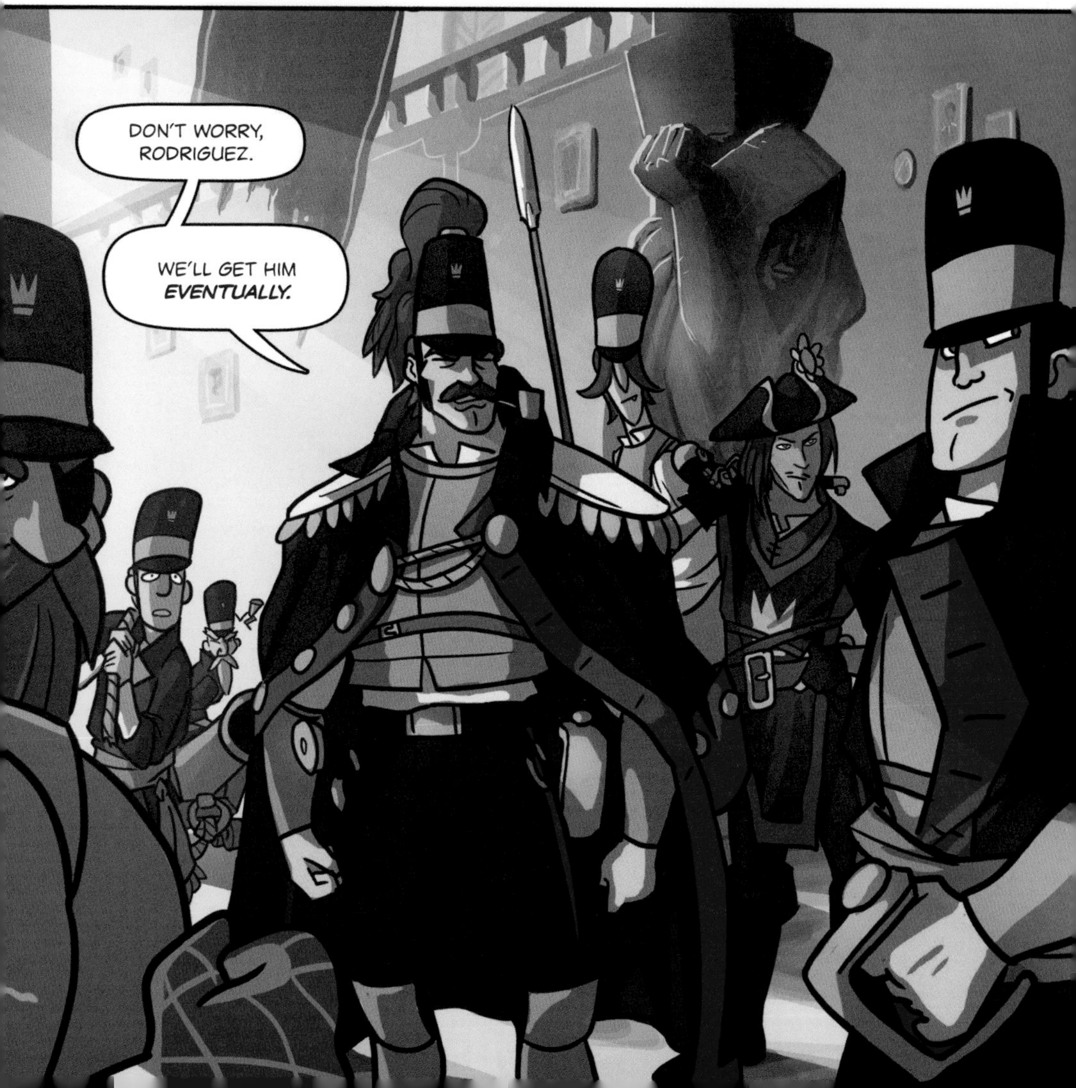
DON'T WORRY, RODRIGUEZ.
WE'LL GET HIM *EVENTUALLY.*

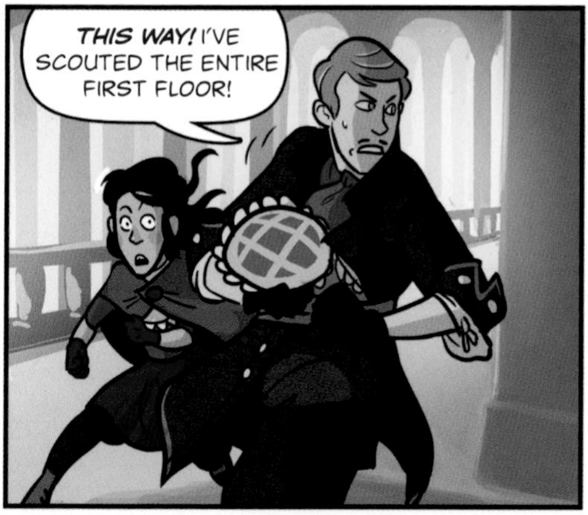
THIS WAY! I'VE SCOUTED THE ENTIRE FIRST FLOOR!

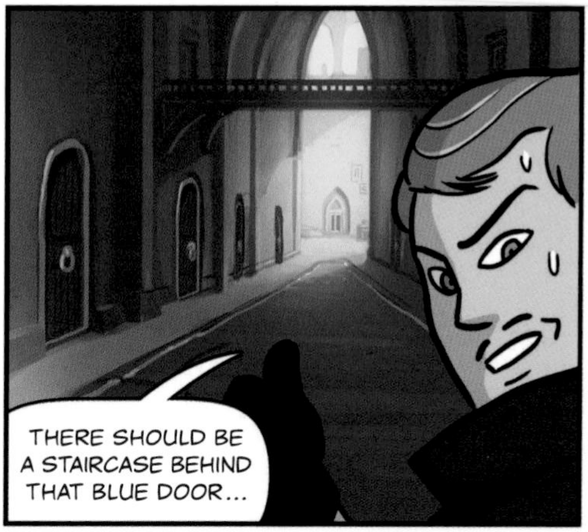
THERE SHOULD BE A STAIRCASE BEHIND THAT BLUE DOOR...

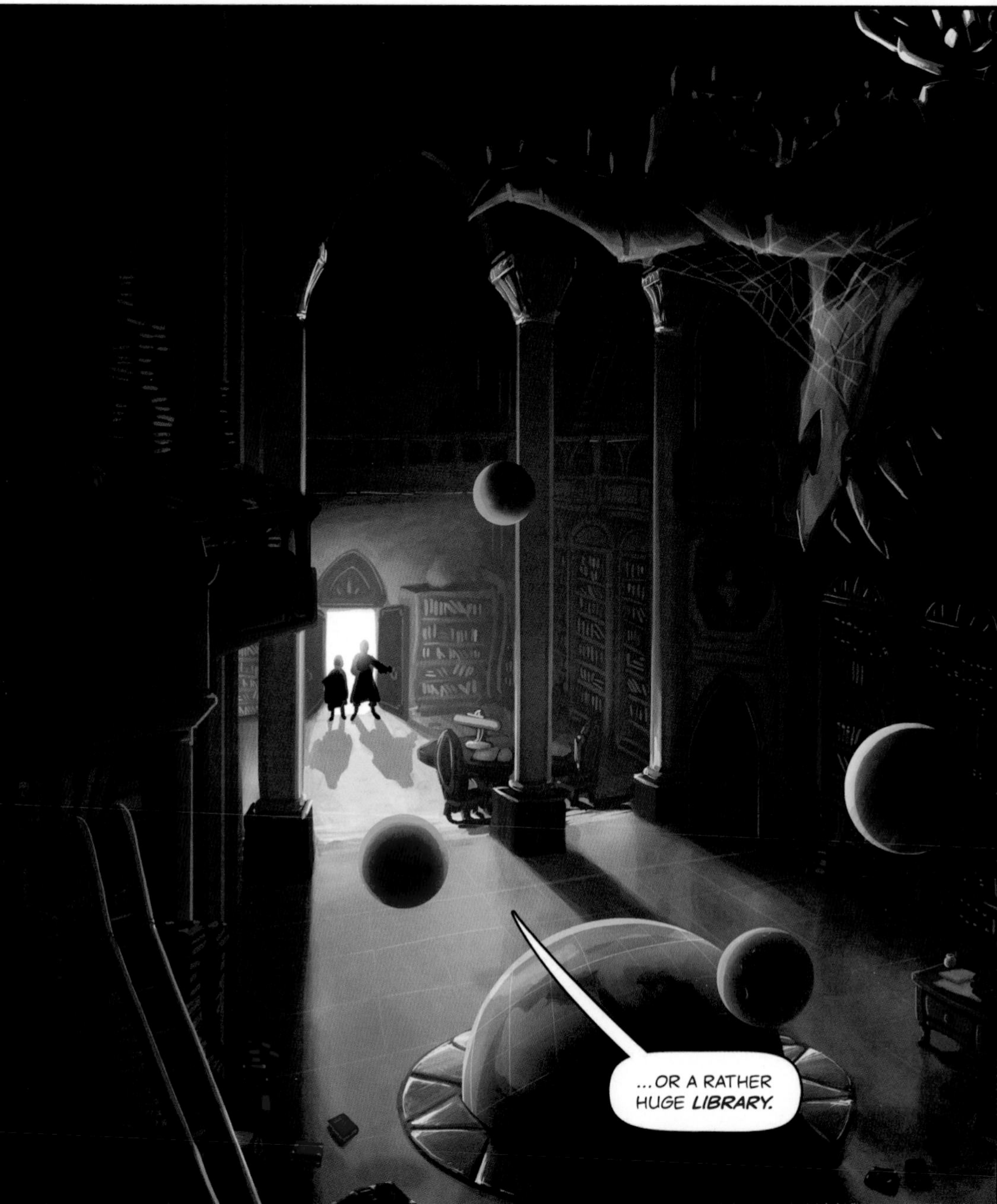
...OR A RATHER HUGE LIBRARY.

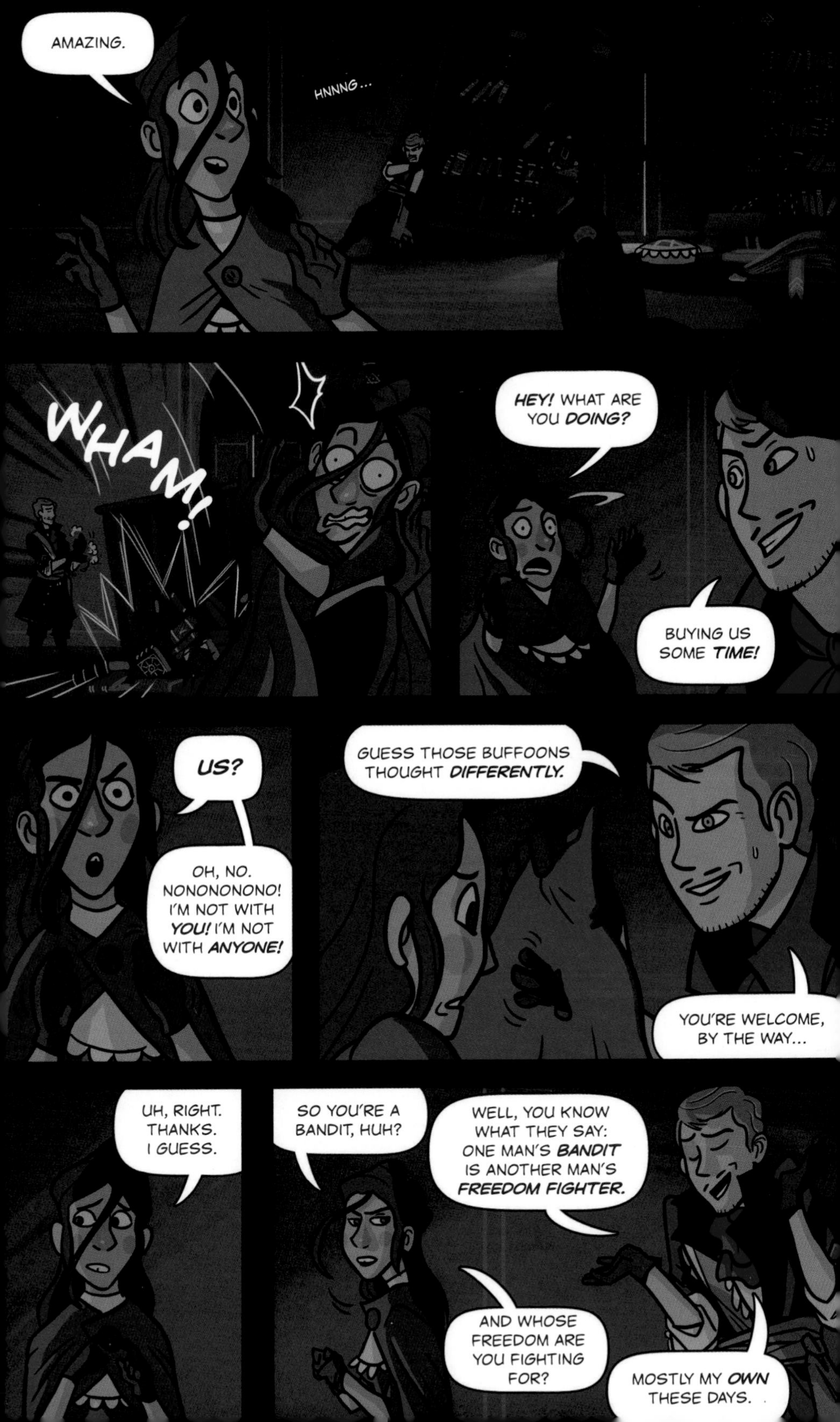
AMAZING.
HNNNG...
WHAM!
HEY! WHAT ARE YOU DOING?
BUYING US SOME TIME!
US?
OH, NO. NONONONONO! I'M NOT WITH YOU! I'M NOT WITH ANYONE!
GUESS THOSE BUFFOONS THOUGHT DIFFERENTLY.
YOU'RE WELCOME, BY THE WAY...
UH, RIGHT. THANKS. I GUESS.
SO YOU'RE A BANDIT, HUH?
WELL, YOU KNOW WHAT THEY SAY: ONE MAN'S BANDIT IS ANOTHER MAN'S FREEDOM FIGHTER.
AND WHOSE FREEDOM ARE YOU FIGHTING FOR?
MOSTLY MY OWN THESE DAYS.

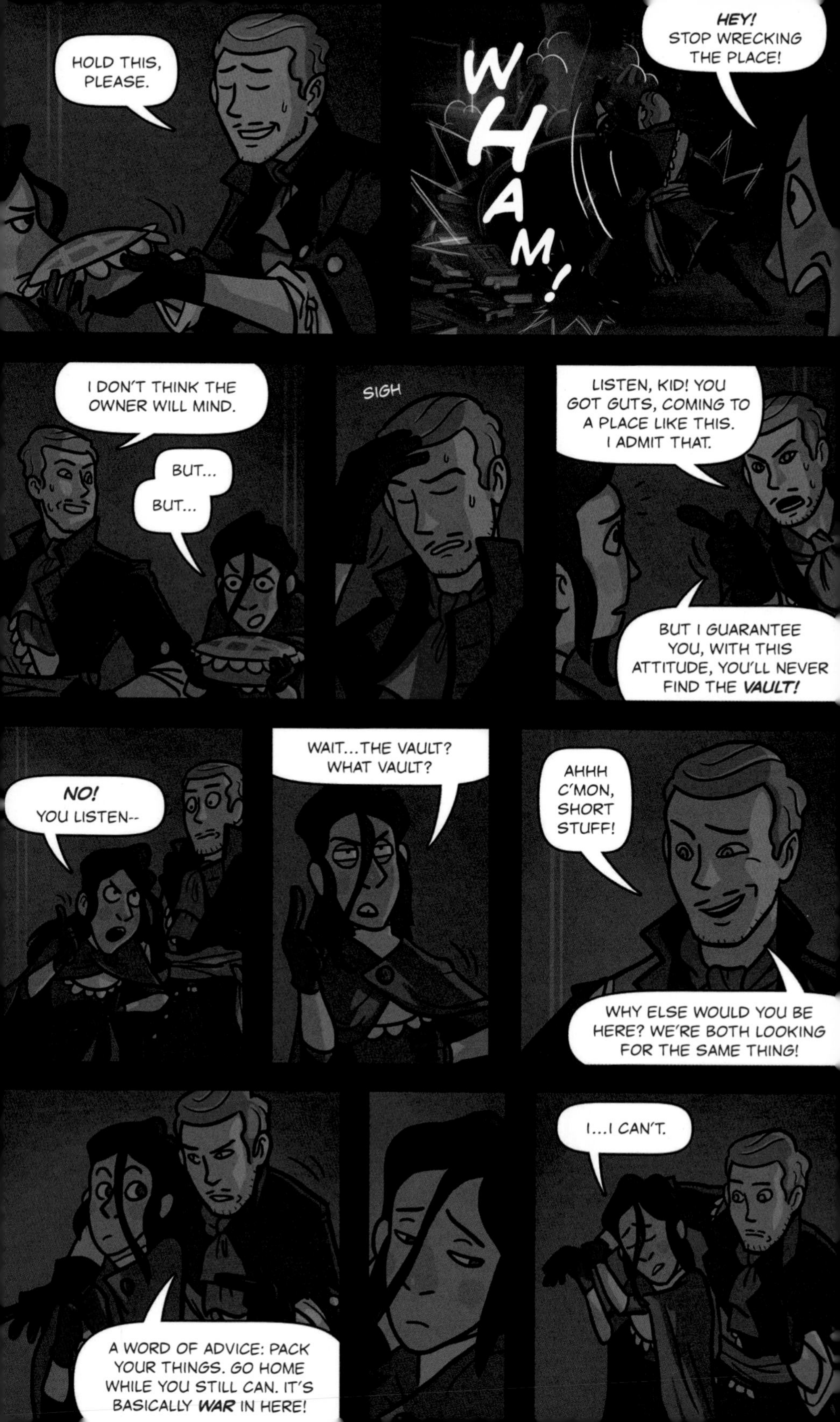
HOLD THIS, PLEASE.
WHAM!
HEY! STOP WRECKING THE PLACE!
I DON'T THINK THE OWNER WILL MIND.
BUT...
BUT...
SIGH
LISTEN, KID! YOU GOT GUTS, COMING TO A PLACE LIKE THIS. I ADMIT THAT.
BUT I GUARANTEE YOU, WITH THIS ATTITUDE, YOU'LL NEVER FIND THE VAULT!
NO! YOU LISTEN--
WAIT...THE VAULT? WHAT VAULT?
AHHH C'MON, SHORT STUFF!
WHY ELSE WOULD YOU BE HERE? WE'RE BOTH LOOKING FOR THE SAME THING!
A WORD OF ADVICE: PACK YOUR THINGS. GO HOME WHILE YOU STILL CAN. IT'S BASICALLY WAR IN HERE!
I...I CAN'T.

YOU'RE A *RUNAWAY*, HUH?

TOUGH LUCK THEN.

NOW HOW DO I GET OUT OF HERE?

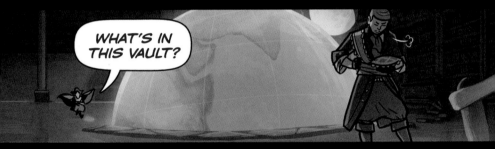
WHAT'S IN THIS VAULT?

YOU'RE PROBABLY TOO YOUNG TO REMEMBER THE LAST DAYS OF THE GRAND WAR...

NO, I'M *NOT!*

OH-KAAAY...

WELL THEN.

PUFF

PUFF

IN THE LAST DAYS OF THE WAR, THINGS LOOKED BAD FOR US.

I MEAN *REALLY* BAD.

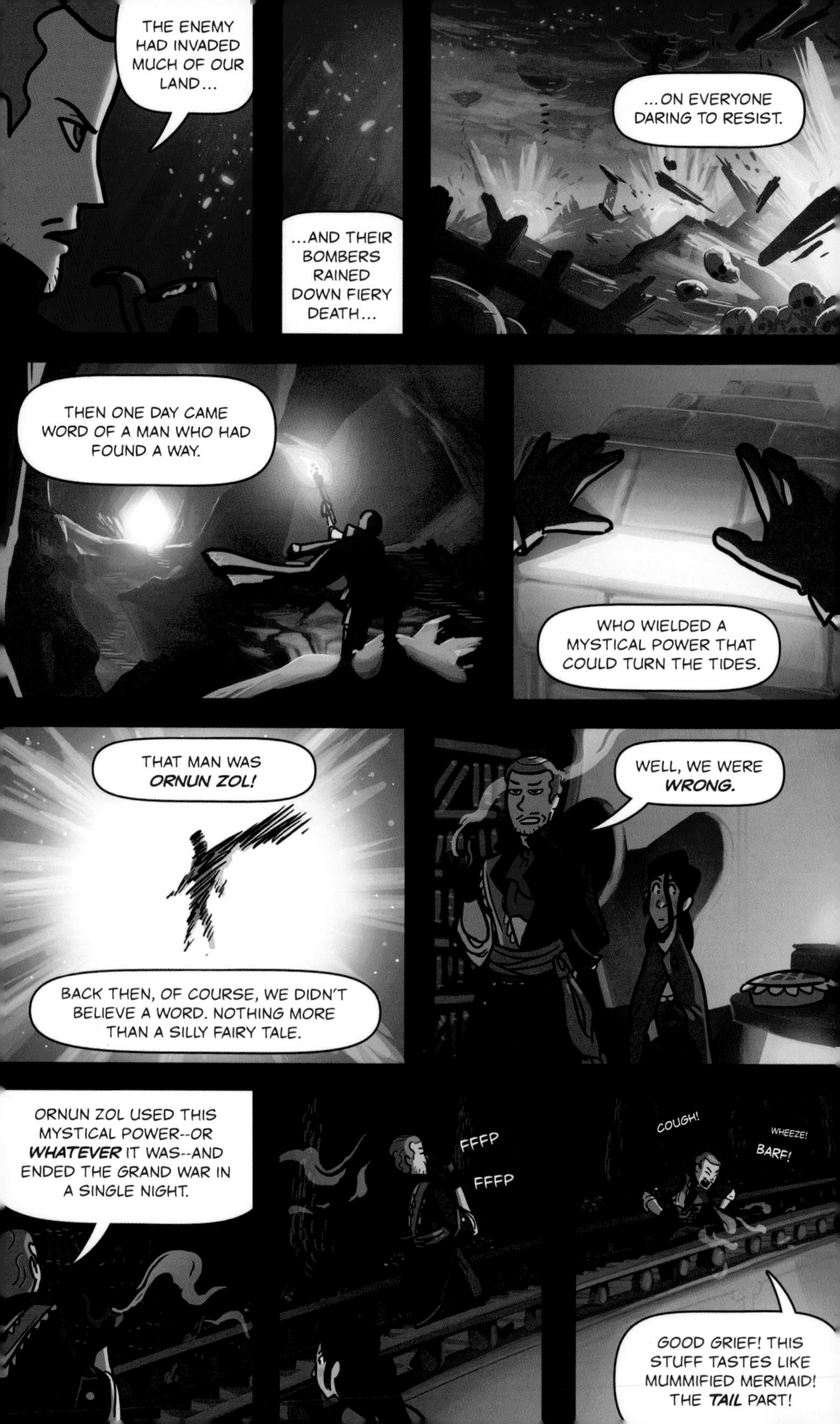

THE ENEMY HAD INVADED MUCH OF OUR LAND...
...AND THEIR BOMBERS RAINED DOWN FIERY DEATH...
...ON EVERYONE DARING TO RESIST.
THEN ONE DAY CAME WORD OF A MAN WHO HAD FOUND A WAY.
WHO WIELDED A MYSTICAL POWER THAT COULD TURN THE TIDES.
THAT MAN WAS ORNUN ZOL!
BACK THEN, OF COURSE, WE DIDN'T BELIEVE A WORD. NOTHING MORE THAN A SILLY FAIRY TALE.
WELL, WE WERE WRONG.
ORNUN ZOL USED THIS MYSTICAL POWER--OR WHATEVER IT WAS--AND ENDED THE GRAND WAR IN A SINGLE NIGHT.
FFFP
FFFP
COUGH!
WHEEZE!
BARF!
GOOD GRIEF! THIS STUFF TASTES LIKE MUMMIFIED MERMAID! THE TAIL PART!

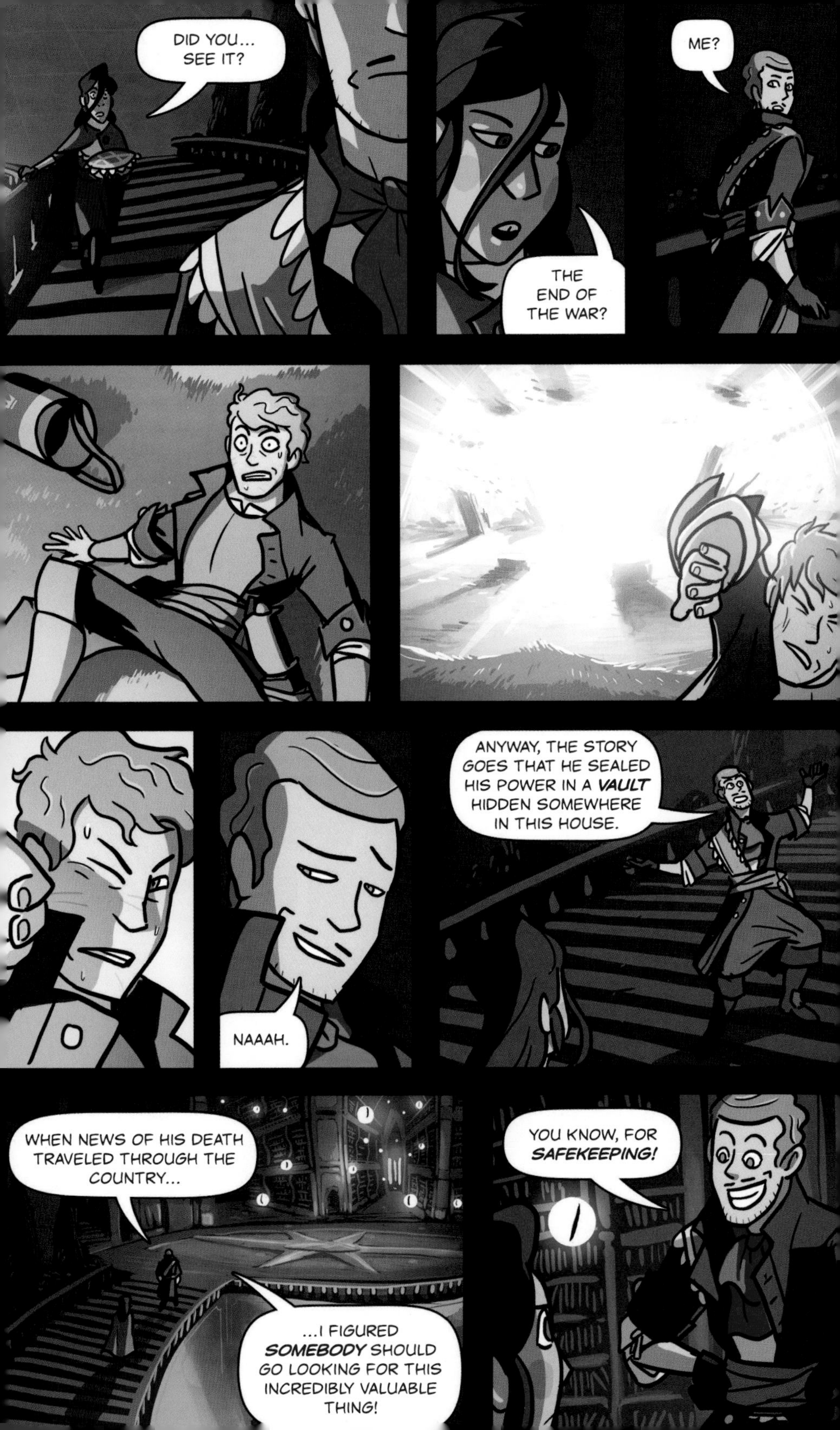

DID YOU... SEE IT?
ME?
THE END OF THE WAR?
ANYWAY, THE STORY GOES THAT HE SEALED HIS POWER IN A ***VAULT*** HIDDEN SOMEWHERE IN THIS HOUSE.
NAAAH.
WHEN NEWS OF HIS DEATH TRAVELED THROUGH THE COUNTRY...
...I FIGURED ***SOMEBODY*** SHOULD GO LOOKING FOR THIS INCREDIBLY VALUABLE THING!
YOU KNOW, FOR ***SAFEKEEPING!***

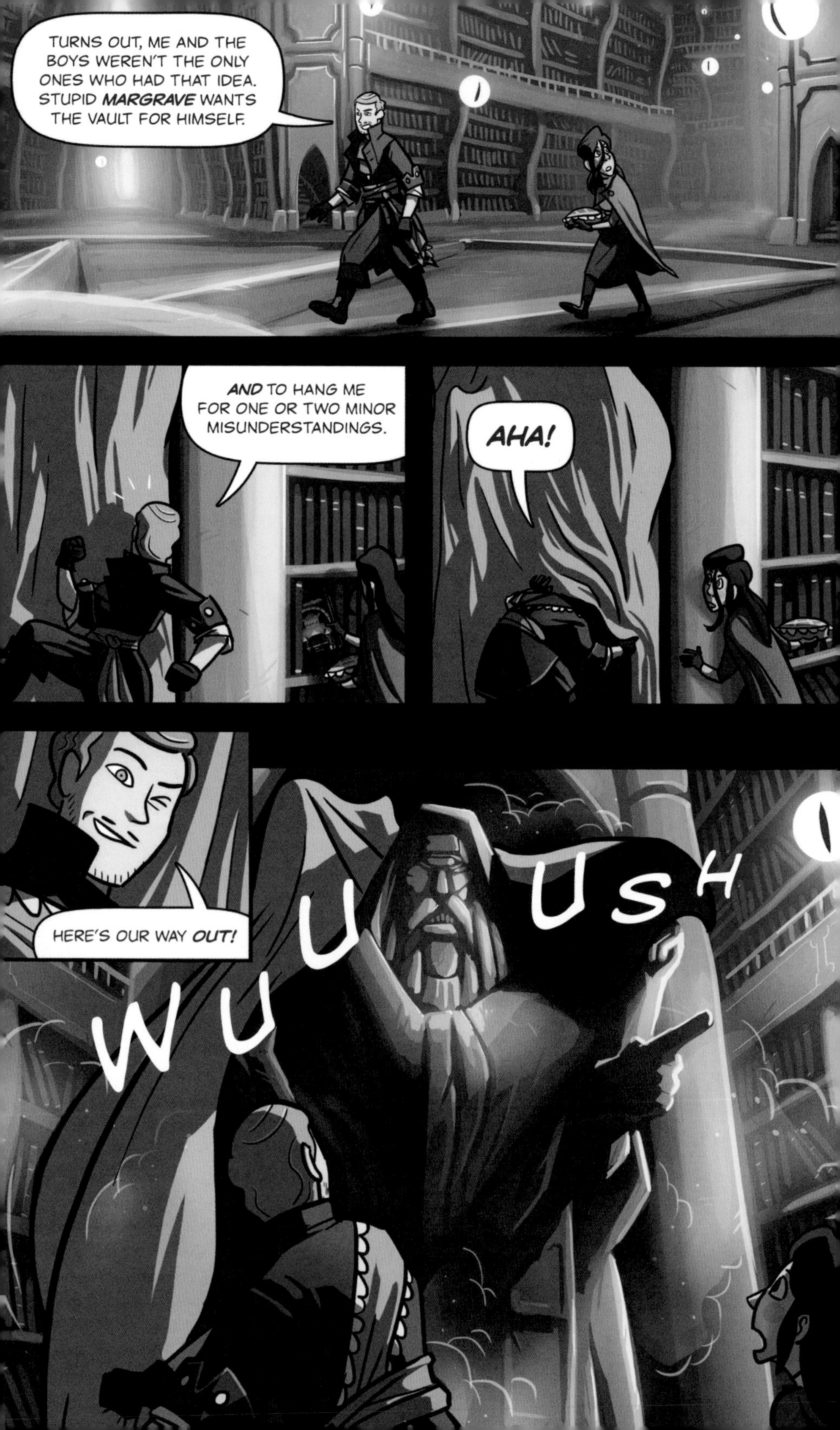
TURNS OUT, ME AND THE BOYS WEREN'T THE ONLY ONES WHO HAD THAT IDEA. STUPID MARGRAVE WANTS THE VAULT FOR HIMSELF.
AND TO HANG ME FOR ONE OR TWO MINOR MISUNDERSTANDINGS.
AHA!
HERE'S OUR WAY OUT!
WUUUSH

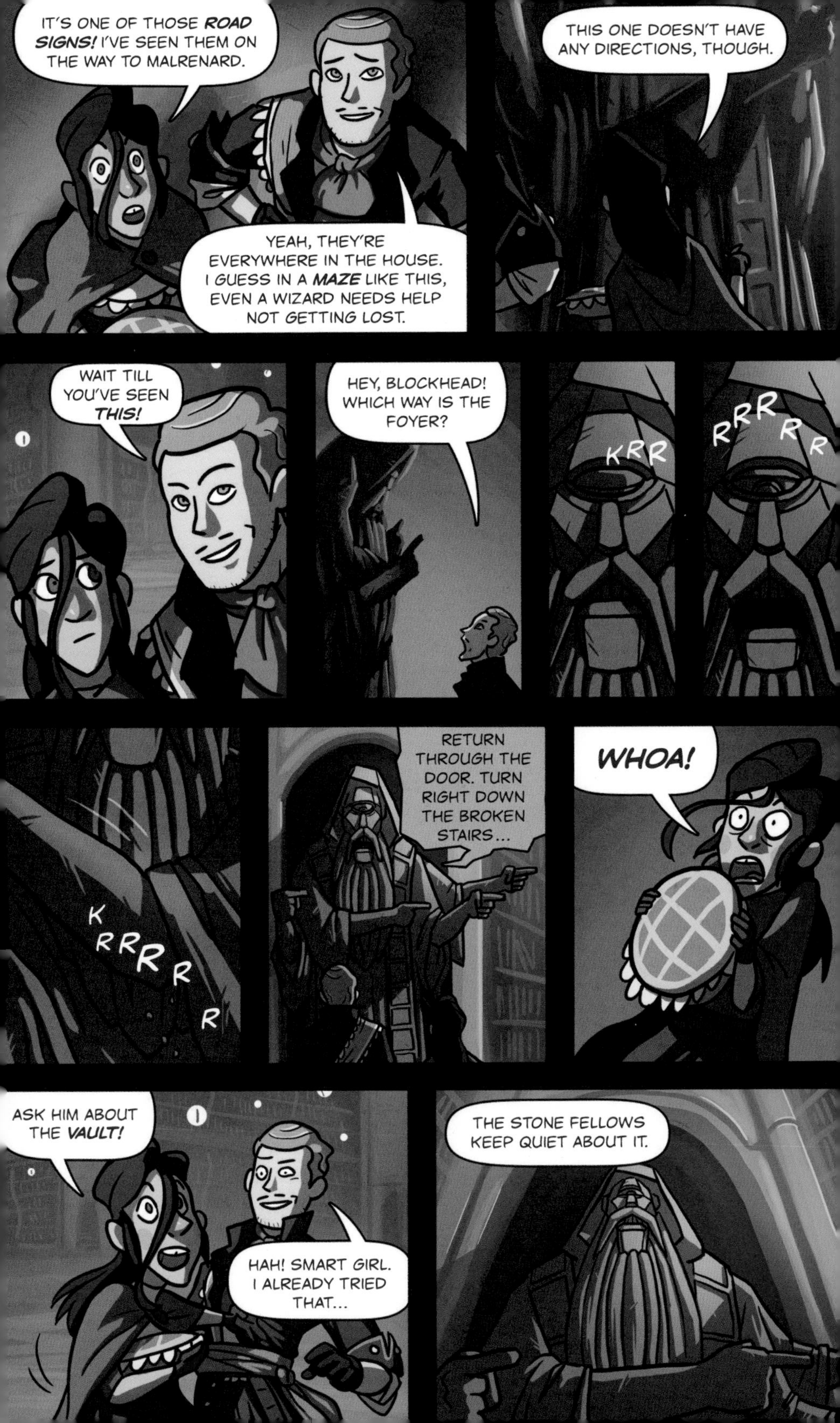
IT'S ONE OF THOSE ROAD SIGNS! I'VE SEEN THEM ON THE WAY TO MALRENARD.
YEAH, THEY'RE EVERYWHERE IN THE HOUSE. I GUESS IN A MAZE LIKE THIS, EVEN A WIZARD NEEDS HELP NOT GETTING LOST.
THIS ONE DOESN'T HAVE ANY DIRECTIONS, THOUGH.
WAIT TILL YOU'VE SEEN THIS!
HEY, BLOCKHEAD! WHICH WAY IS THE FOYER?
KRR
RRRRR
KRRRRRR
RETURN THROUGH THE DOOR. TURN RIGHT DOWN THE BROKEN STAIRS...
WHOA!
ASK HIM ABOUT THE VAULT!
HAH! SMART GIRL. I ALREADY TRIED THAT...
THE STONE FELLOWS KEEP QUIET ABOUT IT.

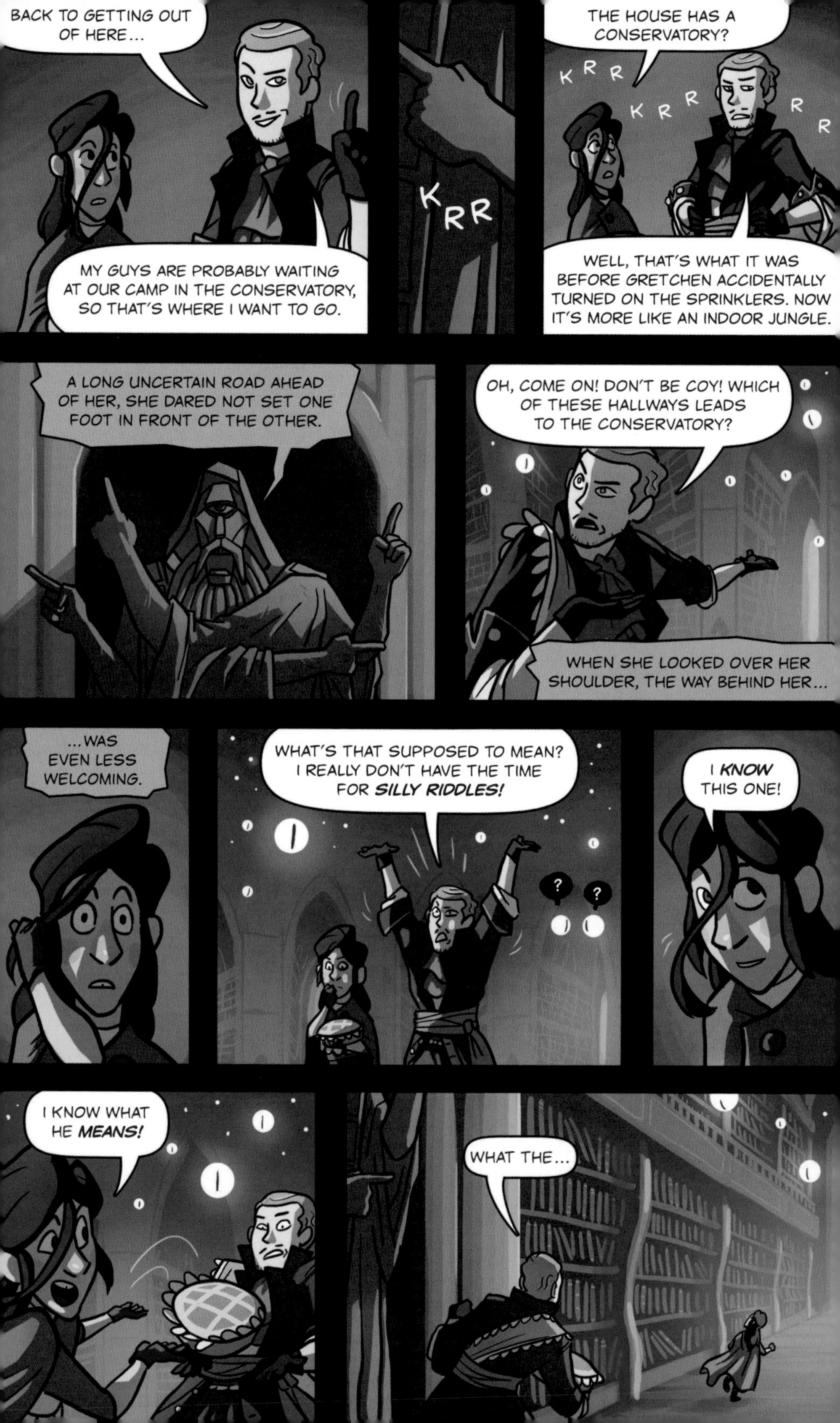
BACK TO GETTING OUT OF HERE...
MY GUYS ARE PROBABLY WAITING AT OUR CAMP IN THE CONSERVATORY, SO THAT'S WHERE I WANT TO GO.
KRR
THE HOUSE HAS A CONSERVATORY?
KRR KRR RR
WELL, THAT'S WHAT IT WAS BEFORE GRETCHEN ACCIDENTALLY TURNED ON THE SPRINKLERS. NOW IT'S MORE LIKE AN INDOOR JUNGLE.
A LONG UNCERTAIN ROAD AHEAD OF HER, SHE DARED NOT SET ONE FOOT IN FRONT OF THE OTHER.
OH, COME ON! DON'T BE COY! WHICH OF THESE HALLWAYS LEADS TO THE CONSERVATORY?
WHEN SHE LOOKED OVER HER SHOULDER, THE WAY BEHIND HER...
...WAS EVEN LESS WELCOMING.
WHAT'S THAT SUPPOSED TO MEAN? I REALLY DON'T HAVE THE TIME FOR ***SILLY RIDDLES!***
? ?
I ***KNOW*** THIS ONE!
I KNOW WHAT HE ***MEANS!***
WHAT THE...

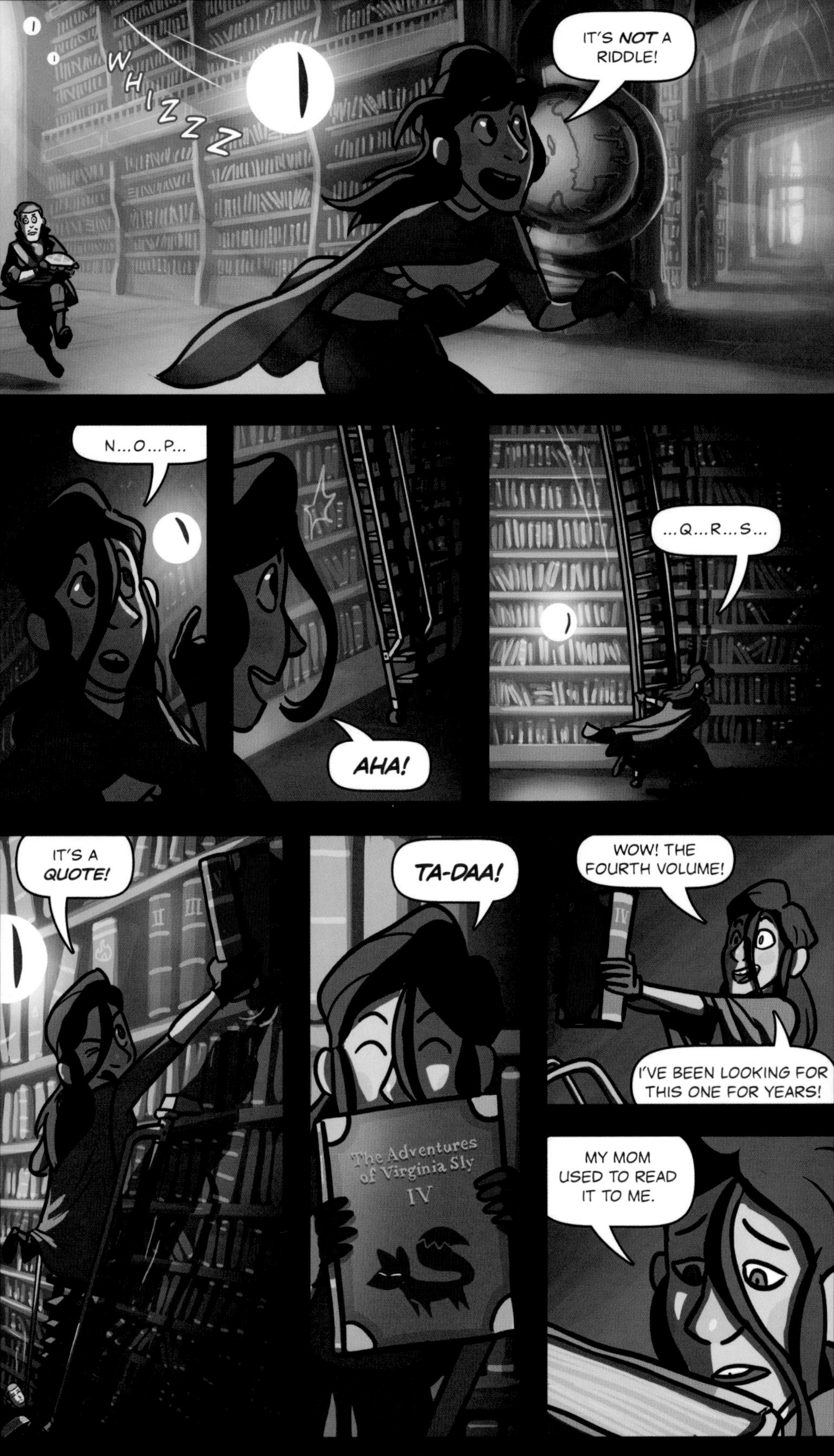
WHIZZZ
IT'S NOT A RIDDLE!
N...O...P...
AHA!
...Q...R...S...
IT'S A QUOTE!
TA-DAA!
The Adventures of Virginia Sly IV
WOW! THE FOURTH VOLUME!
I'VE BEEN LOOKING FOR THIS ONE FOR YEARS!
MY MOM USED TO READ IT TO ME.

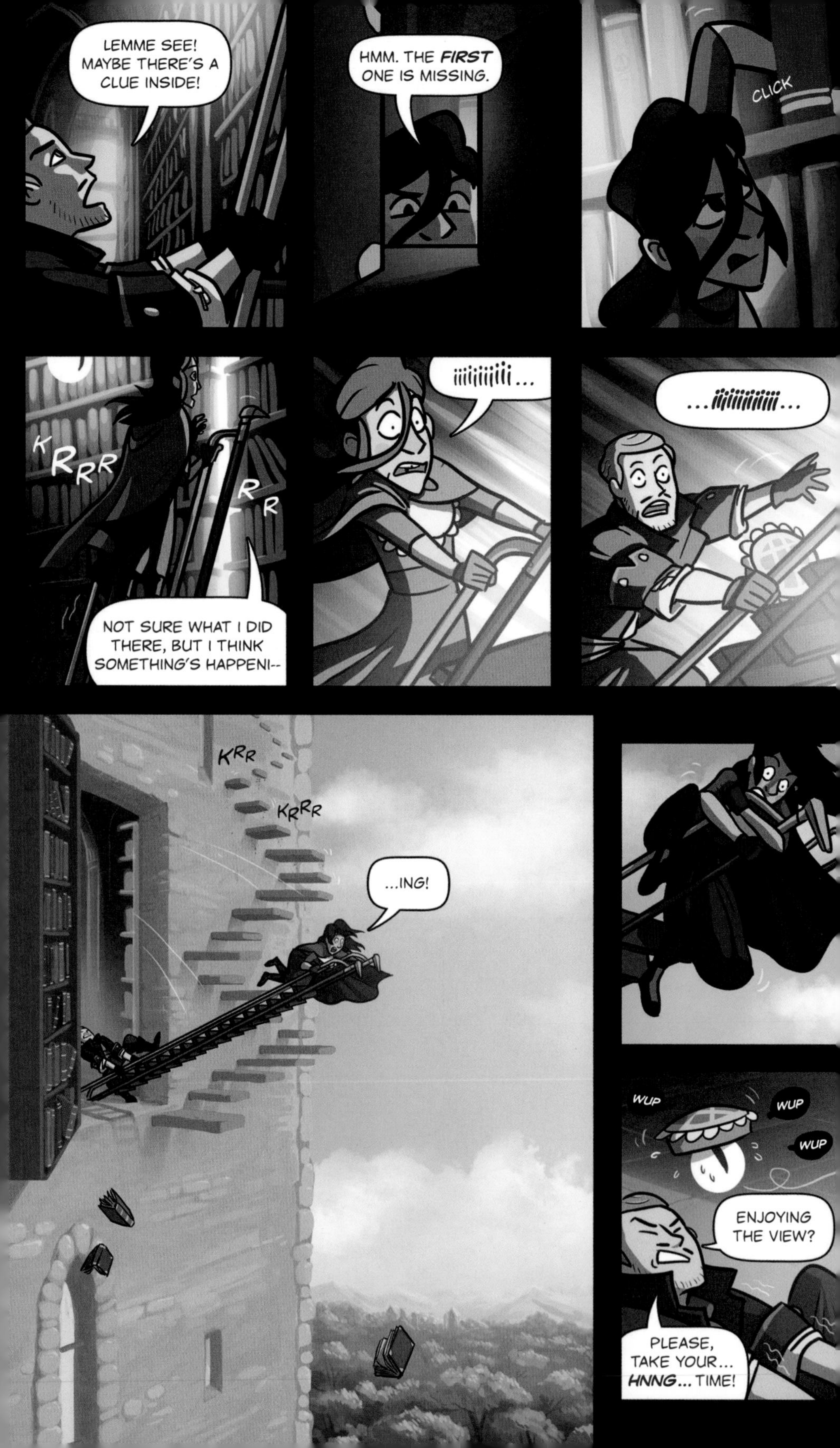
LEMME SEE! MAYBE THERE'S A CLUE INSIDE!
HMM. THE **FIRST** ONE IS MISSING.
CLICK
KRRR
RR
NOT SURE WHAT I DID THERE, BUT I THINK SOMETHING'S HAPPENI--
iiiiiiiiii...
...iiiiiiiiiii...
KRR
KRRR
...ING!
WUP
WUP
WUP
ENJOYING THE VIEW?
PLEASE, TAKE YOUR... **HNNG...** TIME!

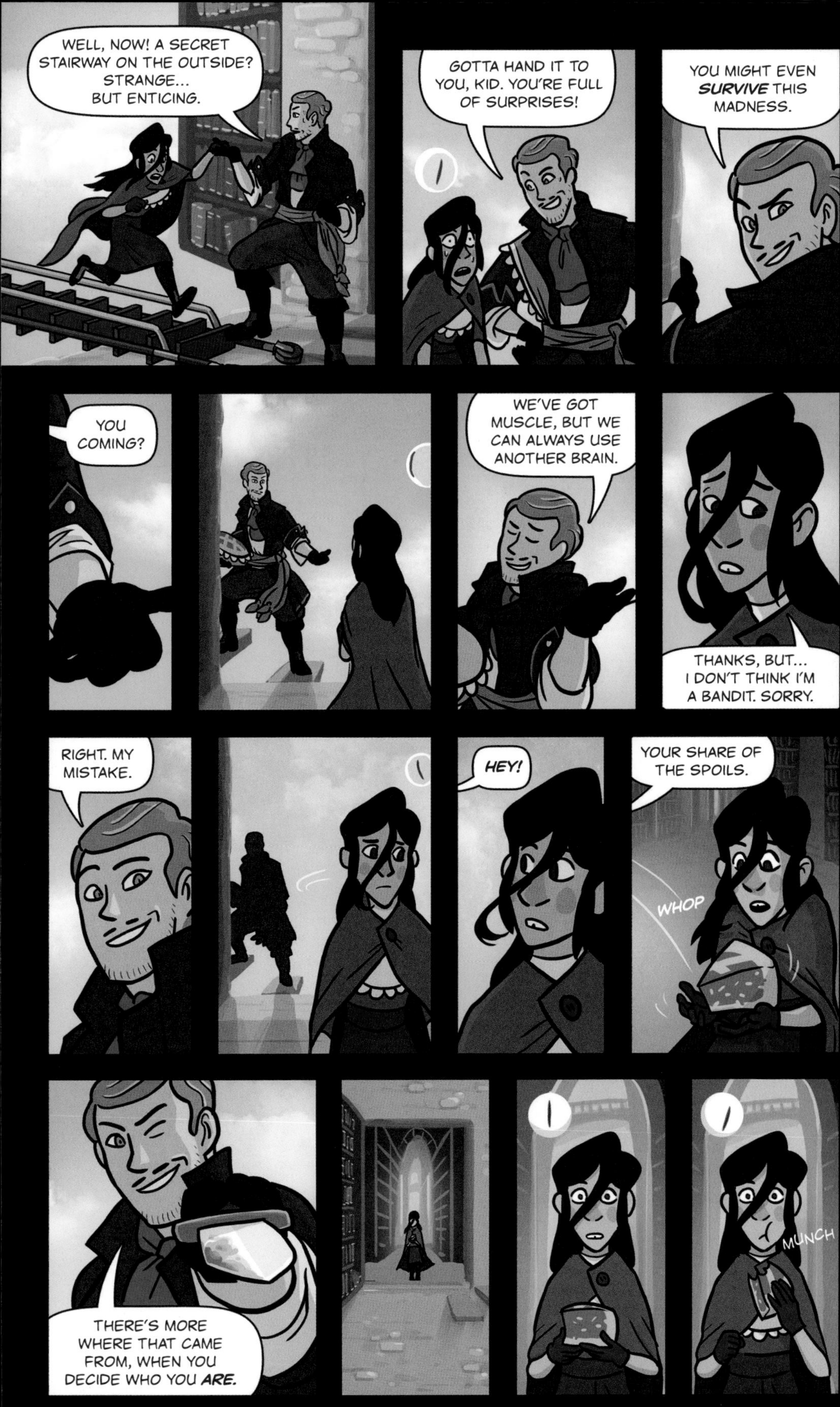
WELL, NOW! A SECRET STAIRWAY ON THE OUTSIDE? STRANGE... BUT ENTICING.
GOTTA HAND IT TO YOU, KID. YOU'RE FULL OF SURPRISES!
YOU MIGHT EVEN SURVIVE THIS MADNESS.
YOU COMING?
WE'VE GOT MUSCLE, BUT WE CAN ALWAYS USE ANOTHER BRAIN.
THANKS, BUT... I DON'T THINK I'M A BANDIT. SORRY.
RIGHT. MY MISTAKE.
HEY!
YOUR SHARE OF THE SPOILS.
WHOP
THERE'S MORE WHERE THAT CAME FROM, WHEN YOU DECIDE WHO YOU ARE.
MUNCH

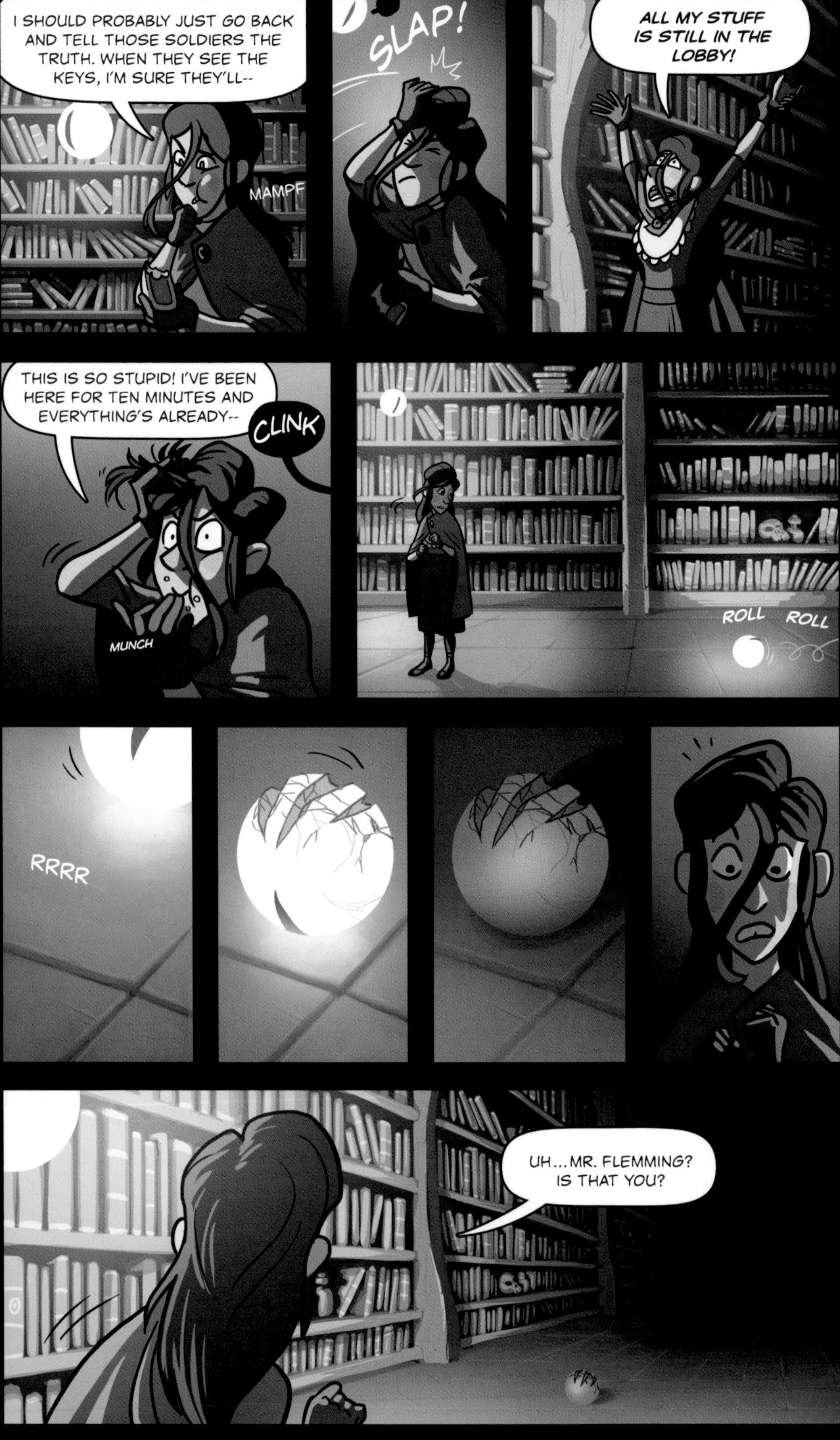

I SHOULD PROBABLY JUST GO BACK AND TELL THOSE SOLDIERS THE TRUTH. WHEN THEY SEE THE KEYS, I'M SURE THEY'LL--
MAMPF
SLAP!
ALL MY STUFF IS STILL IN THE LOBBY!
THIS IS SO STUPID! I'VE BEEN HERE FOR TEN MINUTES AND EVERYTHING'S ALREADY--
CLINK
MUNCH
ROLL
ROLL
RRRR
UH...MR. FLEMMING? IS THAT YOU?

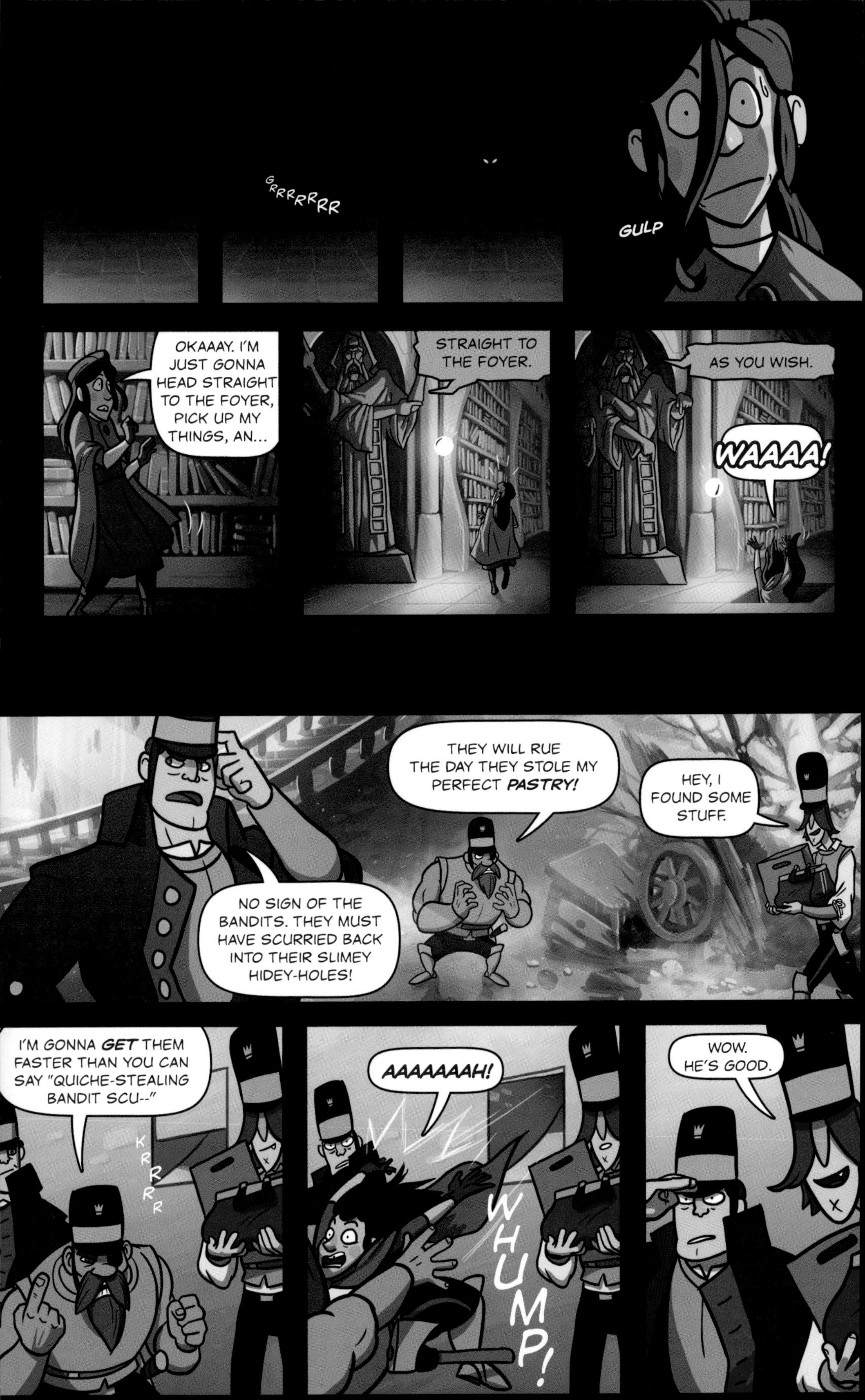
GRRRRRRR
GULP
OKAAAY. I'M JUST GONNA HEAD STRAIGHT TO THE FOYER, PICK UP MY THINGS, AN...
STRAIGHT TO THE FOYER.
AS YOU WISH.
WAAAA!
THEY WILL RUE THE DAY THEY STOLE MY PERFECT PASTRY!
NO SIGN OF THE BANDITS. THEY MUST HAVE SCURRIED BACK INTO THEIR SLIMEY HIDEY-HOLES!
HEY, I FOUND SOME STUFF.
I'M GONNA GET THEM FASTER THAN YOU CAN SAY "QUICHE-STEALING BANDIT SCU--"
KRRRR
AAAAAAAH!
WHUMP!
WOW. HE'S GOOD.

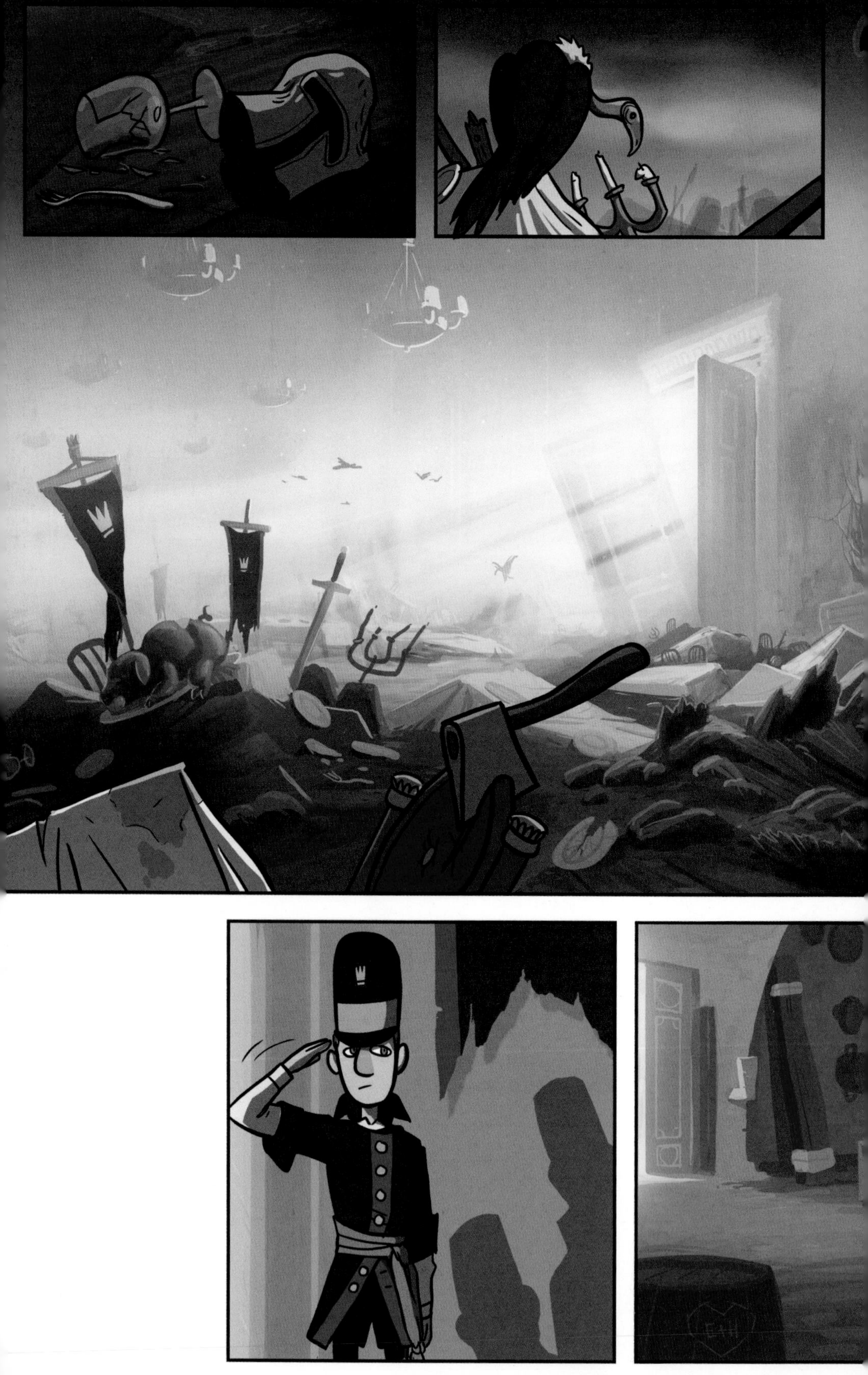

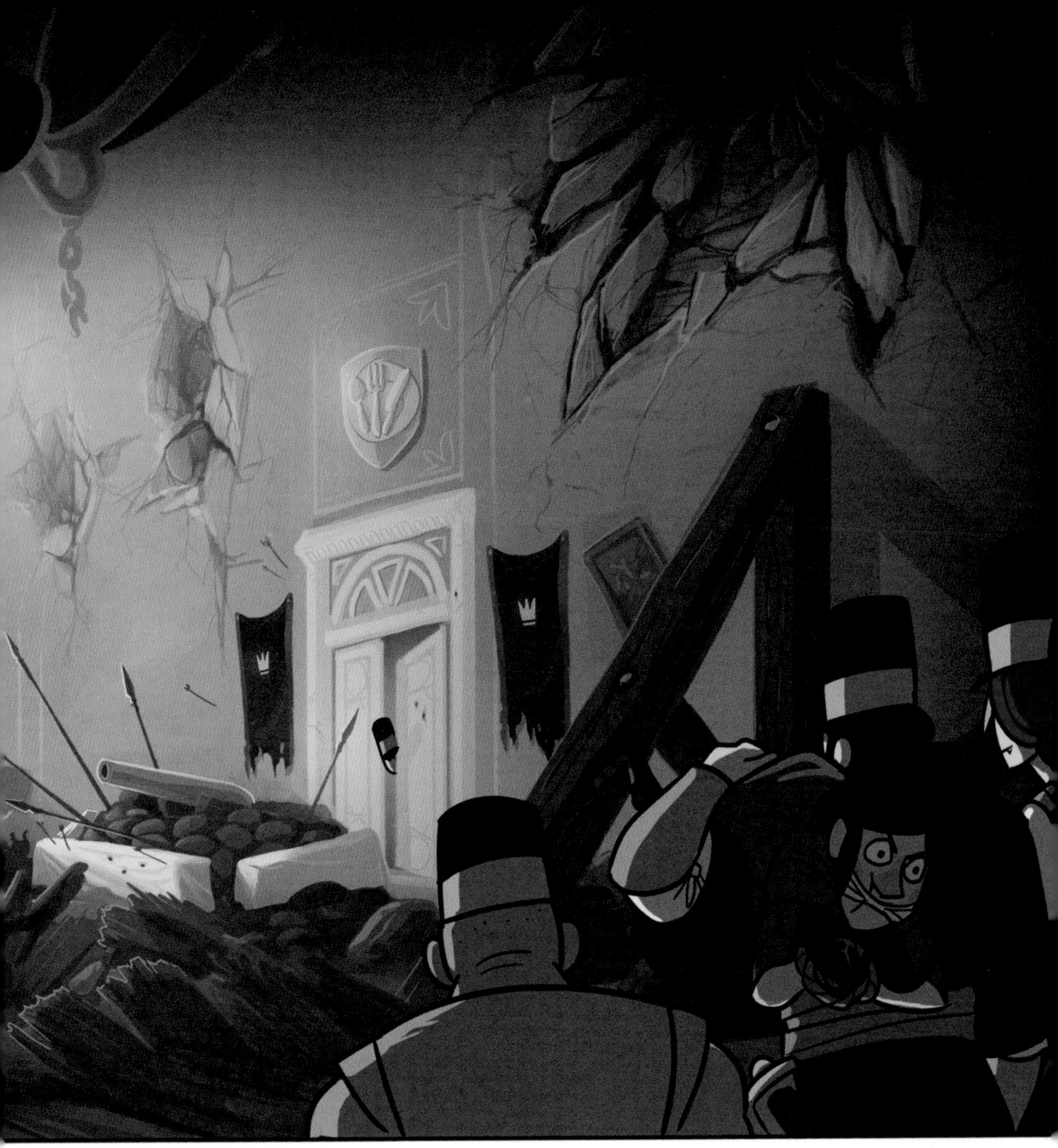

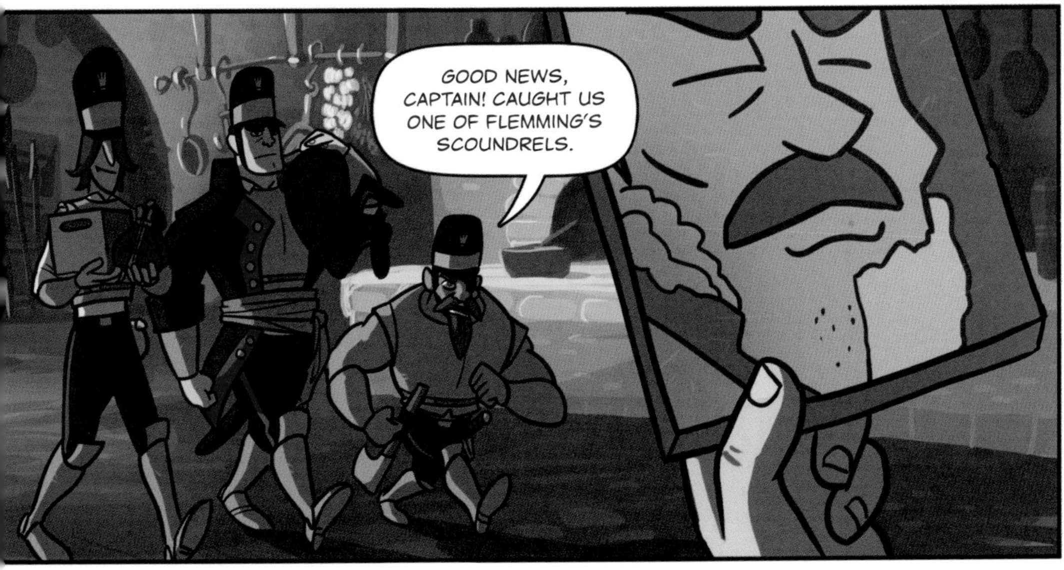
GOOD NEWS, CAPTAIN! CAUGHT US ONE OF FLEMMING'S SCOUNDRELS.

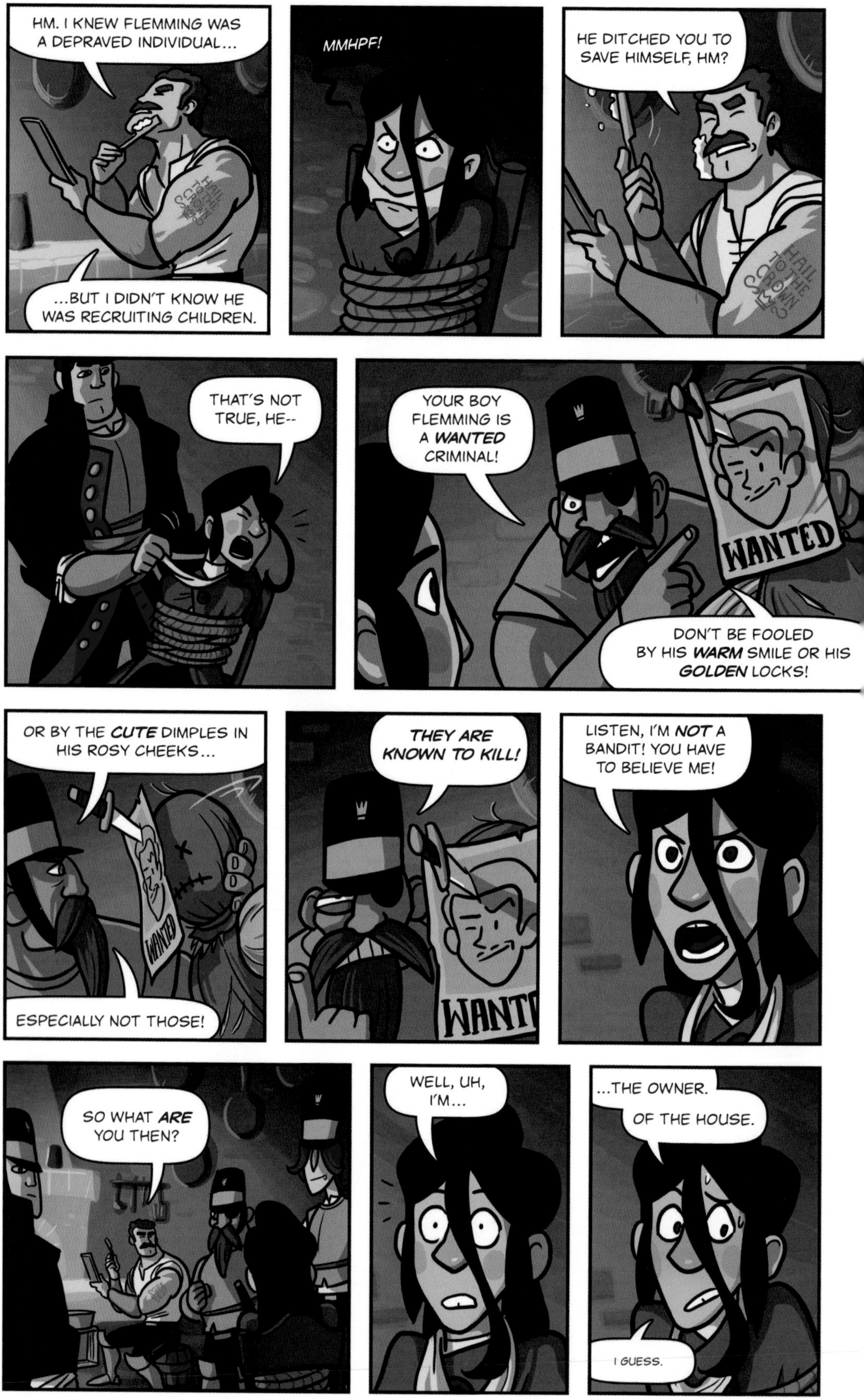
HM. I KNEW FLEMMING WAS A DEPRAVED INDIVIDUAL...
...BUT I DIDN'T KNOW HE WAS RECRUITING CHILDREN.
MMHPF!
HE DITCHED YOU TO SAVE HIMSELF, HM?
HAIL TO THE CROWN
THAT'S NOT TRUE, HE--
YOUR BOY FLEMMING IS A WANTED CRIMINAL!
WANTED
DON'T BE FOOLED BY HIS WARM SMILE OR HIS GOLDEN LOCKS!
OR BY THE CUTE DIMPLES IN HIS ROSY CHEEKS...
ESPECIALLY NOT THOSE!
THEY ARE KNOWN TO KILL!
LISTEN, I'M NOT A BANDIT! YOU HAVE TO BELIEVE ME!
SO WHAT ARE YOU THEN?
WELL, UH, I'M...
...THE OWNER.
OF THE HOUSE.
I GUESS.

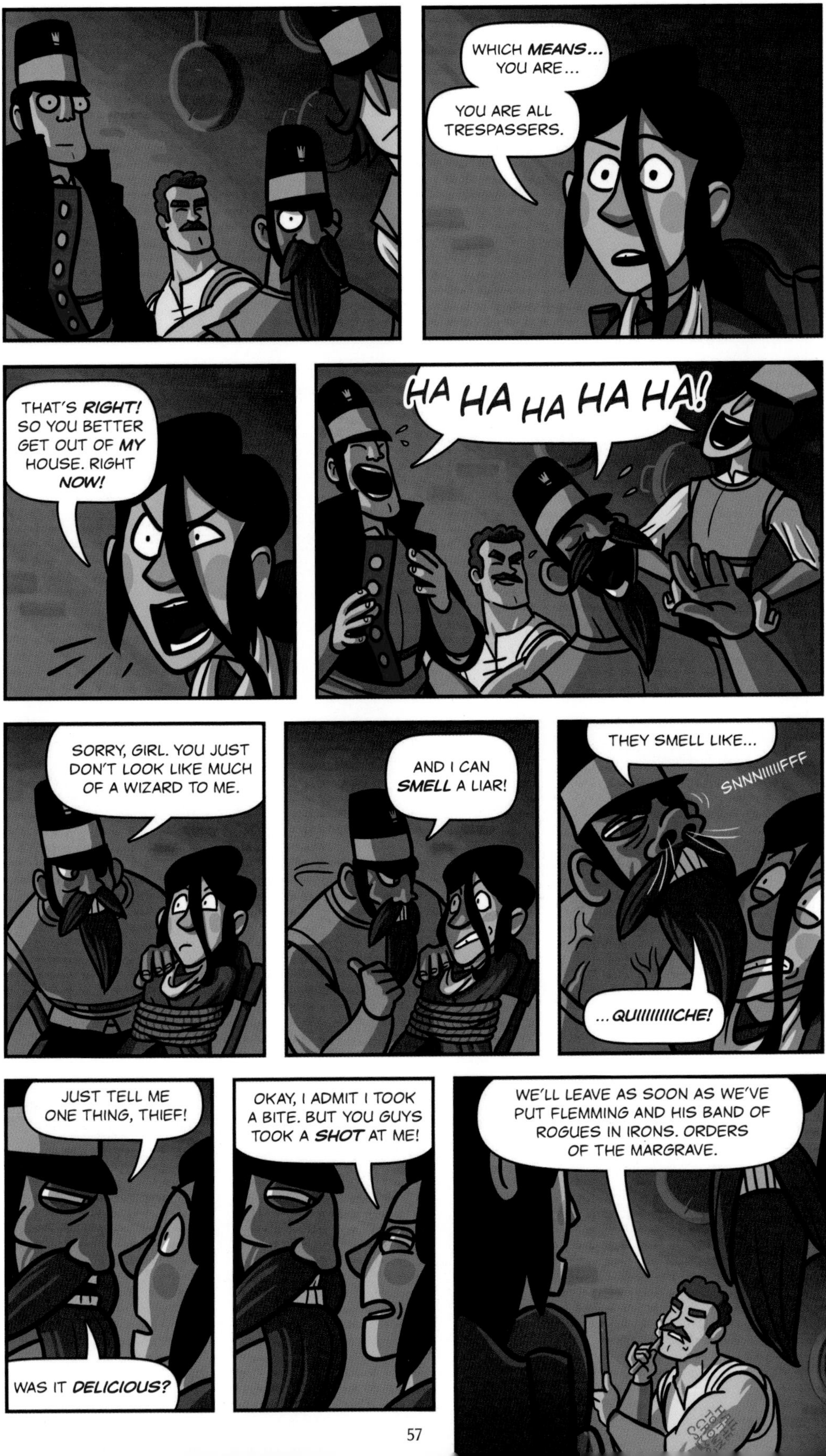

WHICH MEANS... YOU ARE...
YOU ARE ALL TRESPASSERS.
THAT'S RIGHT! SO YOU BETTER GET OUT OF MY HOUSE. RIGHT NOW!
HA HA HA HA HA!
SORRY, GIRL. YOU JUST DON'T LOOK LIKE MUCH OF A WIZARD TO ME.
AND I CAN SMELL A LIAR!
THEY SMELL LIKE...
SNNNIIIIIFFF
...QUIIIIIIIICHE!
JUST TELL ME ONE THING, THIEF!
WAS IT DELICIOUS?
OKAY, I ADMIT I TOOK A BITE. BUT YOU GUYS TOOK A SHOT AT ME!
WE'LL LEAVE AS SOON AS WE'VE PUT FLEMMING AND HIS BAND OF ROGUES IN IRONS. ORDERS OF THE MARGRAVE.

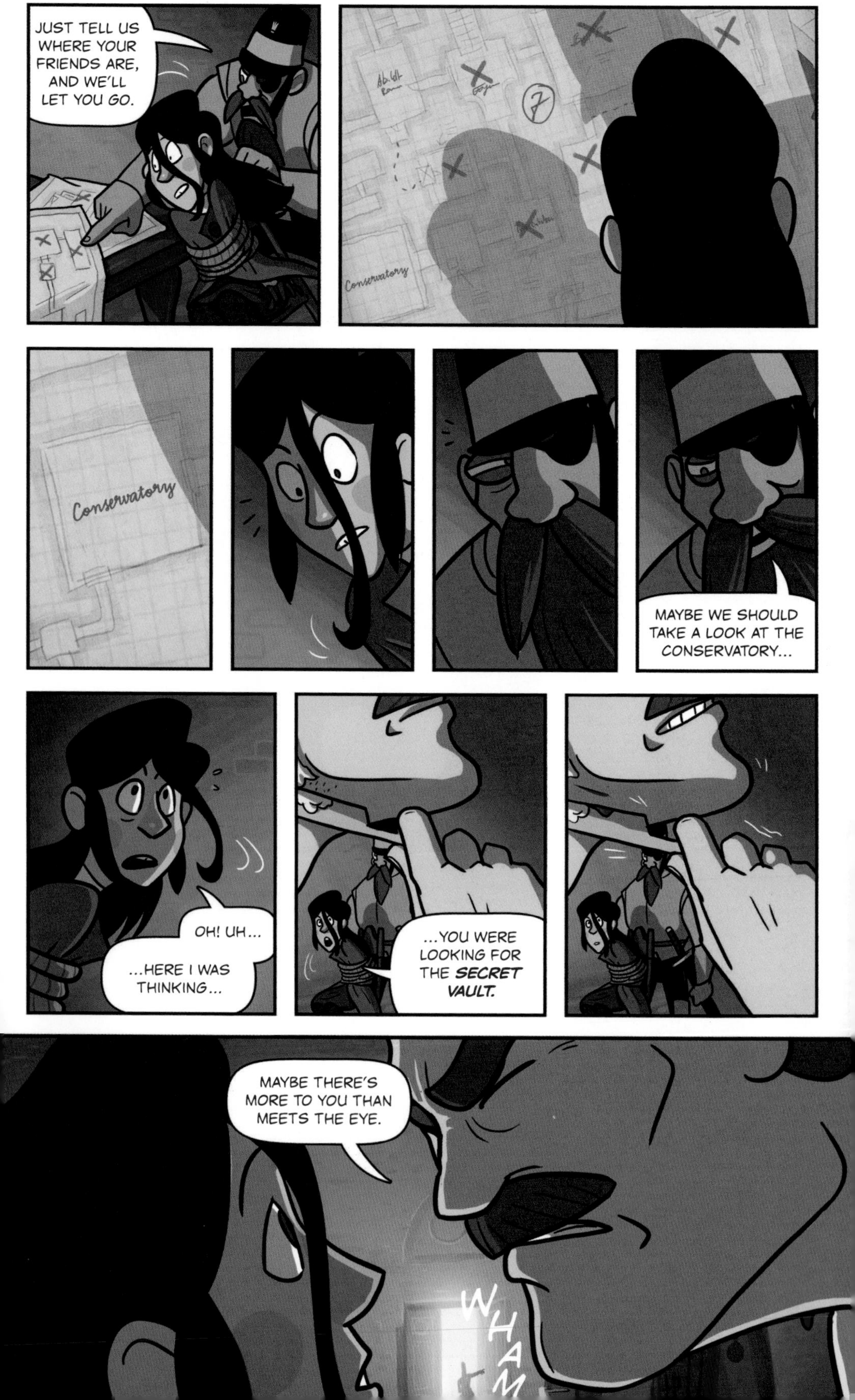
JUST TELL US WHERE YOUR FRIENDS ARE, AND WE'LL LET YOU GO.
Conservatory
Conservatory
MAYBE WE SHOULD TAKE A LOOK AT THE CONSERVATORY...
OH! UH...
...HERE I WAS THINKING...
...YOU WERE LOOKING FOR THE ***SECRET VAULT.***
MAYBE THERE'S MORE TO YOU THAN MEETS THE EYE.
WHAM

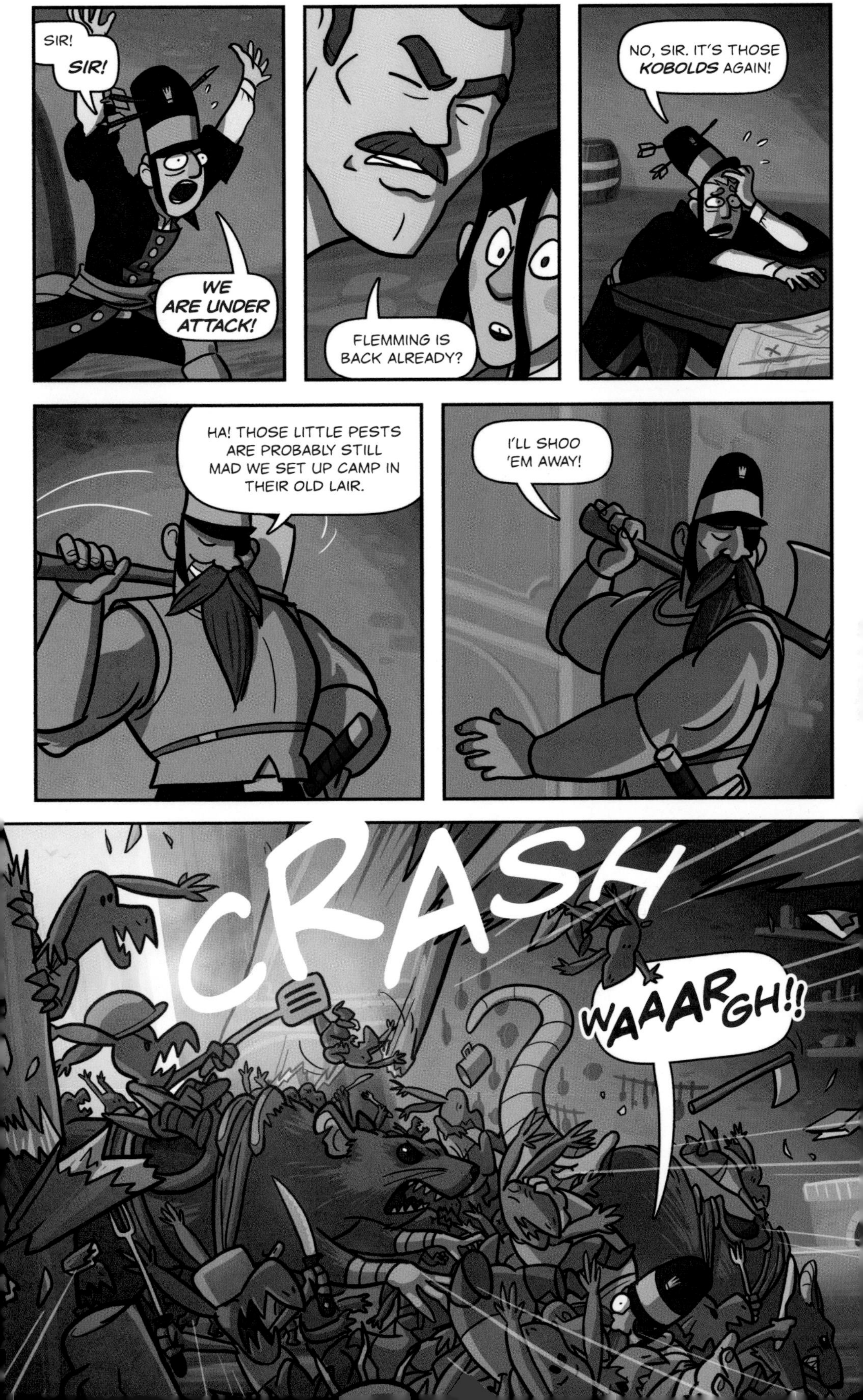
SIR!
SIR!
WE ARE UNDER ATTACK!
FLEMMING IS BACK ALREADY?
NO, SIR. IT'S THOSE KOBOLDS AGAIN!
HA! THOSE LITTLE PESTS ARE PROBABLY STILL MAD WE SET UP CAMP IN THEIR OLD LAIR.
I'LL SHOO 'EM AWAY!
CRASH
WAAARGH!!

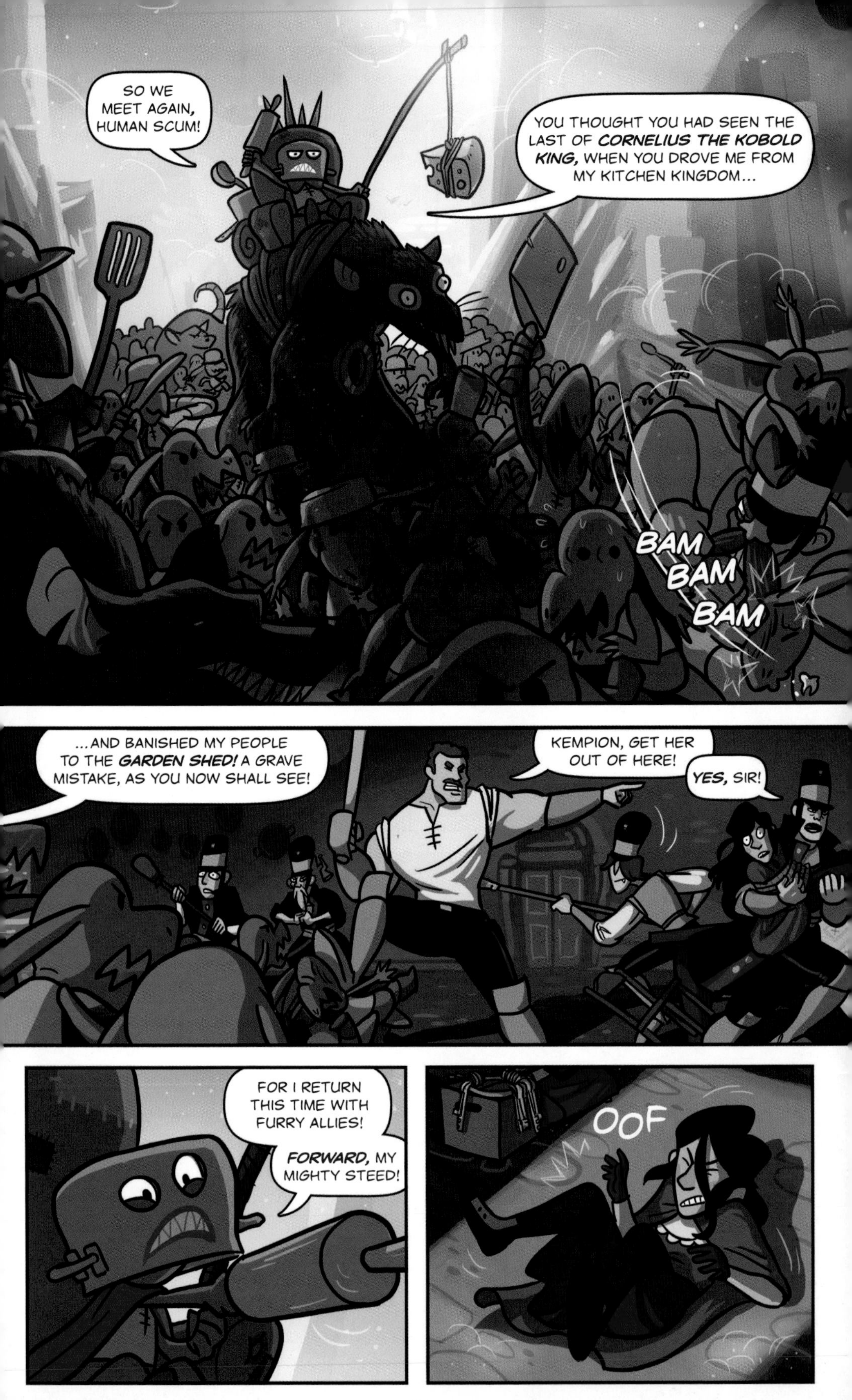

SO WE MEET AGAIN, HUMAN SCUM!
YOU THOUGHT YOU HAD SEEN THE LAST OF CORNELIUS THE KOBOLD KING, WHEN YOU DROVE ME FROM MY KITCHEN KINGDOM...
BAM BAM BAM
...AND BANISHED MY PEOPLE TO THE GARDEN SHED! A GRAVE MISTAKE, AS YOU NOW SHALL SEE!
KEMPION, GET HER OUT OF HERE!
YES, SIR!
FOR I RETURN THIS TIME WITH FURRY ALLIES!
FORWARD, MY MIGHTY STEED!
OOF

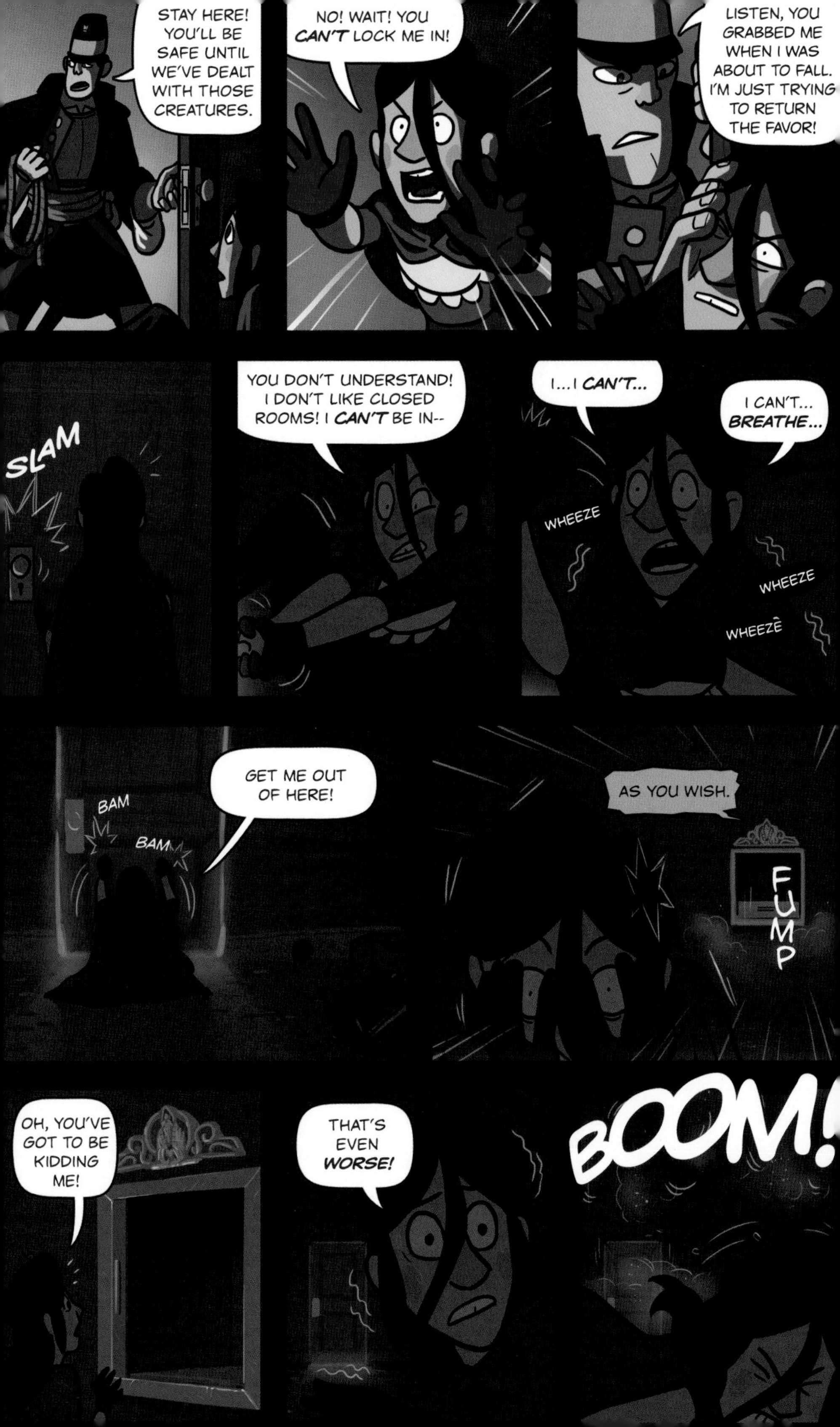
STAY HERE! YOU'LL BE SAFE UNTIL WE'VE DEALT WITH THOSE CREATURES.
NO! WAIT! YOU CAN'T LOCK ME IN!
LISTEN, YOU GRABBED ME WHEN I WAS ABOUT TO FALL. I'M JUST TRYING TO RETURN THE FAVOR!
SLAM
YOU DON'T UNDERSTAND! I DON'T LIKE CLOSED ROOMS! I CAN'T BE IN--
I...I CAN'T...
I CAN'T... BREATHE...
WHEEZE
WHEEZE
WHEEZE
GET ME OUT OF HERE!
BAM
BAM
AS YOU WISH.
FUMP
OH, YOU'VE GOT TO BE KIDDING ME!
THAT'S EVEN WORSE!
BOOM!

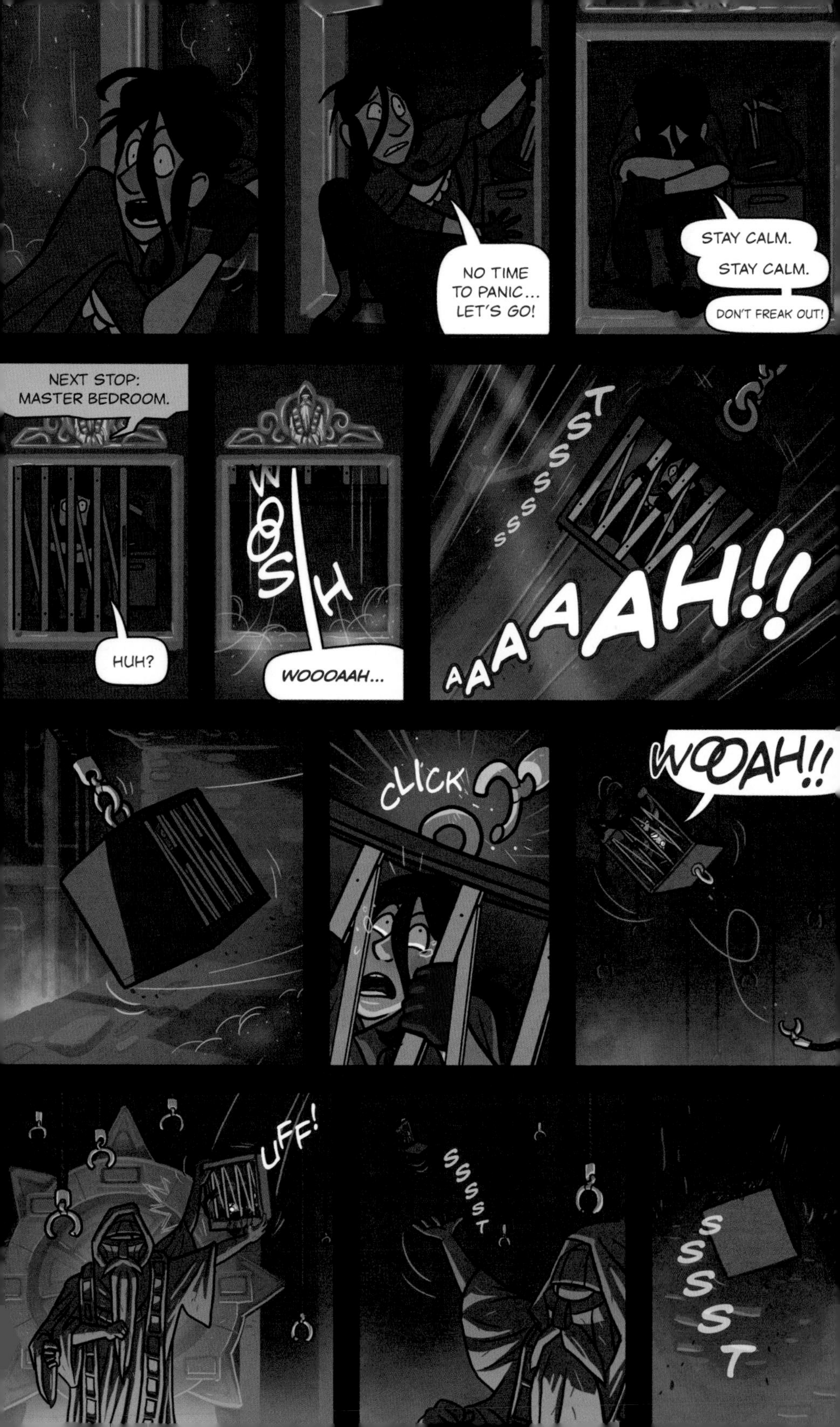
NO TIME TO PANIC... LET'S GO!
STAY CALM.
STAY CALM.
DON'T FREAK OUT!
NEXT STOP: MASTER BEDROOM.
HUH?
WOOSH
WOOOAAH...
SSSSSST
AAAAAAH!!
CLICK
WOOAH!!
UFF!
SSSST
SSSST

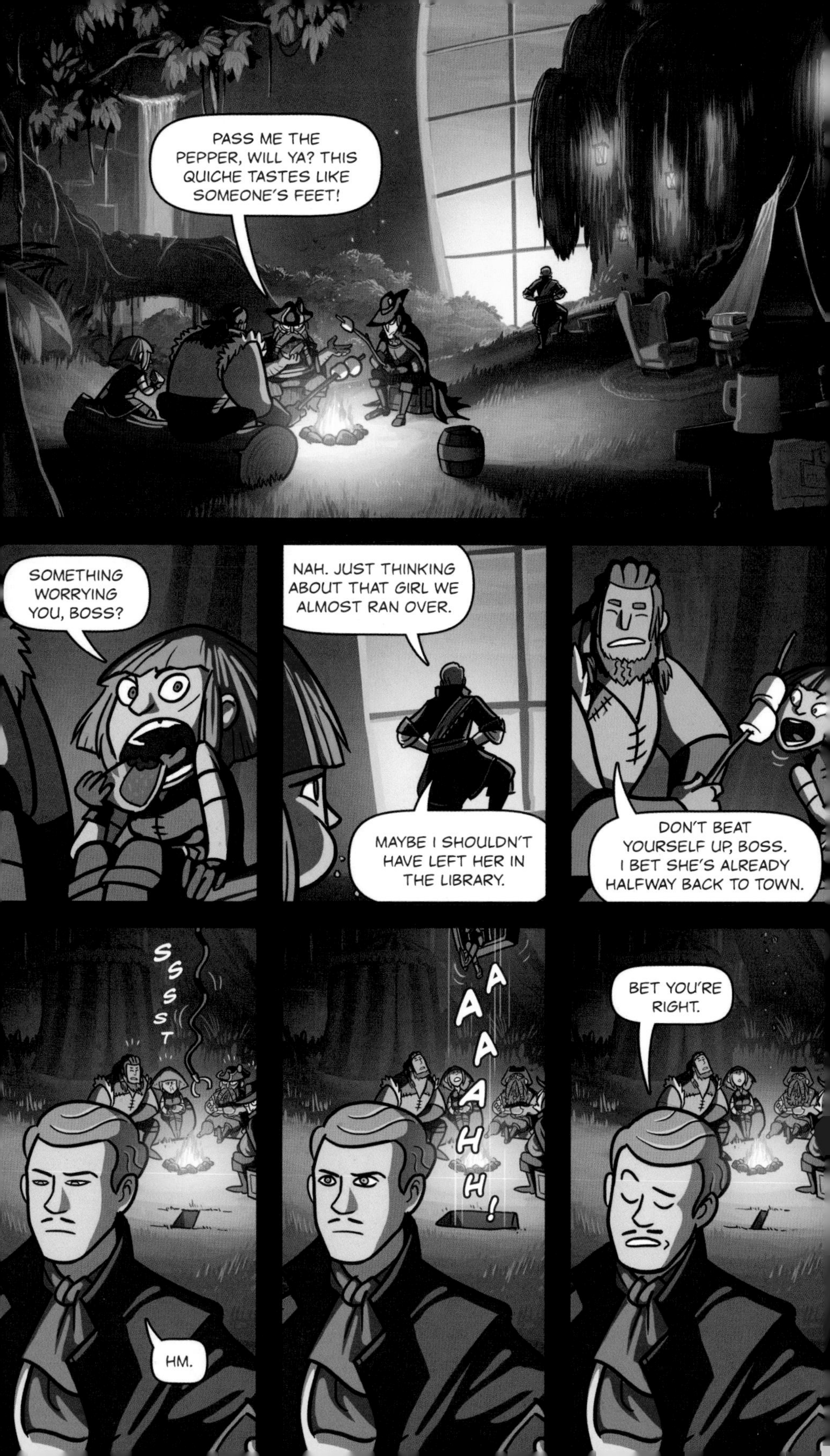
PASS ME THE PEPPER, WILL YA? THIS QUICHE TASTES LIKE SOMEONE'S FEET!
SOMETHING WORRYING YOU, BOSS?
NAH. JUST THINKING ABOUT THAT GIRL WE ALMOST RAN OVER.
MAYBE I SHOULDN'T HAVE LEFT HER IN THE LIBRARY.
DON'T BEAT YOURSELF UP, BOSS. I BET SHE'S ALREADY HALFWAY BACK TO TOWN.
SSSST
HM.
AAAAHH!
BET YOU'RE RIGHT.

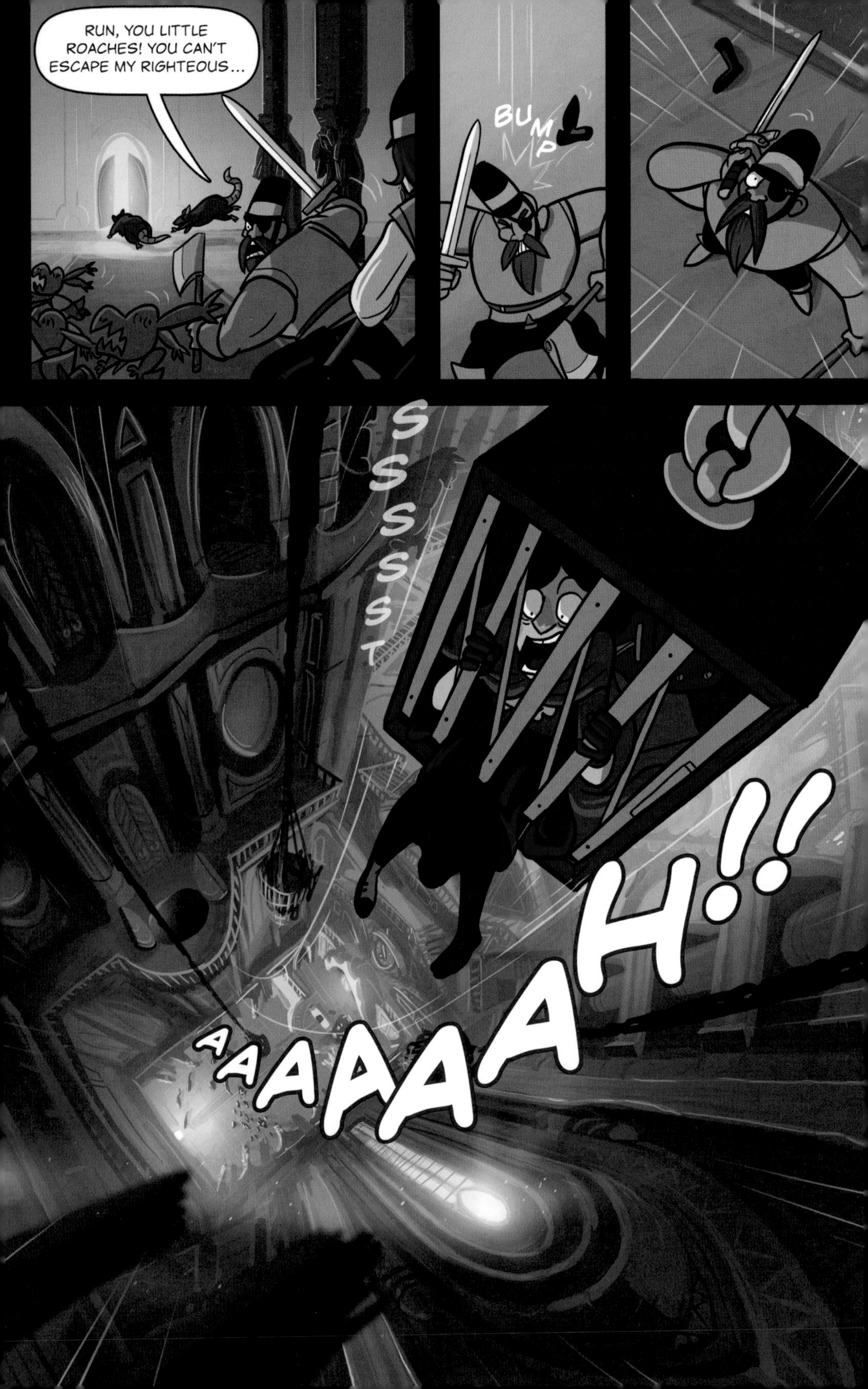
RUN, YOU LITTLE ROACHES! YOU CAN'T ESCAPE MY RIGHTEOUS...
BUMP
SSSSSST
AAAAAAH!!!

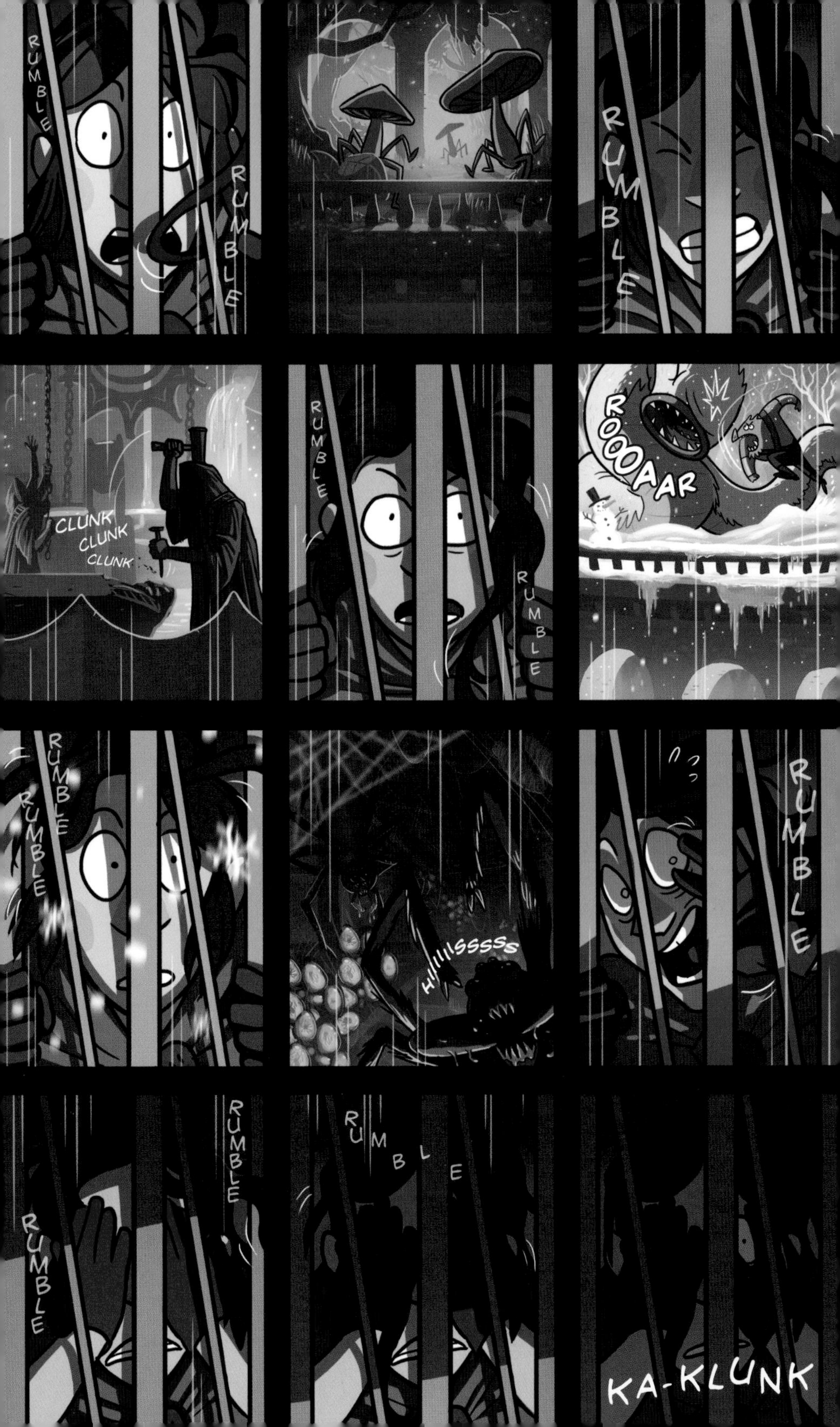
RUMBLE
RUMBLE
RUMBLE
CLUNK
CLUNK
CLUNK
RUMBLE
RUMBLE
ROOOAAR
RUMBLE
RUMBLE
HIIIISSSSS
RUMBLE
RUMBLE
RUMBLE
RUMBLE
KA-KLUNK

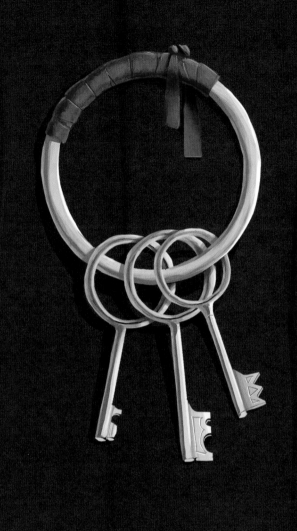

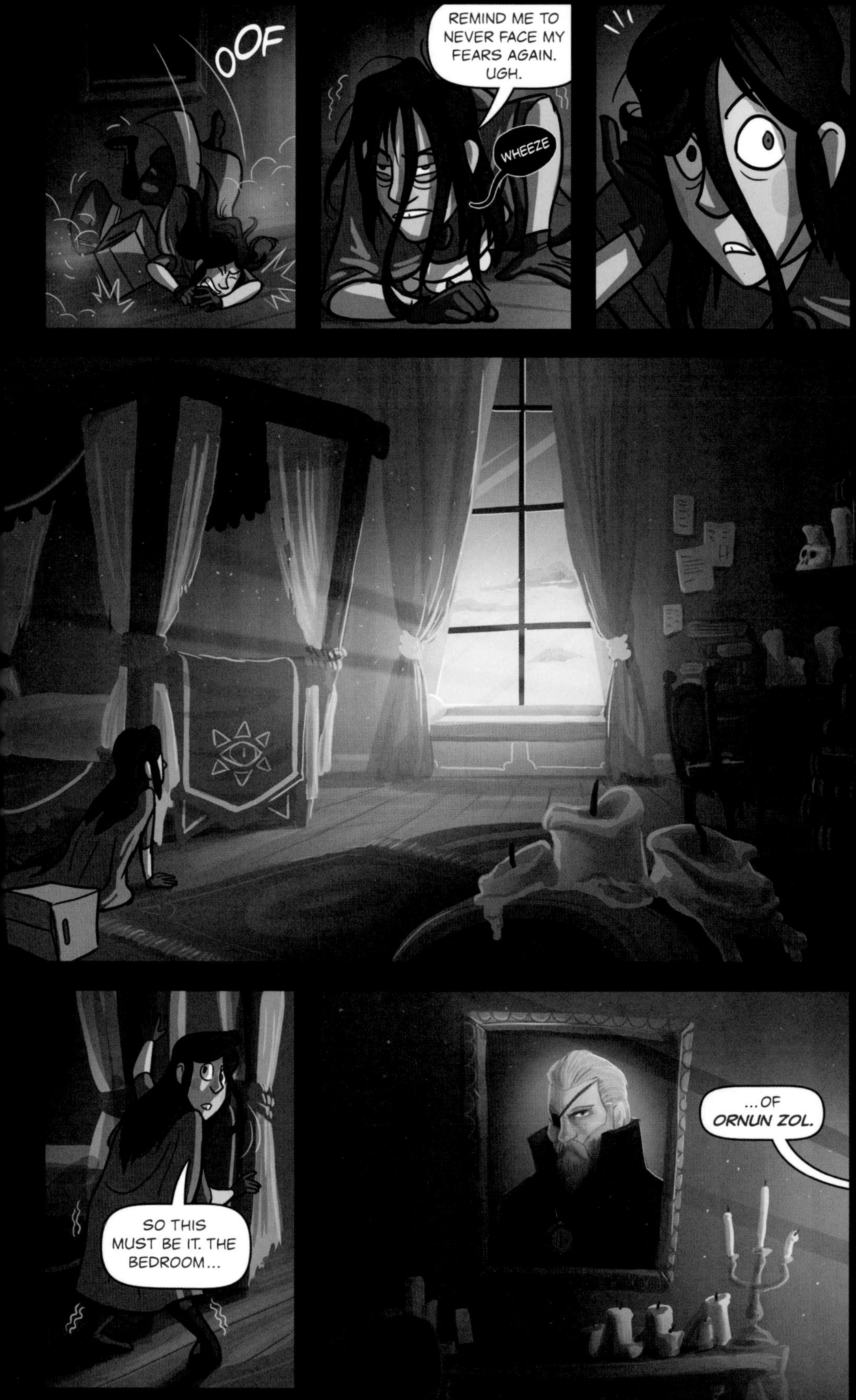
OOF
REMIND ME TO NEVER FACE MY FEARS AGAIN. UGH.
WHEEZE
SO THIS MUST BE IT. THE BEDROOM...
...OF ORNUN ZOL.

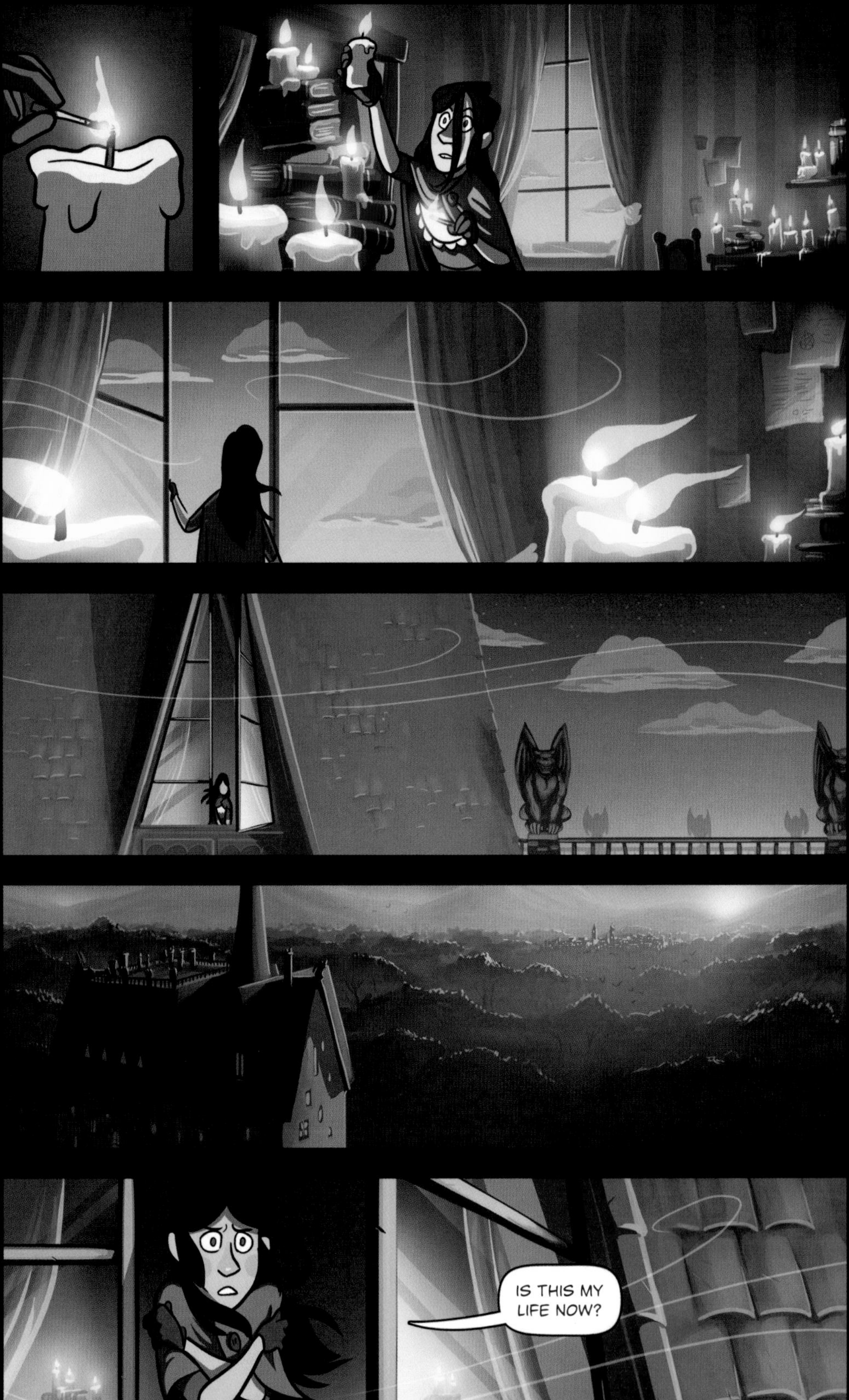
IS THIS MY LIFE NOW?

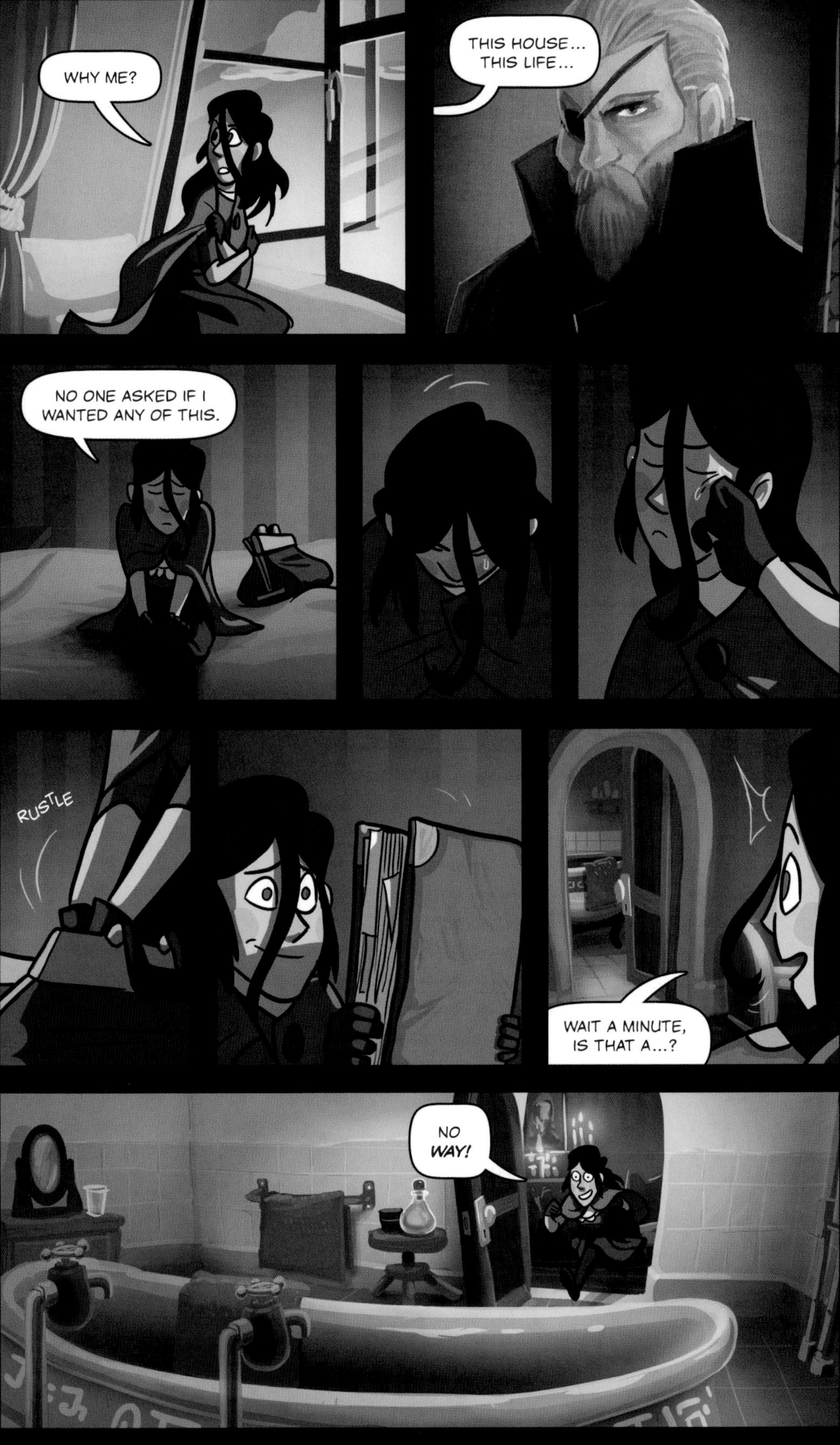
WHY ME?
THIS HOUSE... THIS LIFE...
NO ONE ASKED IF I WANTED ANY OF THIS.
RUSTLE
WAIT A MINUTE, IS THAT A...?
NO WAY!

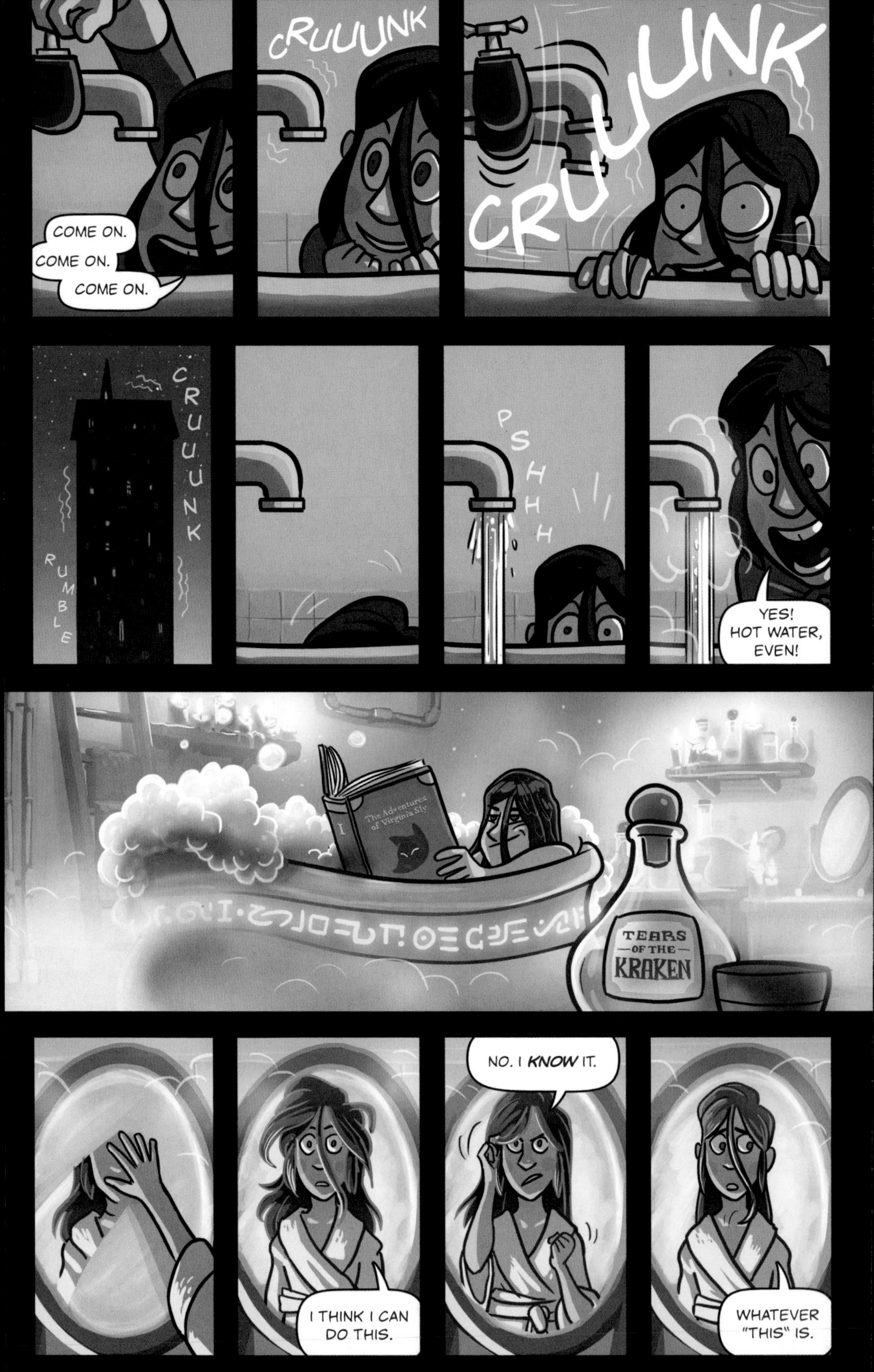
COME ON.
COME ON.
COME ON.
CRUUUNK
CRUUUNK
CRUUUNK
RUMBLE
PSHHH
YES! HOT WATER, EVEN!
The Adventures of Virginia Sly
TEARS OF THE KRAKEN
I THINK I CAN DO THIS.
NO. I KNOW IT.
WHATEVER "THIS" IS.

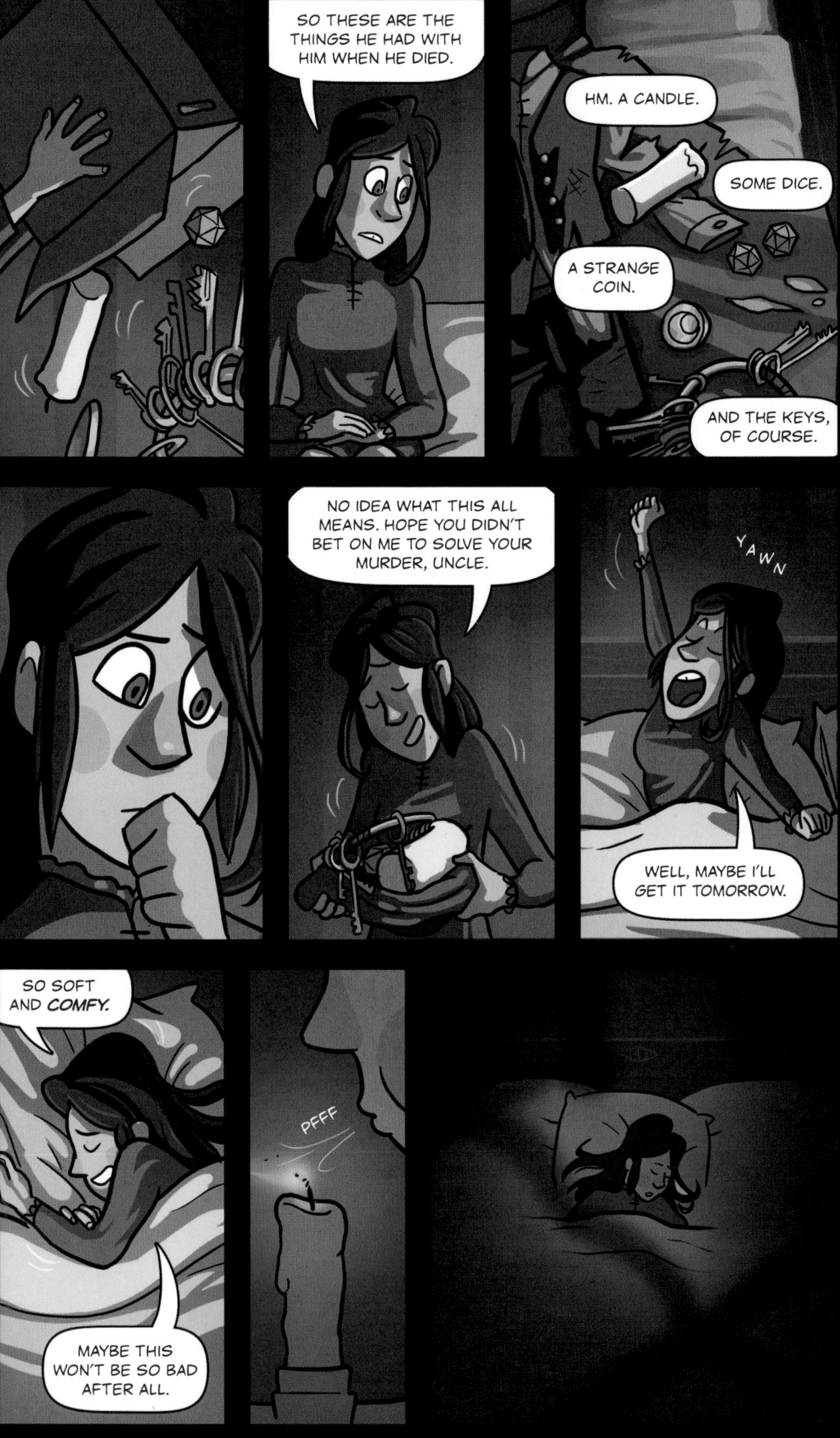
SO THESE ARE THE THINGS HE HAD WITH HIM WHEN HE DIED.
HM. A CANDLE.
SOME DICE.
A STRANGE COIN.
AND THE KEYS, OF COURSE.
NO IDEA WHAT THIS ALL MEANS. HOPE YOU DIDN'T BET ON ME TO SOLVE YOUR MURDER, UNCLE.
YAWN
WELL, MAYBE I'LL GET IT TOMORROW.
SO SOFT AND COMFY.
MAYBE THIS WON'T BE SO BAD AFTER ALL.
PFFF

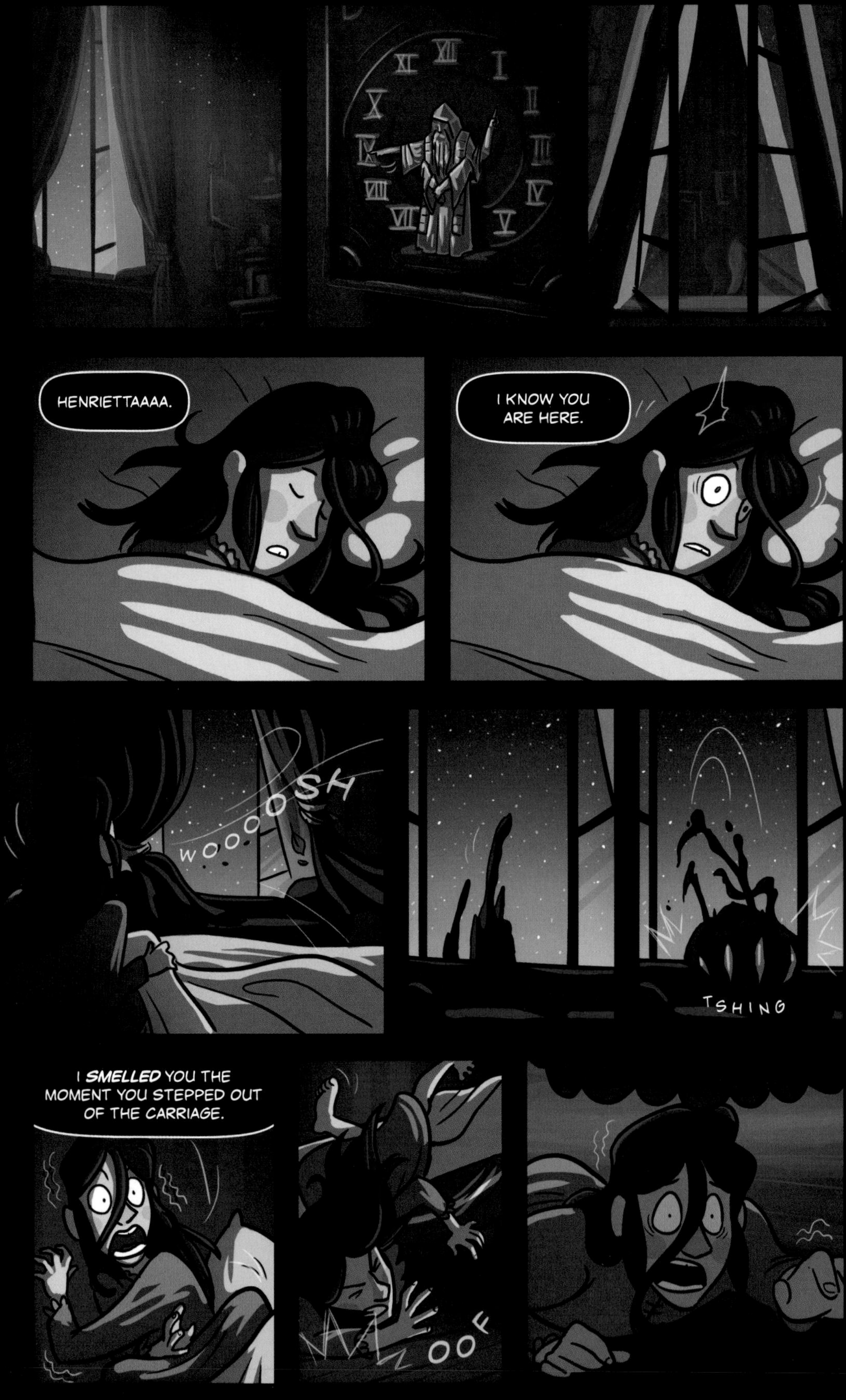
HENRIETTAAAA.
I KNOW YOU ARE HERE.
WOOOOOSH
TSHING
I SMELLED YOU THE MOMENT YOU STEPPED OUT OF THE CARRIAGE.
OOF

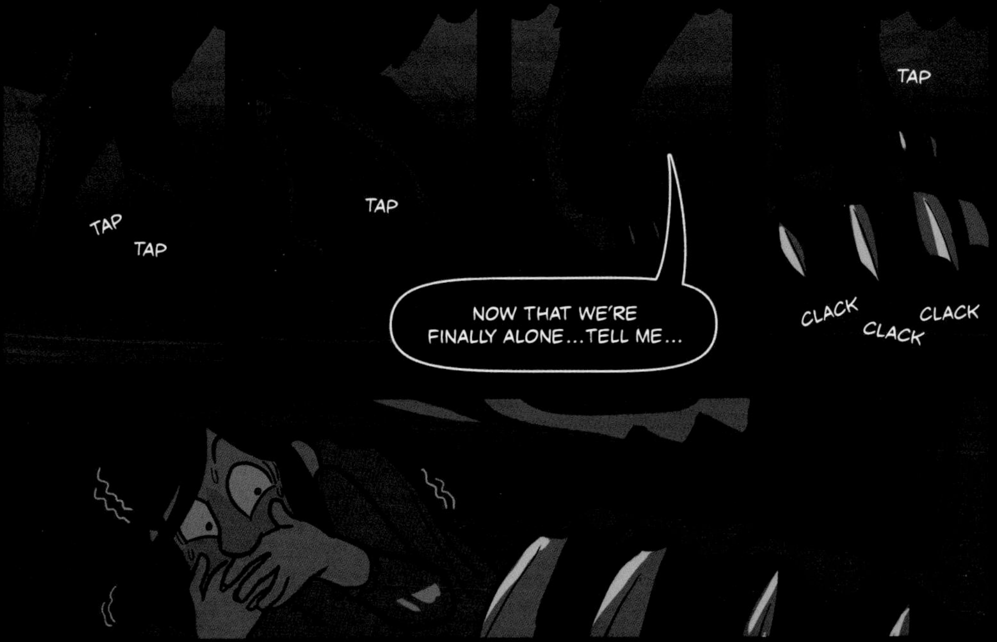
TAP
TAP
TAP
TAP
NOW THAT WE'RE FINALLY ALONE...TELL ME...
CLACK
CLACK
CLACK

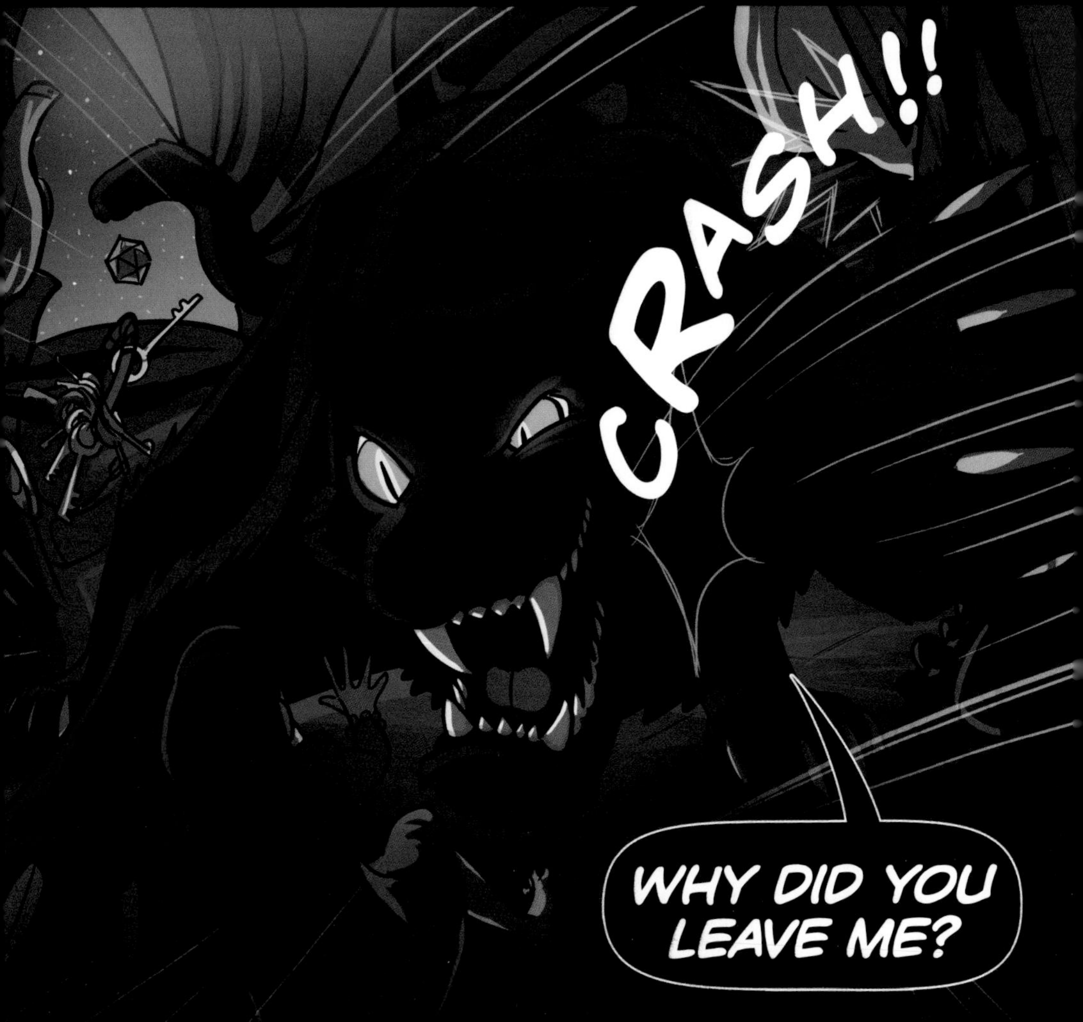
CRASH!!
WHY DID YOU LEAVE ME?

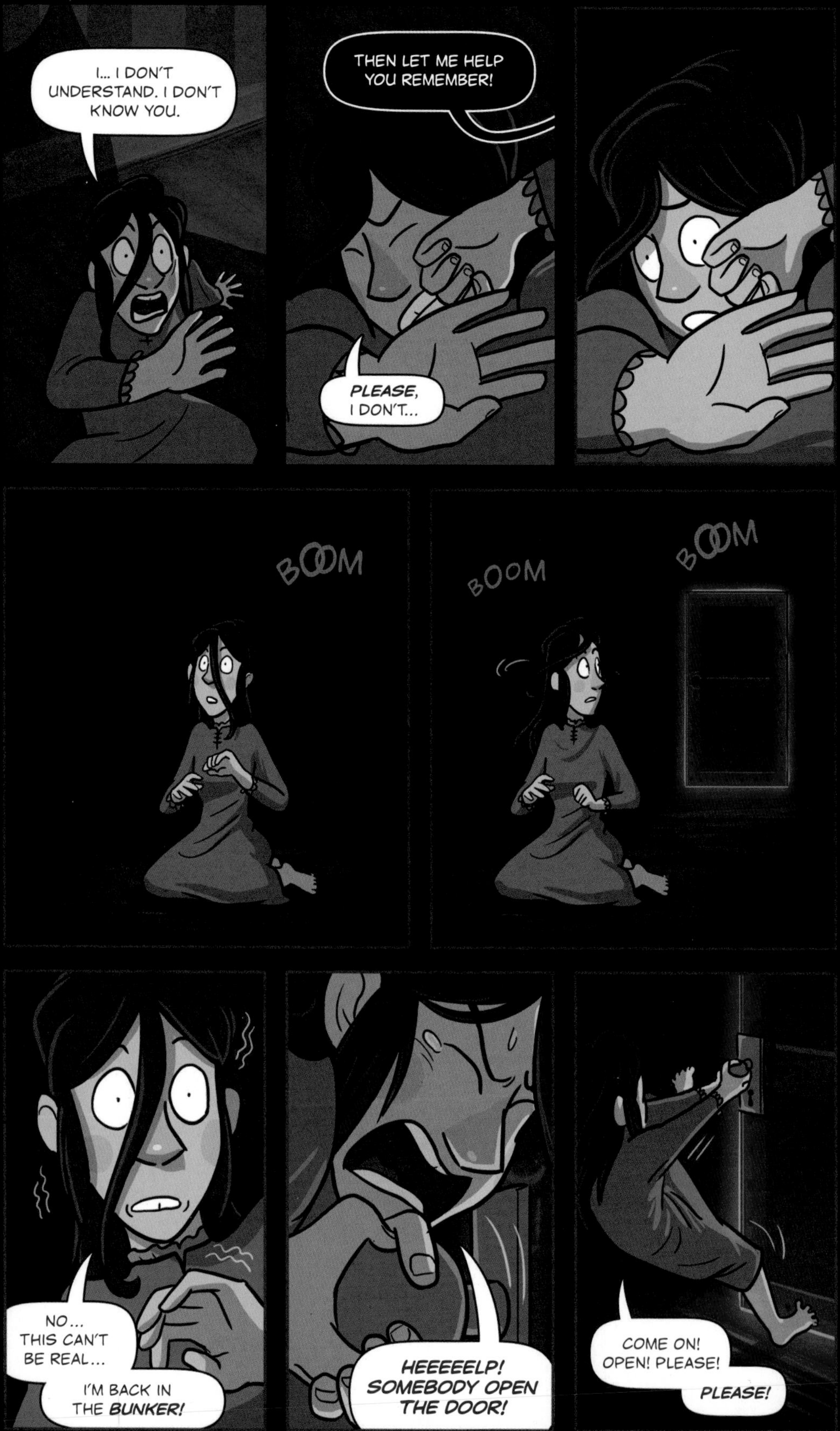
I... I DON'T UNDERSTAND. I DON'T KNOW YOU.
THEN LET ME HELP YOU REMEMBER!
PLEASE, I DON'T...
BOOM
BOOM
BOOM
NO... THIS CAN'T BE REAL...
I'M BACK IN THE BUNKER!
HEEEEELP! SOMEBODY OPEN THE DOOR!
COME ON! OPEN! PLEASE!
PLEASE!

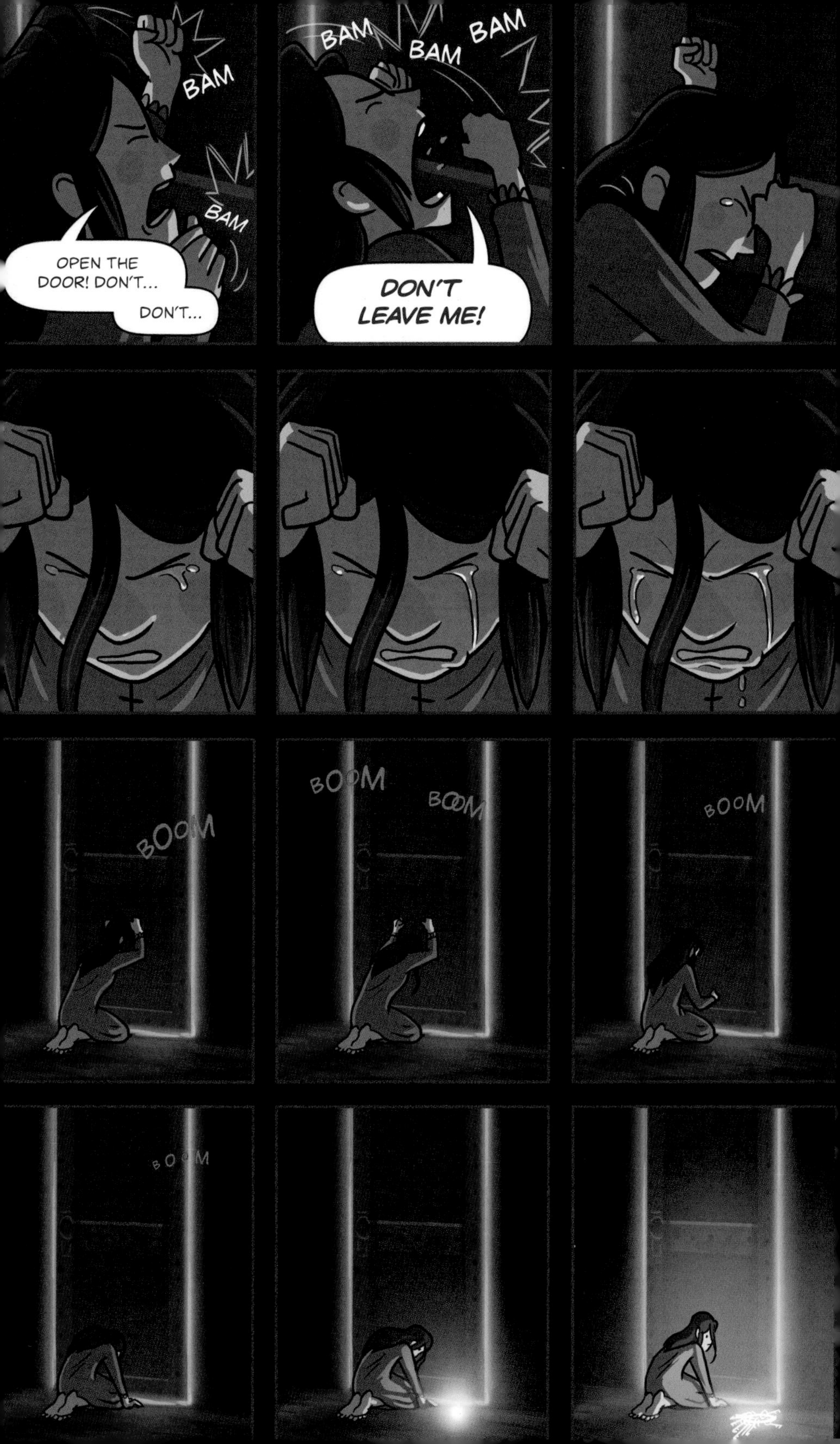

BAM
BAM
OPEN THE DOOR! DON'T... DON'T...
BAM
BAM
BAM
DON'T LEAVE ME!
BOOM
BOOM
BOOM
BOOM
BOOM

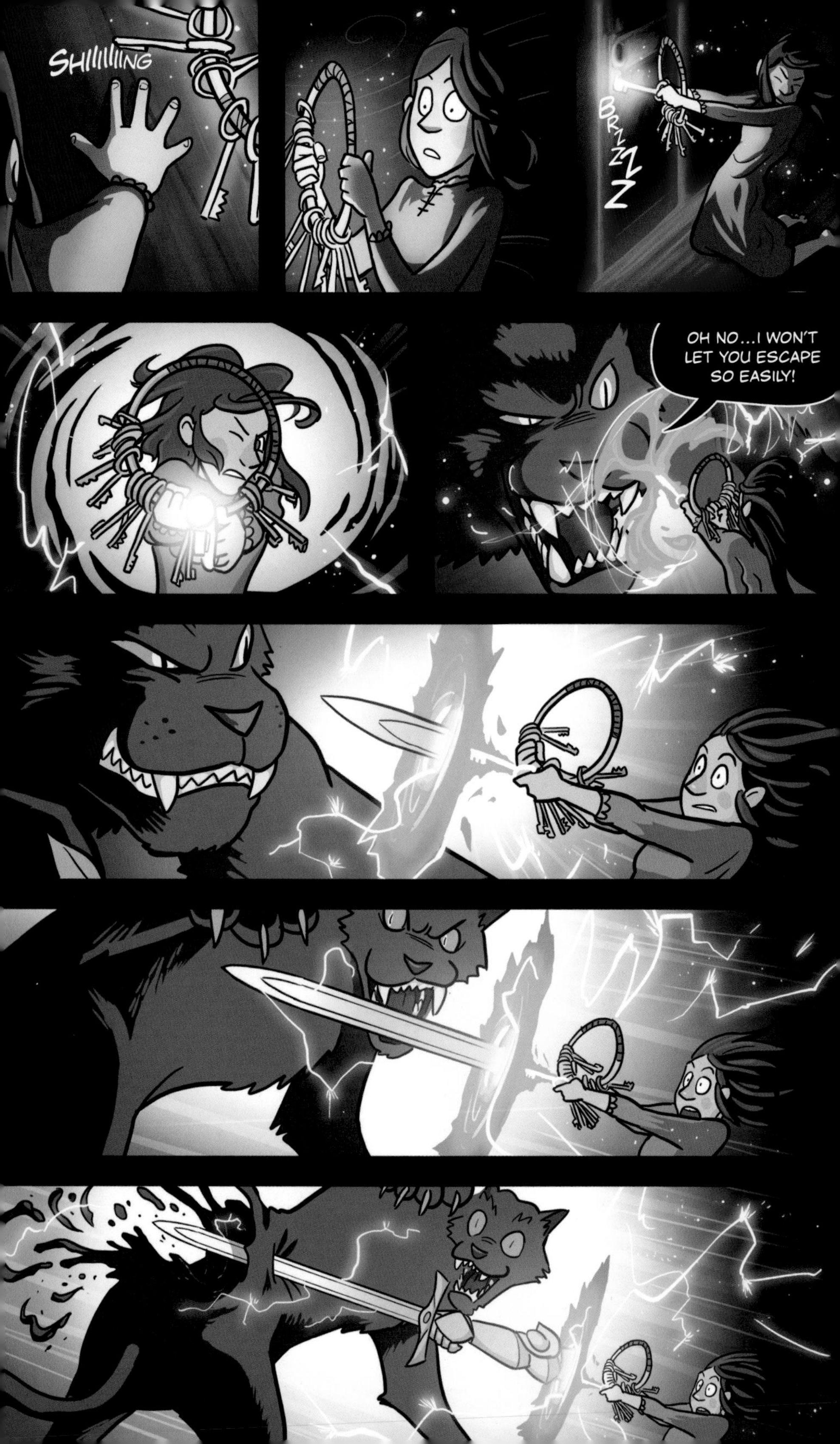
SHIIIIIING
BRZZZZ
OH NO...I WON'T LET YOU ESCAPE SO EASILY!

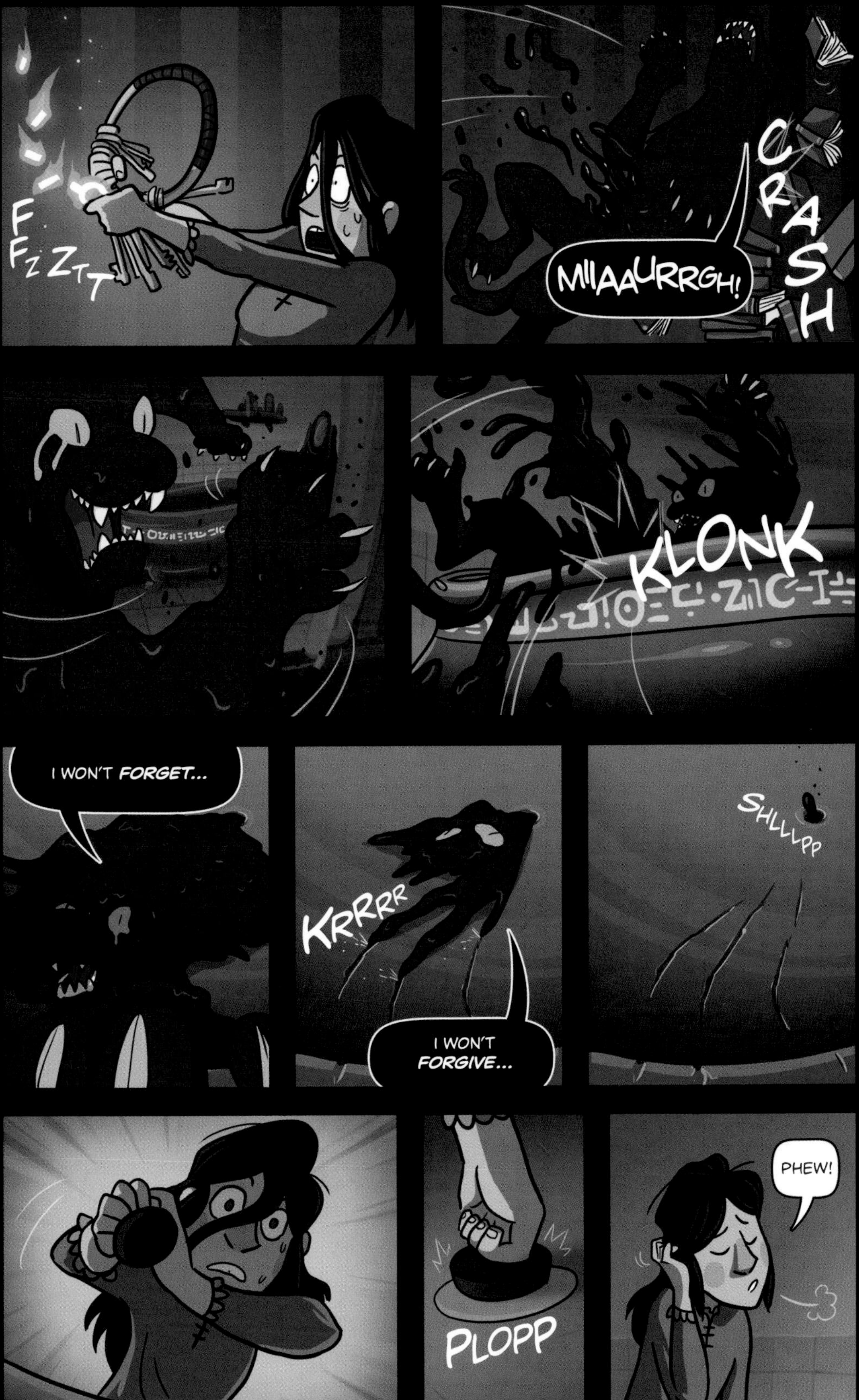
FFZZTT
MIIAAURRGH!
CRASH
KLONK
I WON'T FORGET...
KRRRR
I WON'T FORGIVE...
SHLLLPP
PLOPP
PHEW!

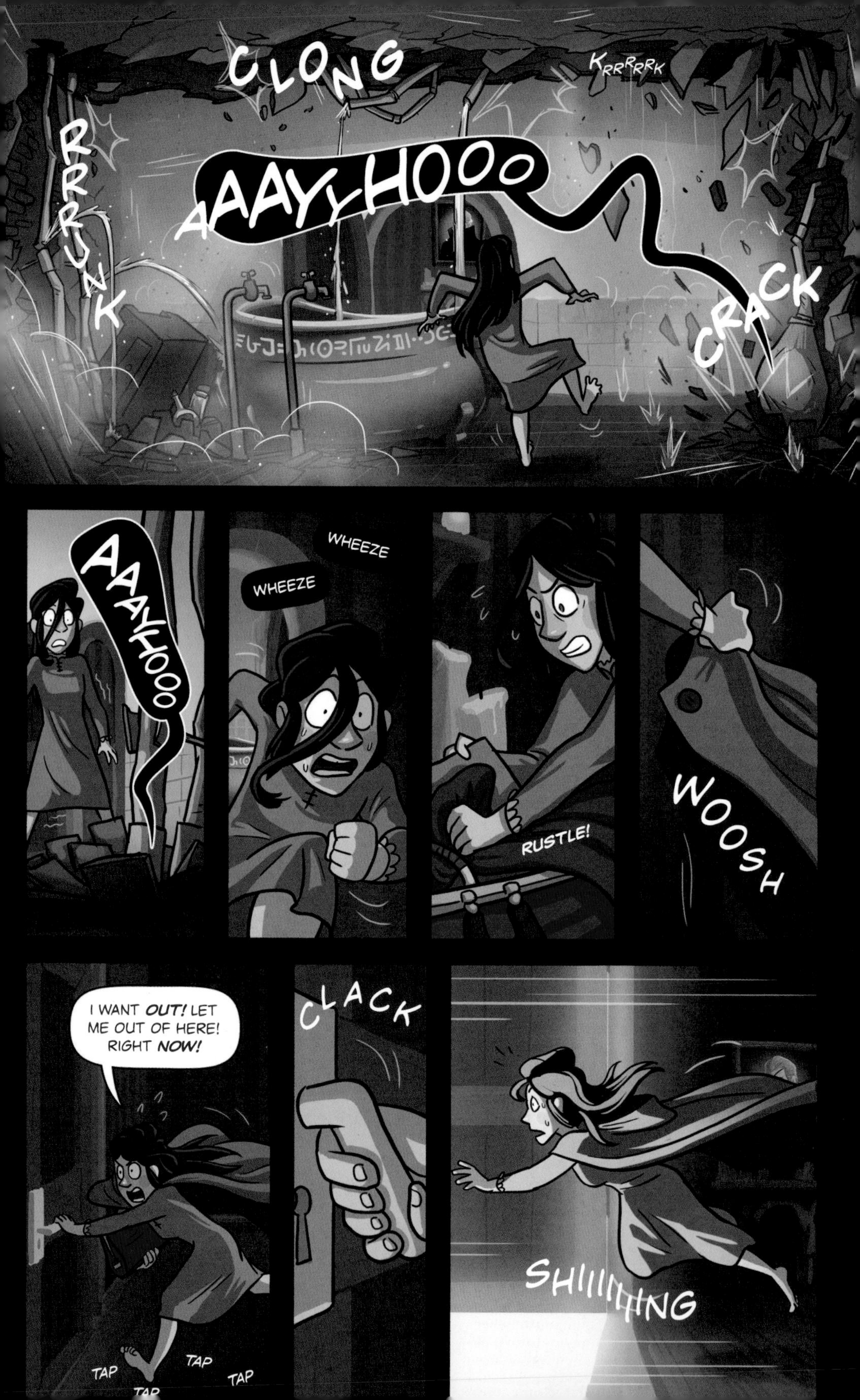
CLONG
KRRRRRK
RRRRUNK
AAAYYHOOO
CRACK
AAAYHOOO
WHEEZE
WHEEZE
RUSTLE!
WOOSH
I WANT *OUT!* LET ME OUT OF HERE! RIGHT *NOW!*
TAP
TAP
TAP
CLACK
SHIIIIIING

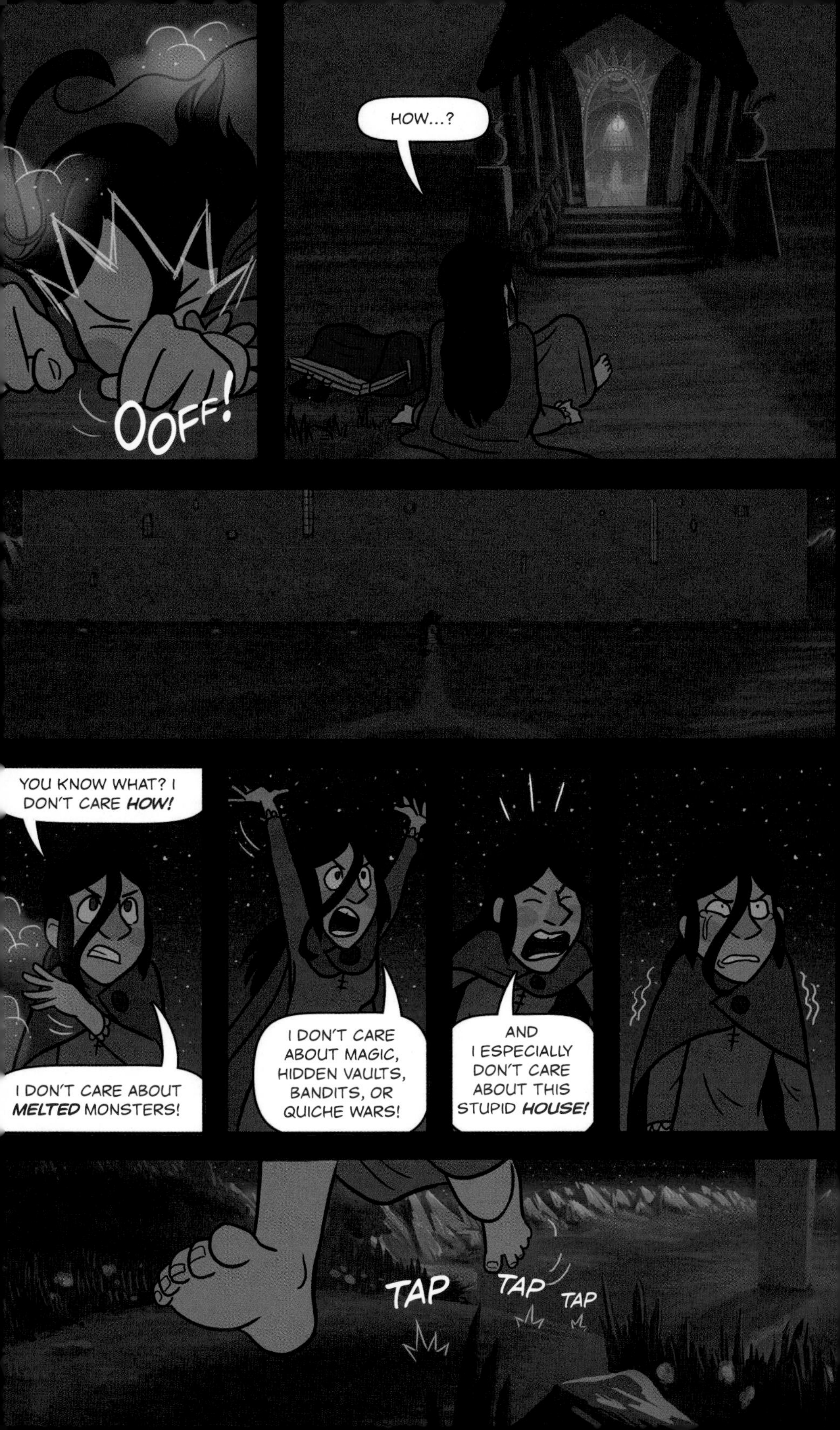
OOFF!
HOW...?
YOU KNOW WHAT? I DON'T CARE *HOW!*
I DON'T CARE ABOUT *MELTED* MONSTERS!
I DON'T CARE ABOUT MAGIC, HIDDEN VAULTS, BANDITS, OR QUICHE WARS!
AND I ESPECIALLY DON'T CARE ABOUT THIS STUPID *HOUSE!*
TAP
TAP
TAP

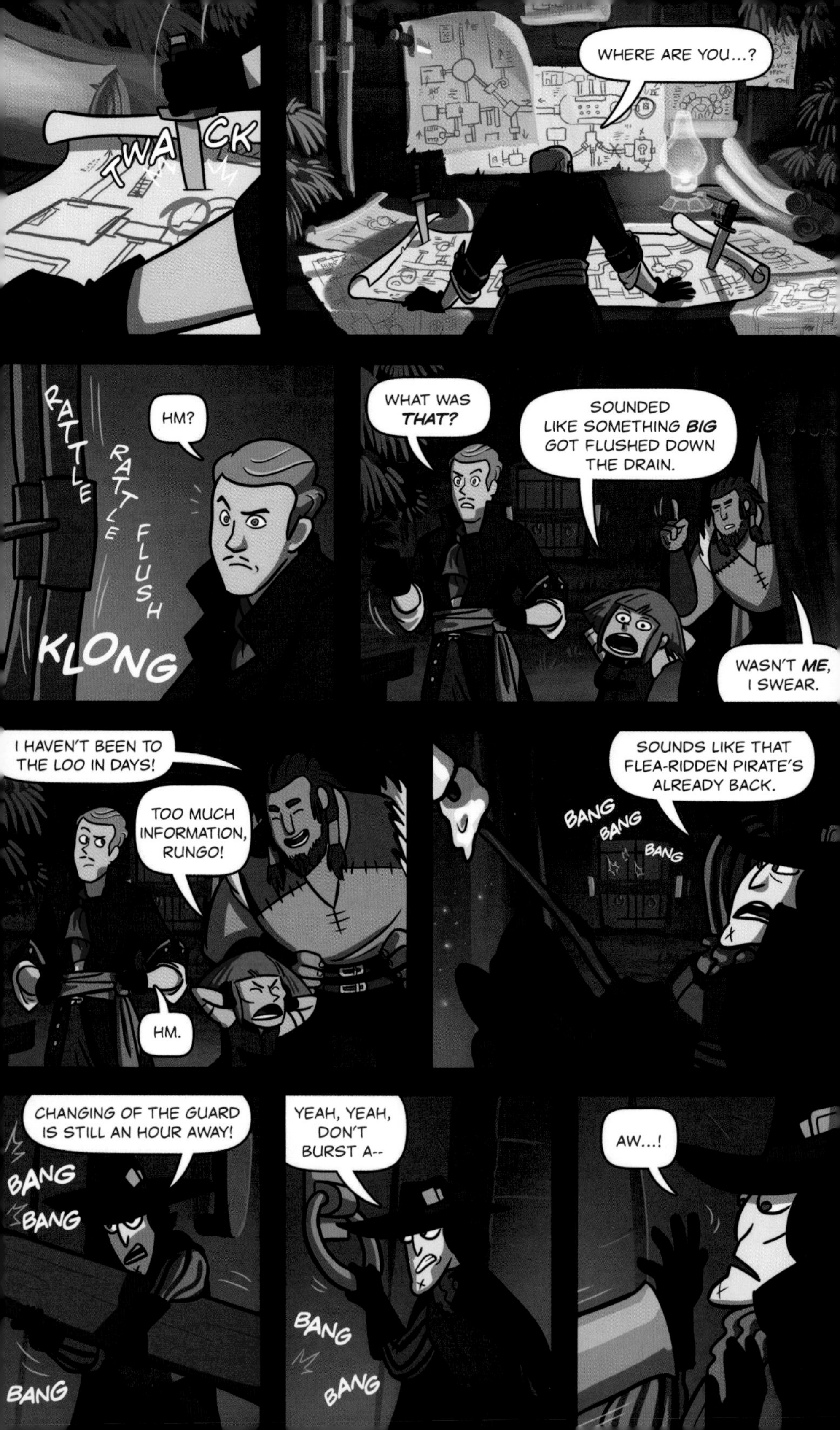
TWACK
WHERE ARE YOU...?
RATTLE
RATTLE
FLUSH
KLONG
HM?
WHAT WAS *THAT?*
SOUNDED LIKE SOMETHING ***BIG*** GOT FLUSHED DOWN THE DRAIN.
WASN'T ***ME***, I SWEAR.
I HAVEN'T BEEN TO THE LOO IN DAYS!
TOO MUCH INFORMATION, RUNGO!
HM.
SOUNDS LIKE THAT FLEA-RIDDEN PIRATE'S ALREADY BACK.
BANG
BANG
BANG
CHANGING OF THE GUARD IS STILL AN HOUR AWAY!
BANG
BANG
BANG
YEAH, YEAH, DON'T BURST A--
BANG
BANG
AW...!

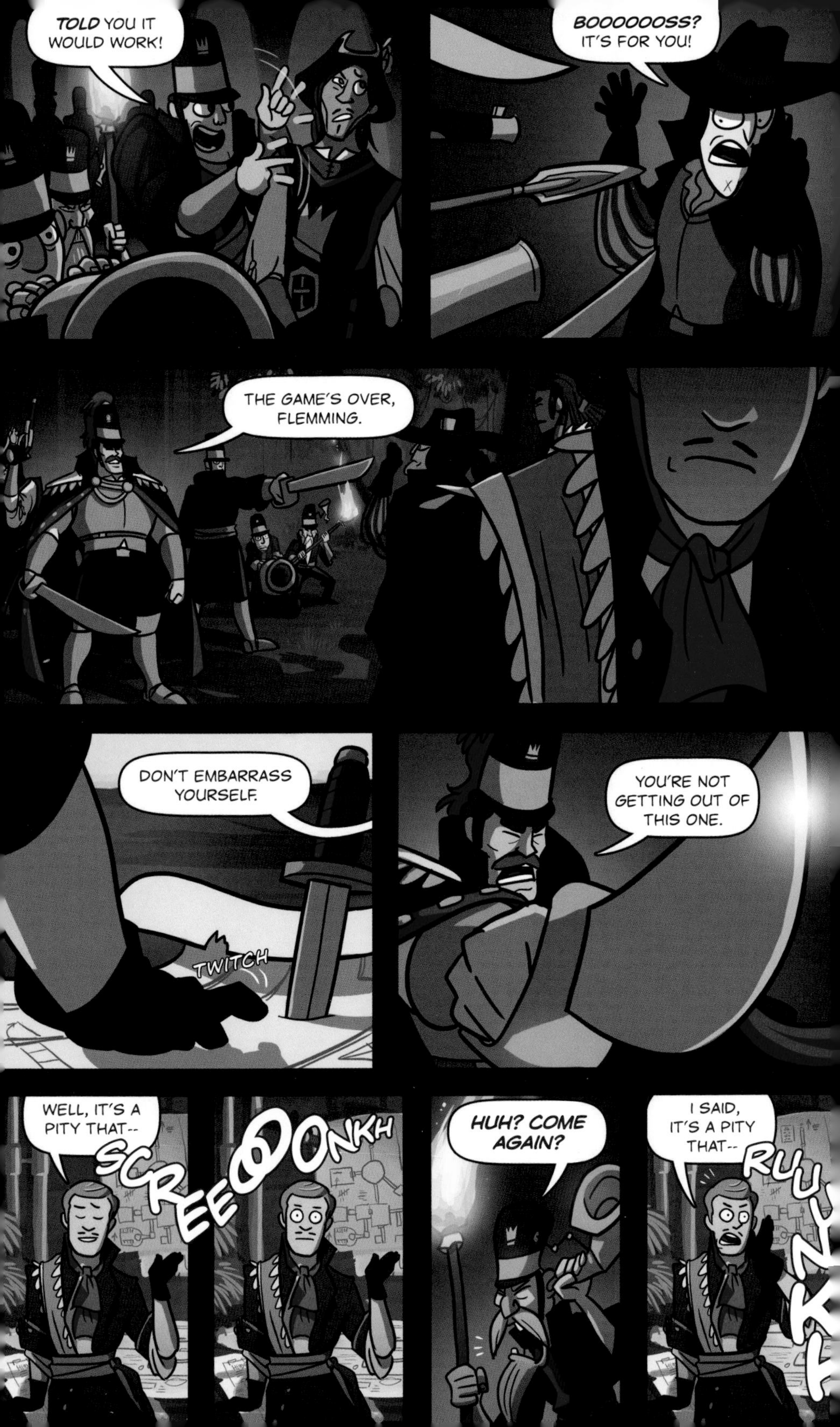
TOLD YOU IT WOULD WORK!
BOOOOOOOSS? IT'S FOR YOU!
THE GAME'S OVER, FLEMMING.
DON'T EMBARRASS YOURSELF.
TWITCH
YOU'RE NOT GETTING OUT OF THIS ONE.
WELL, IT'S A PITY THAT--
SCREEOOONKH
HUH? COME AGAIN?
I SAID, IT'S A PITY THAT--
RUUUNZKT

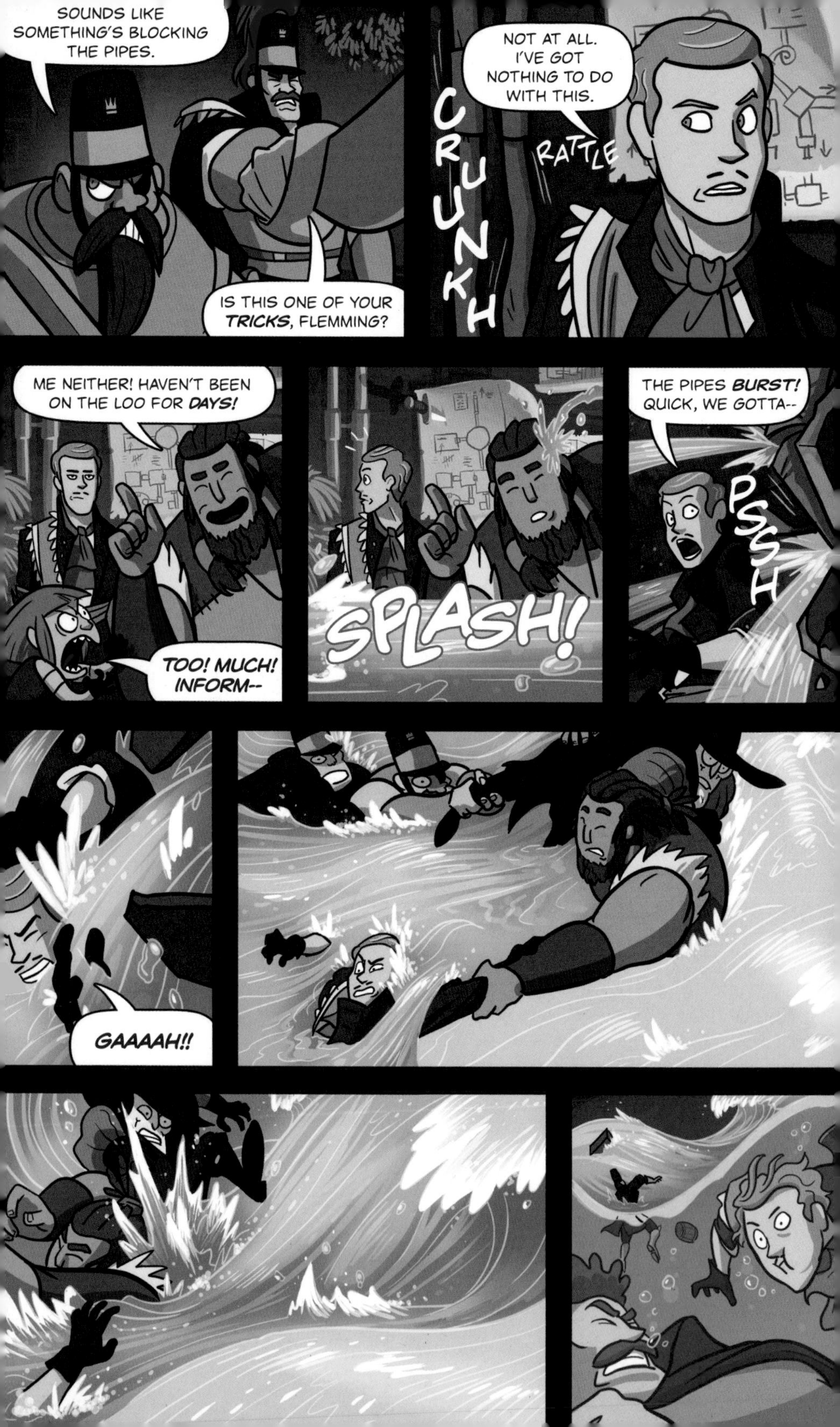
SOUNDS LIKE SOMETHING'S BLOCKING THE PIPES.
IS THIS ONE OF YOUR *TRICKS*, FLEMMING?
CRUNKH
NOT AT ALL. I'VE GOT NOTHING TO DO WITH THIS.
RATTLE
ME NEITHER! HAVEN'T BEEN ON THE LOO FOR *DAYS!*
TOO! MUCH! INFORM--
SPLASH!
THE PIPES *BURST!* QUICK, WE GOTTA--
PSSSH
GAAAAH!!

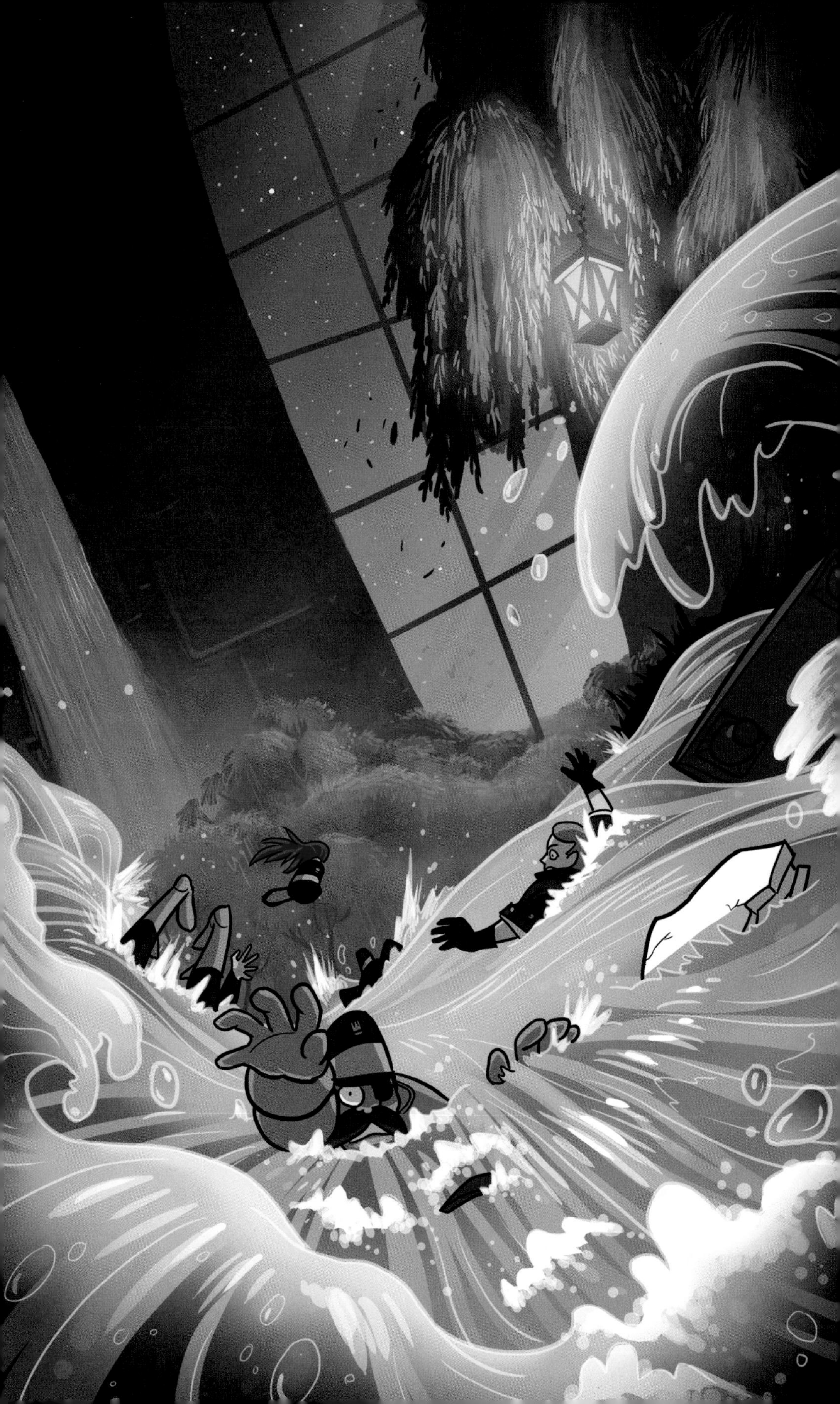

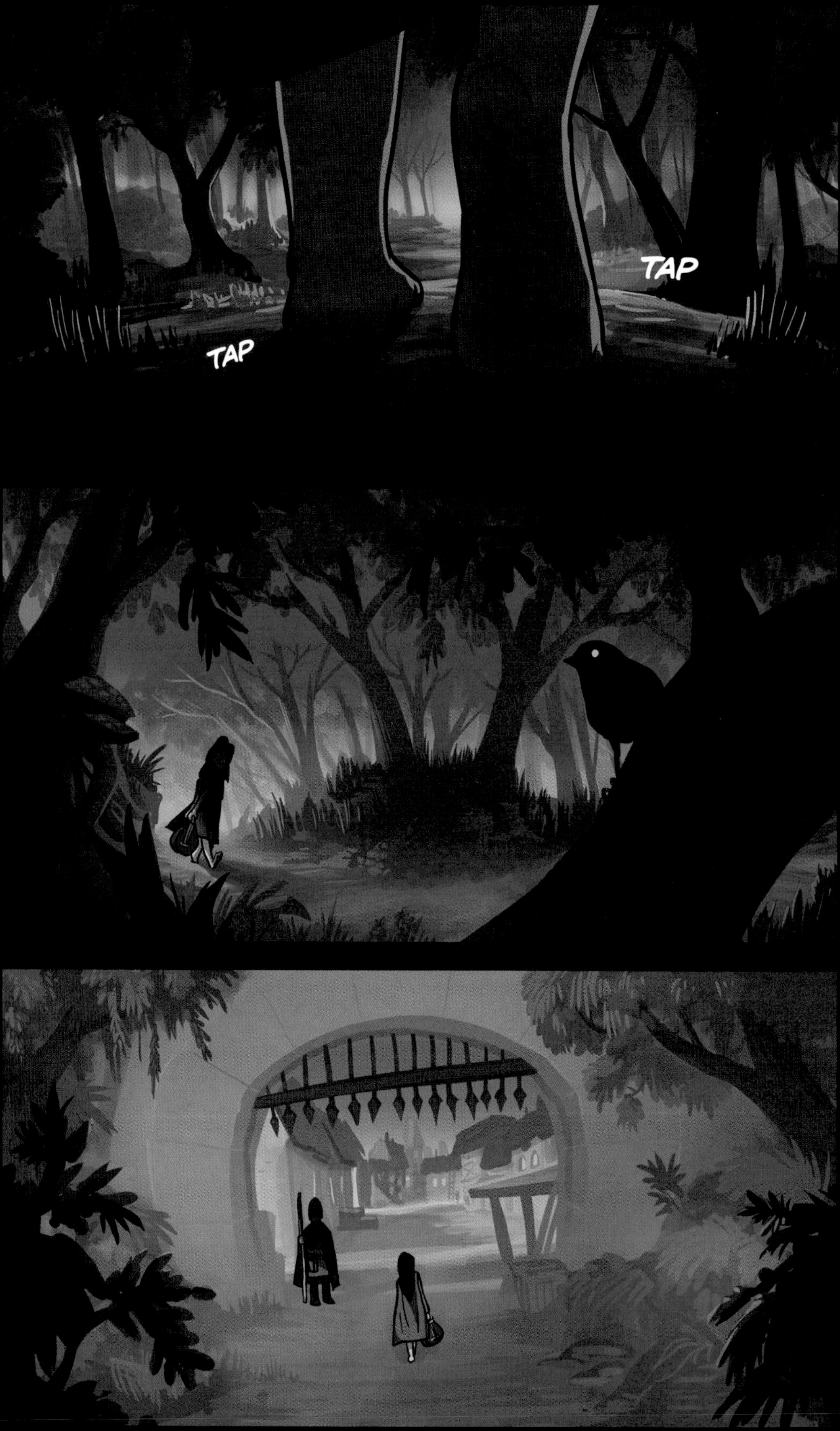
TAP
TAP

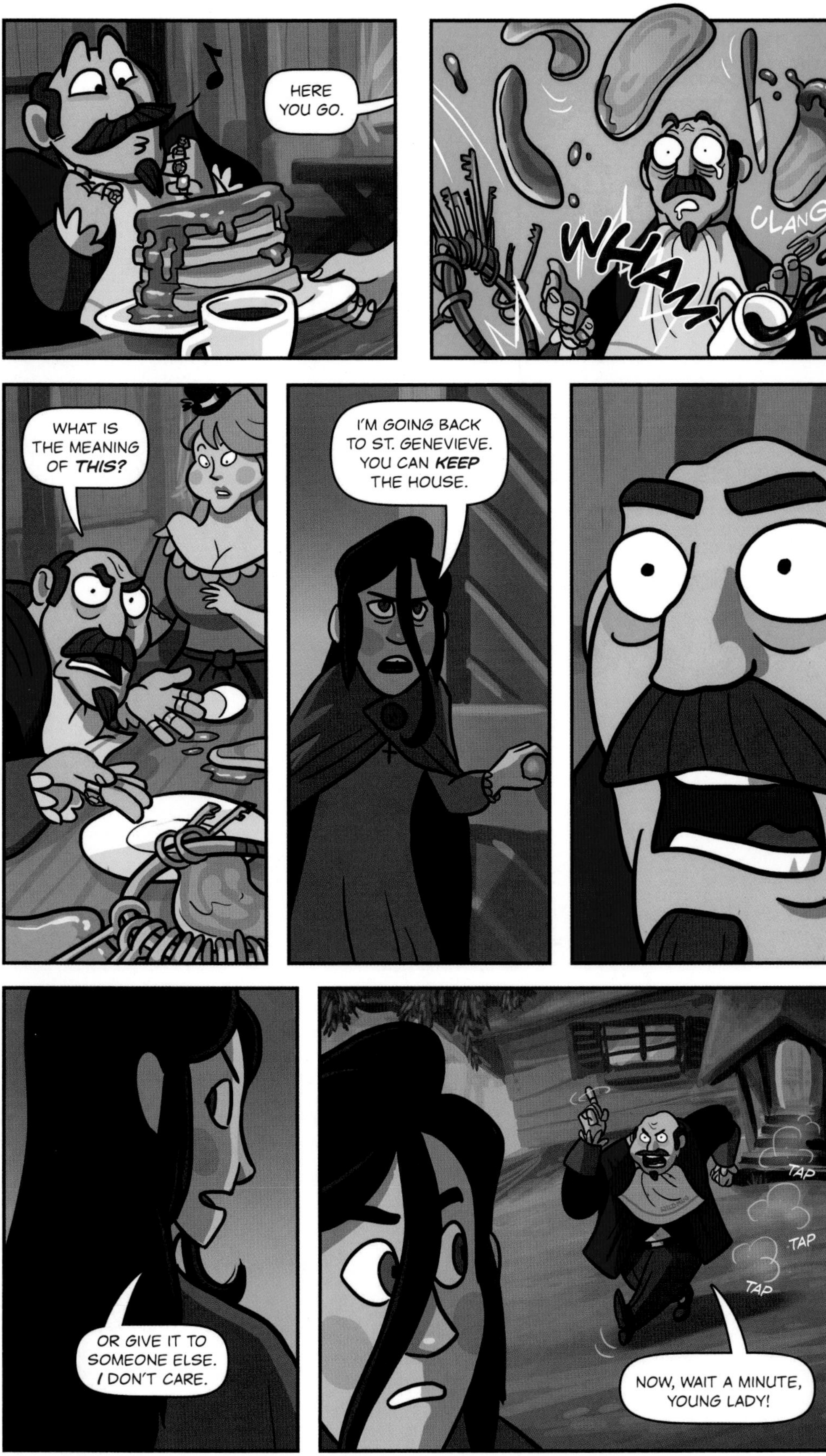
HERE YOU GO.
WHAM
CLANG
WHAT IS THE MEANING OF *THIS?*
I'M GOING BACK TO ST. GENEVIEVE. YOU CAN *KEEP* THE HOUSE.
OR GIVE IT TO SOMEONE ELSE. *I* DON'T CARE.
TAP
TAP
TAP
NOW, WAIT A MINUTE, YOUNG LADY!

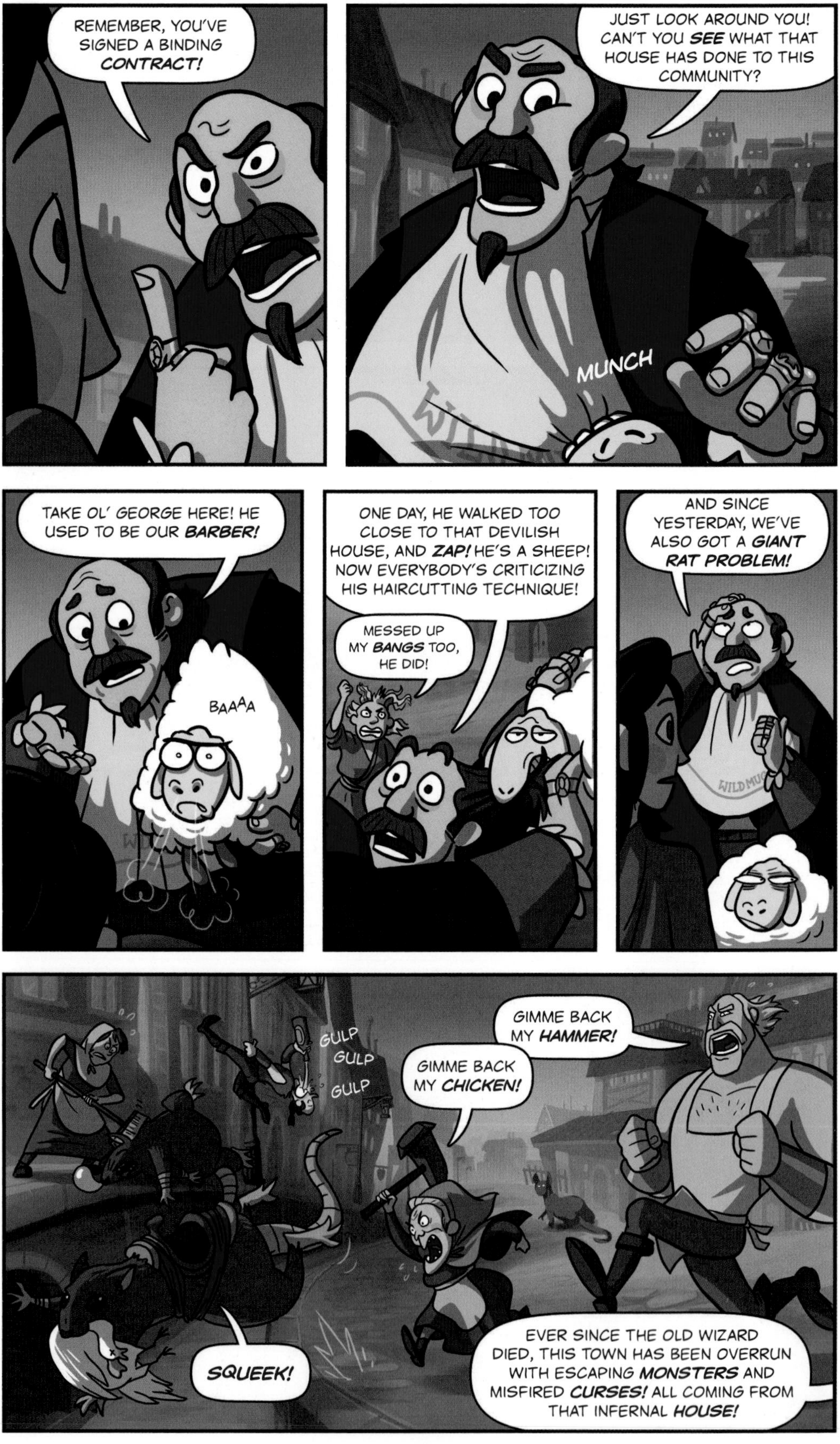
REMEMBER, YOU'VE SIGNED A BINDING *CONTRACT!*
JUST LOOK AROUND YOU! CAN'T YOU *SEE* WHAT THAT HOUSE HAS DONE TO THIS COMMUNITY?
MUNCH
TAKE OL' GEORGE HERE! HE USED TO BE OUR *BARBER!*
BAAAA
ONE DAY, HE WALKED TOO CLOSE TO THAT DEVILISH HOUSE, AND *ZAP!* HE'S A SHEEP! NOW EVERYBODY'S CRITICIZING HIS HAIRCUTTING TECHNIQUE!
MESSED UP MY *BANGS* TOO, HE DID!
AND SINCE YESTERDAY, WE'VE ALSO GOT A *GIANT RAT PROBLEM!*
GULP
GULP
GULP
GIMME BACK MY *HAMMER!*
GIMME BACK MY *CHICKEN!*
SQUEEK!
EVER SINCE THE OLD WIZARD DIED, THIS TOWN HAS BEEN OVERRUN WITH ESCAPING *MONSTERS* AND MISFIRED *CURSES!* ALL COMING FROM THAT INFERNAL *HOUSE!*

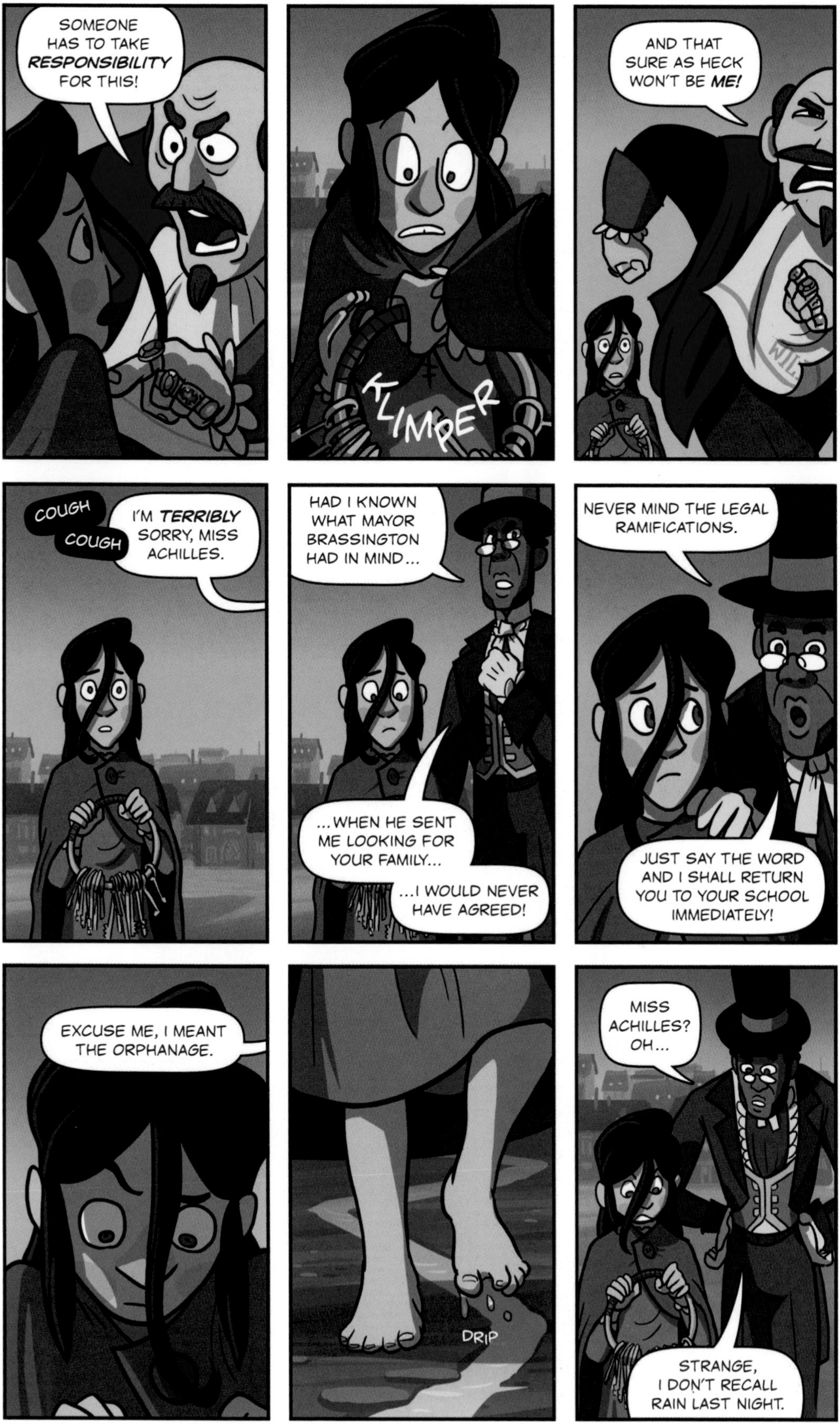
SOMEONE HAS TO TAKE *RESPONSIBILITY* FOR THIS!
KLIMPER
AND THAT SURE AS HECK WON'T BE *ME!*
COUGH
COUGH
I'M *TERRIBLY* SORRY, MISS ACHILLES.
HAD I KNOWN WHAT MAYOR BRASSINGTON HAD IN MIND...
...WHEN HE SENT ME LOOKING FOR YOUR FAMILY...
...I WOULD NEVER HAVE AGREED!
NEVER MIND THE LEGAL RAMIFICATIONS.
JUST SAY THE WORD AND I SHALL RETURN YOU TO YOUR SCHOOL IMMEDIATELY!
EXCUSE ME, I MEANT THE ORPHANAGE.
DRIP
MISS ACHILLES? OH...
STRANGE, I DON'T RECALL RAIN LAST NIGHT.

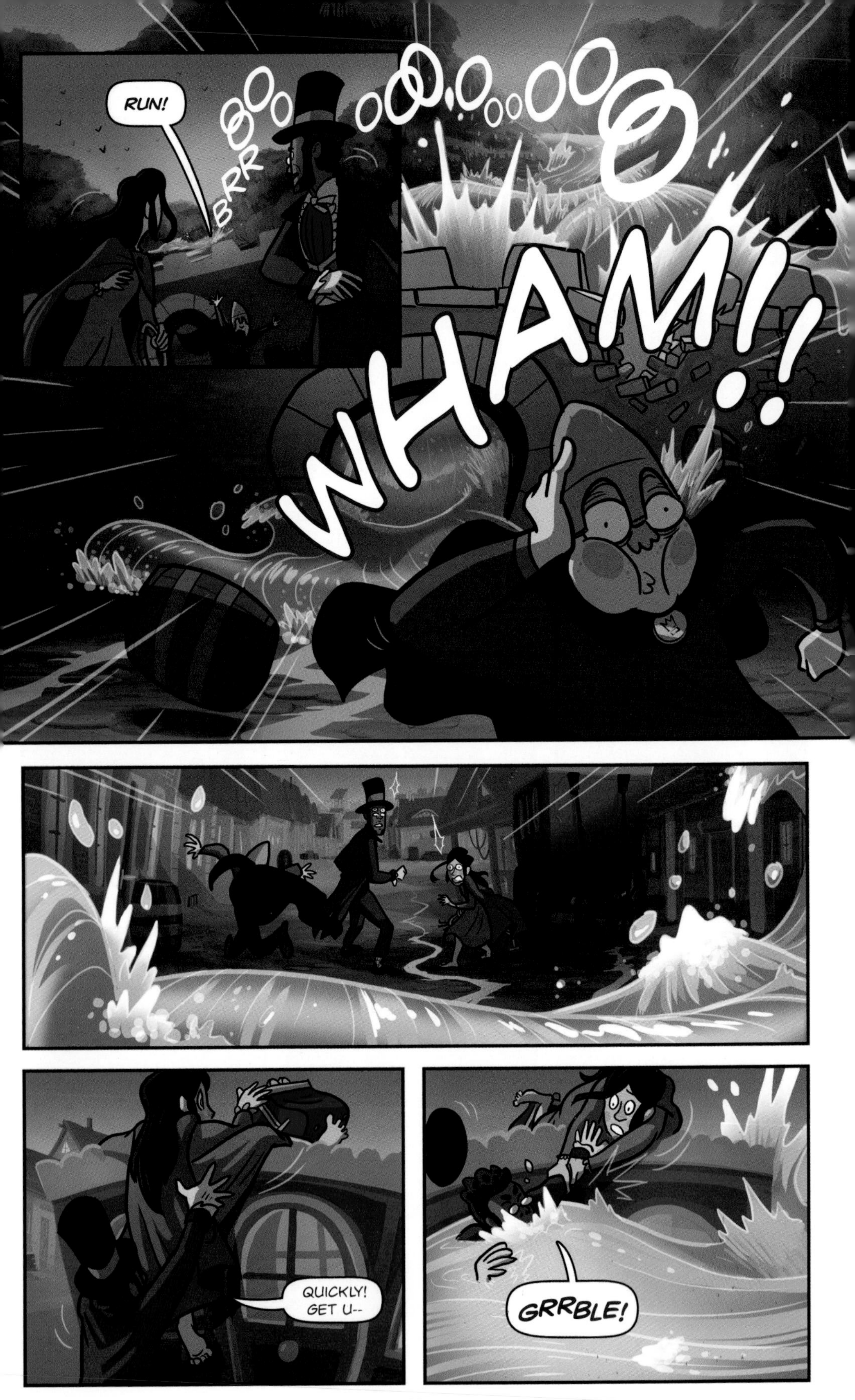
RUN!
BRRBOOOOOOOOOOOO
WHAM!!!
QUICKLY! GET U--
GRRBLE!

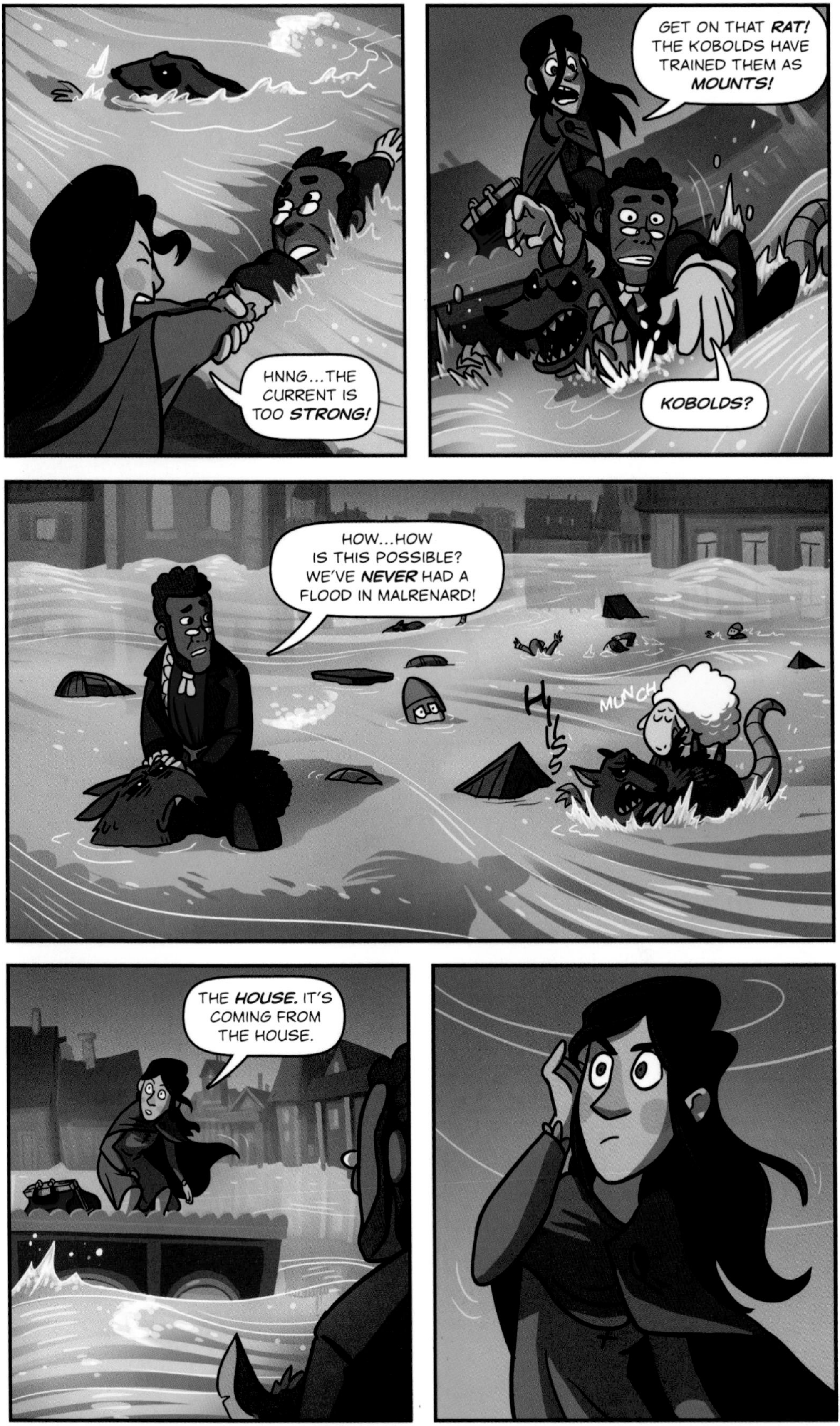
HNNG...THE CURRENT IS TOO STRONG!
GET ON THAT RAT! THE KOBOLDS HAVE TRAINED THEM AS MOUNTS!
KOBOLDS?
HOW...HOW IS THIS POSSIBLE? WE'VE NEVER HAD A FLOOD IN MALRENARD!
HISS
MUNCH
THE HOUSE. IT'S COMING FROM THE HOUSE.

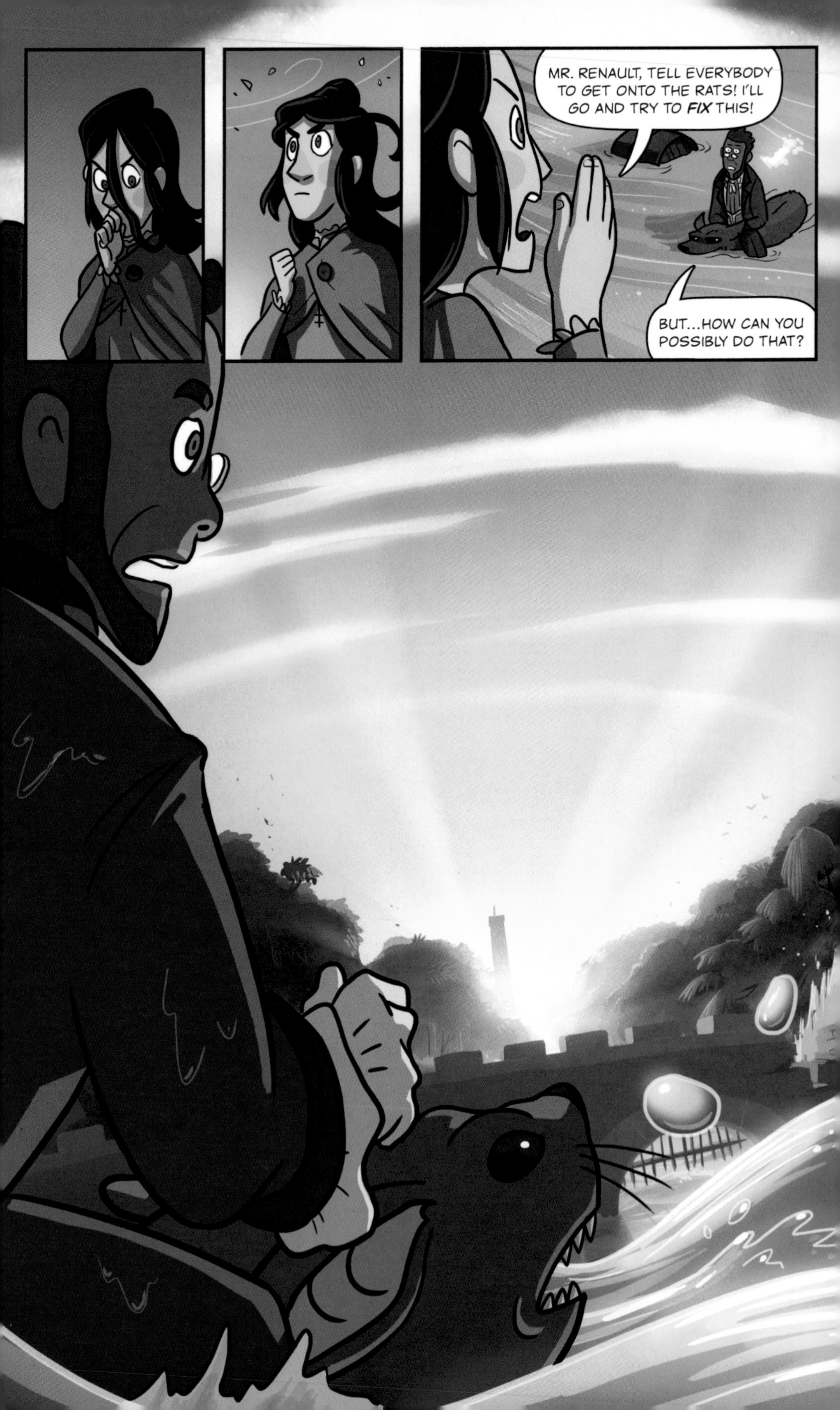
MR. RENAULT, TELL EVERYBODY TO GET ONTO THE RATS! I'LL GO AND TRY TO ***FIX*** THIS!
BUT...HOW CAN YOU POSSIBLY DO THAT?

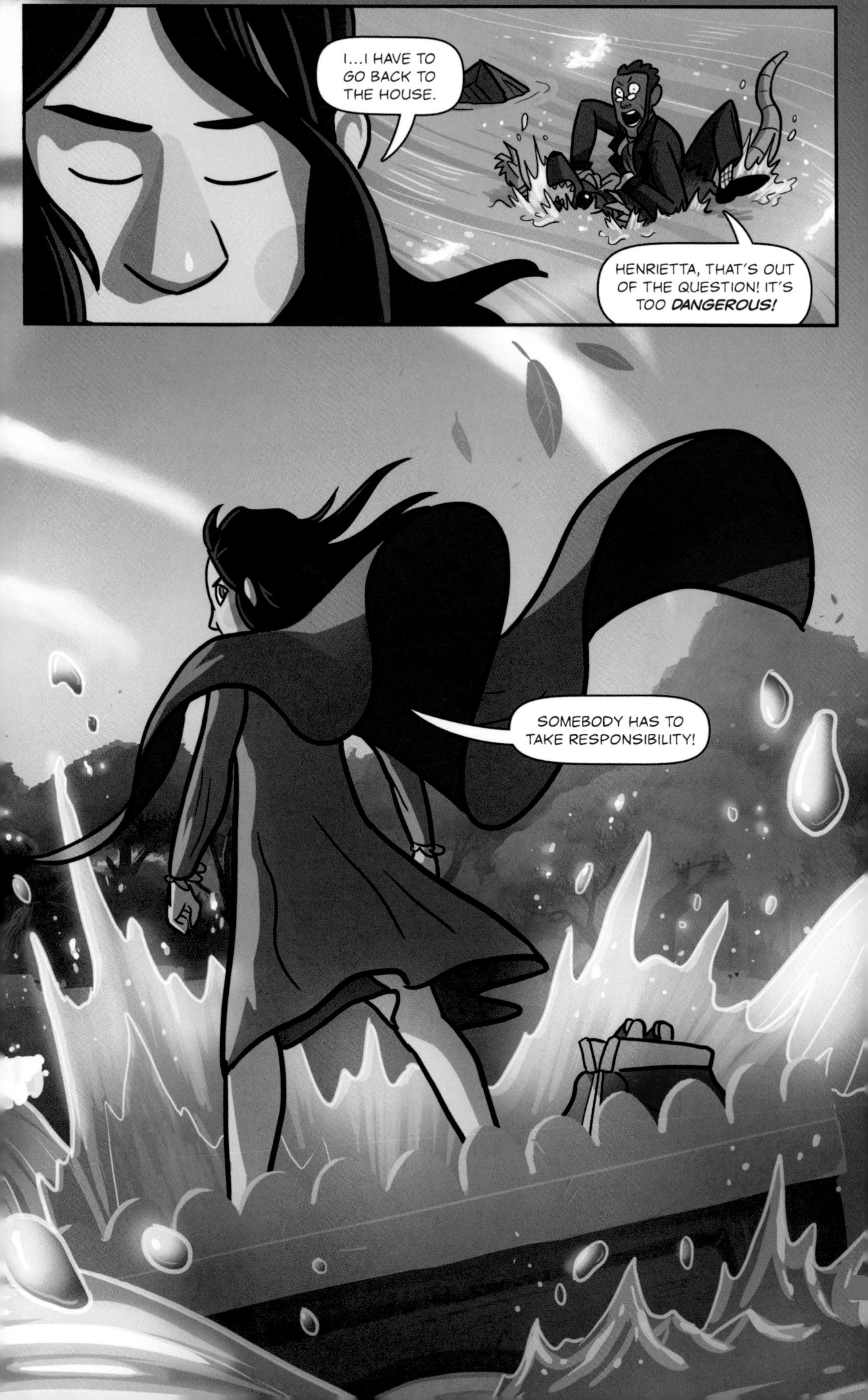

I...I HAVE TO GO BACK TO THE HOUSE.
HENRIETTA, THAT'S OUT OF THE QUESTION! IT'S TOO DANGEROUS!
SOMEBODY HAS TO TAKE RESPONSIBILITY!

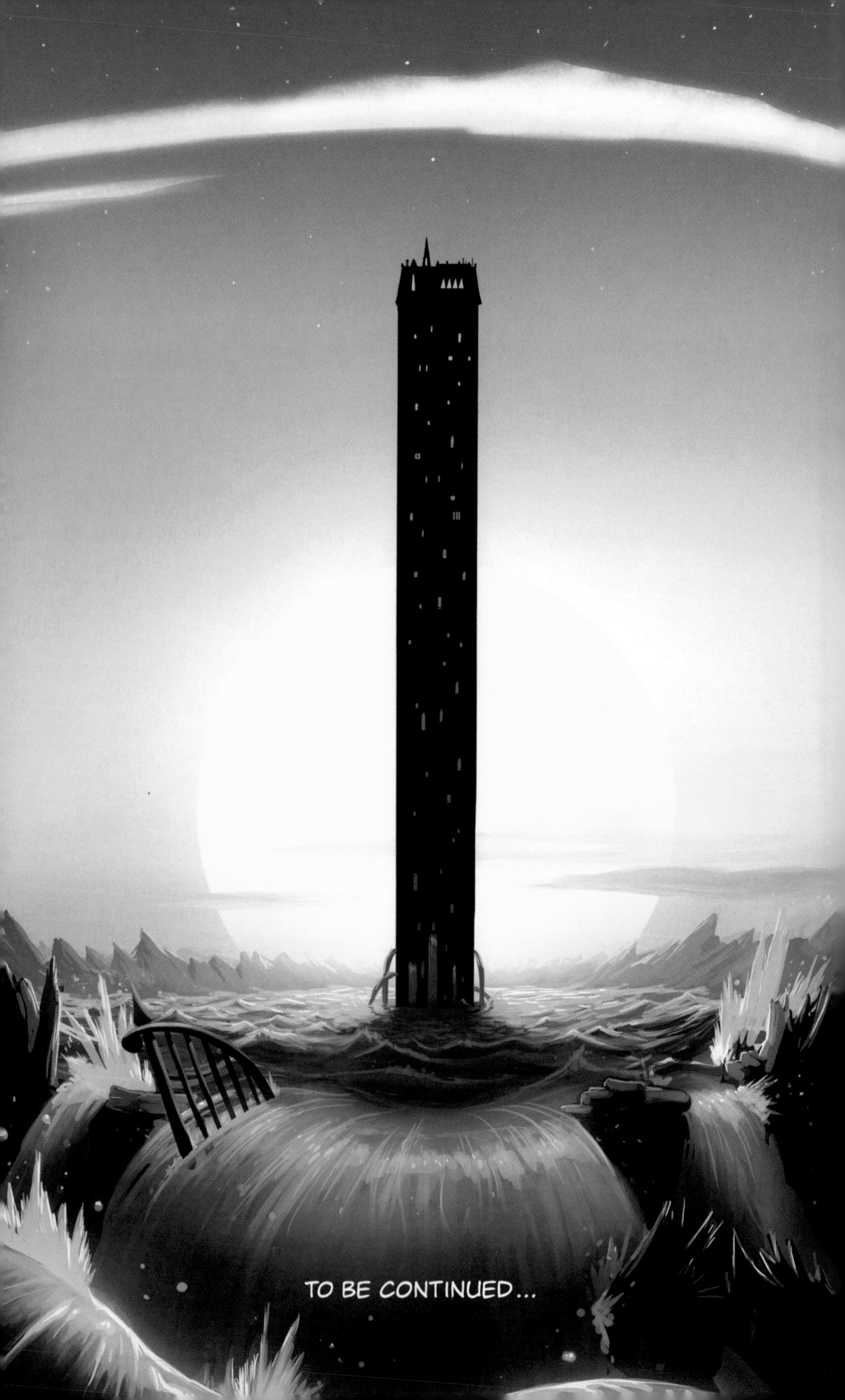
TO BE CONTINUED...

Swain's Quiche

WHAM!

Hands off or I cut them off!!

DOUGH:

- 2 cups plain flour
- ½ teaspoon salt
- 10 tablespoons cold butter
- 3–4 tbsp (50 milliliters) cold water

FILLING:

- 7 oz bacon (4–5 slices thick-cut bacon), cubed
- ½ onion, sliced
- ½ red bell pepper, diced
- 3 tablespoons tomato paste
- 8 ounces (240 ml) heavy whipping cream
- 5 eggs
- 2 cups shredded cheese (half Swiss, half cheddar)
- A pinch of pepper, salt, and nutmeg

ALSO:

- 10-inch (25-centimeter) pie pan
- shortening for the pan
- flour for dusting the counter

Whisk together the flour and salt. Cut the butter into the flour mixture using a fork or pastry blender. Mix in the water with a fork until dough just starts to come together. Knead lightly to form a smooth dough. Pat dough into a circle and refrigerate for 30 minutes.

(You can use this time to make the filling.)

THEN:

Grease baking pan.

Reserve one third of the dough for the lattice crust.

Roll out the remaining dough on a lightly floured surface. Then put dough in the pie pan so it overlaps the edges of the pan by 0.5- to 1-inch (1.3–2.5 cm).

Roll out the reserved dough and cut into ½-inch (1.3 cm) thick ribbons. Set aside.

Preheat the oven to 350°F.

Fry bacon bits until crisp. Sauté onions in a separate pan until soft. Add in diced pepper and sauté together. Mix in tomato paste, then add the bacon. Turn down heat and add half of the cream (½ cup [120 ml]). Stir together, turn off the heat, and let cool.

Whisk eggs in a medium bowl. Mix in remaining ½-cup cream. Stir in salt, pepper, and nutmeg. Add in the onion mixture and fold in the cheese.

Pour the filling evenly into the pan.

Weave the dough ribbons into a lattice pattern on top of the filling. Adhere them to the sides of the crust using a dab of cold water to help the dough stick.

Put quiche in the preheated oven for 45 minutes or until the crust is golden brown and the filling has thickened. To check for doneness, a knife inserted into the middle of the quiche should come out clean.

45 Min

FINAL STEP:

Let it cool down and serve it either warm or cold.

Bon Appetit!

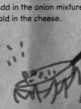

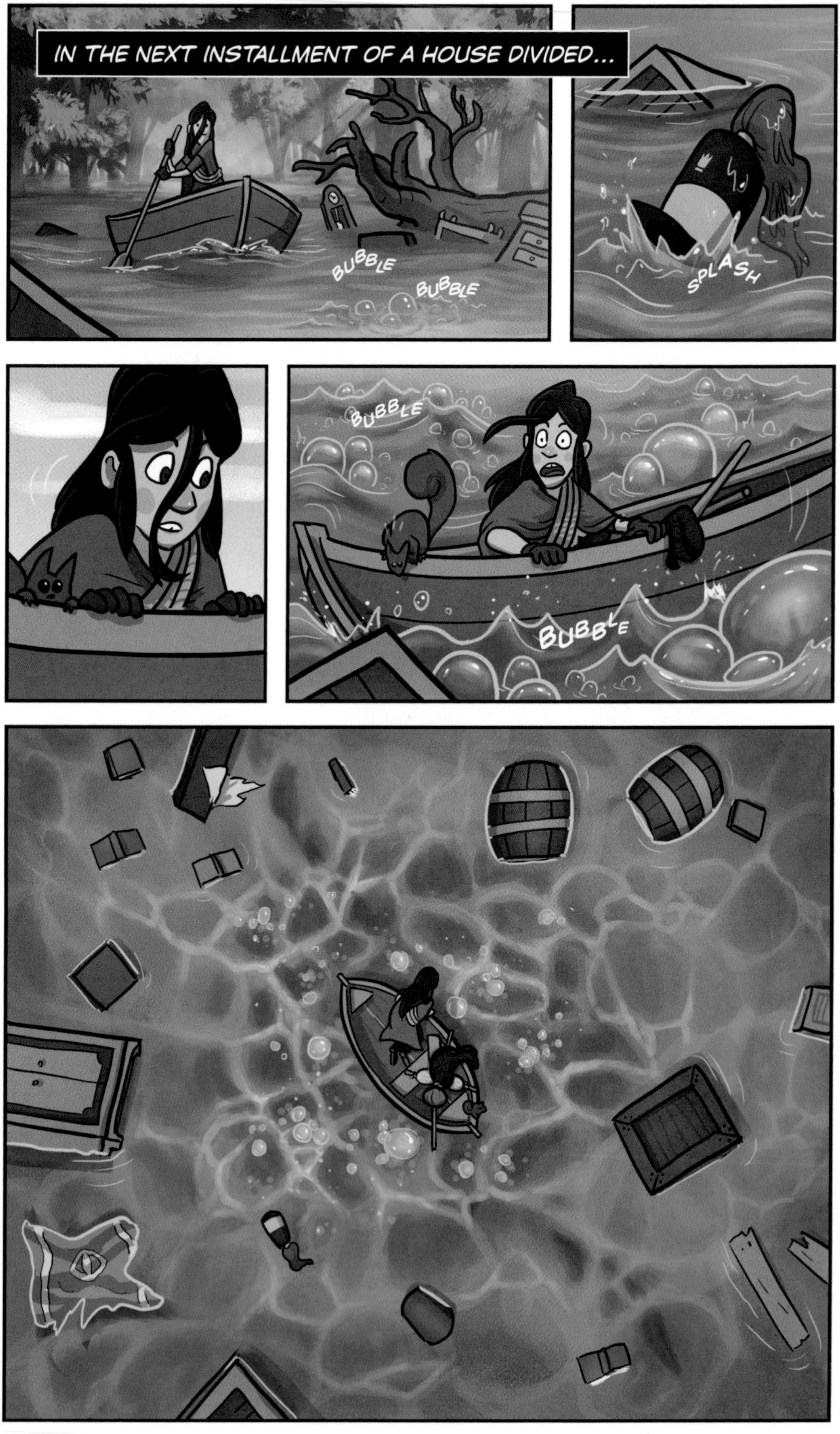
IN THE NEXT INSTALLMENT OF A HOUSE DIVIDED...
BUBBLE
BUBBLE
SPLASH
BUBBLE
BUBBLE

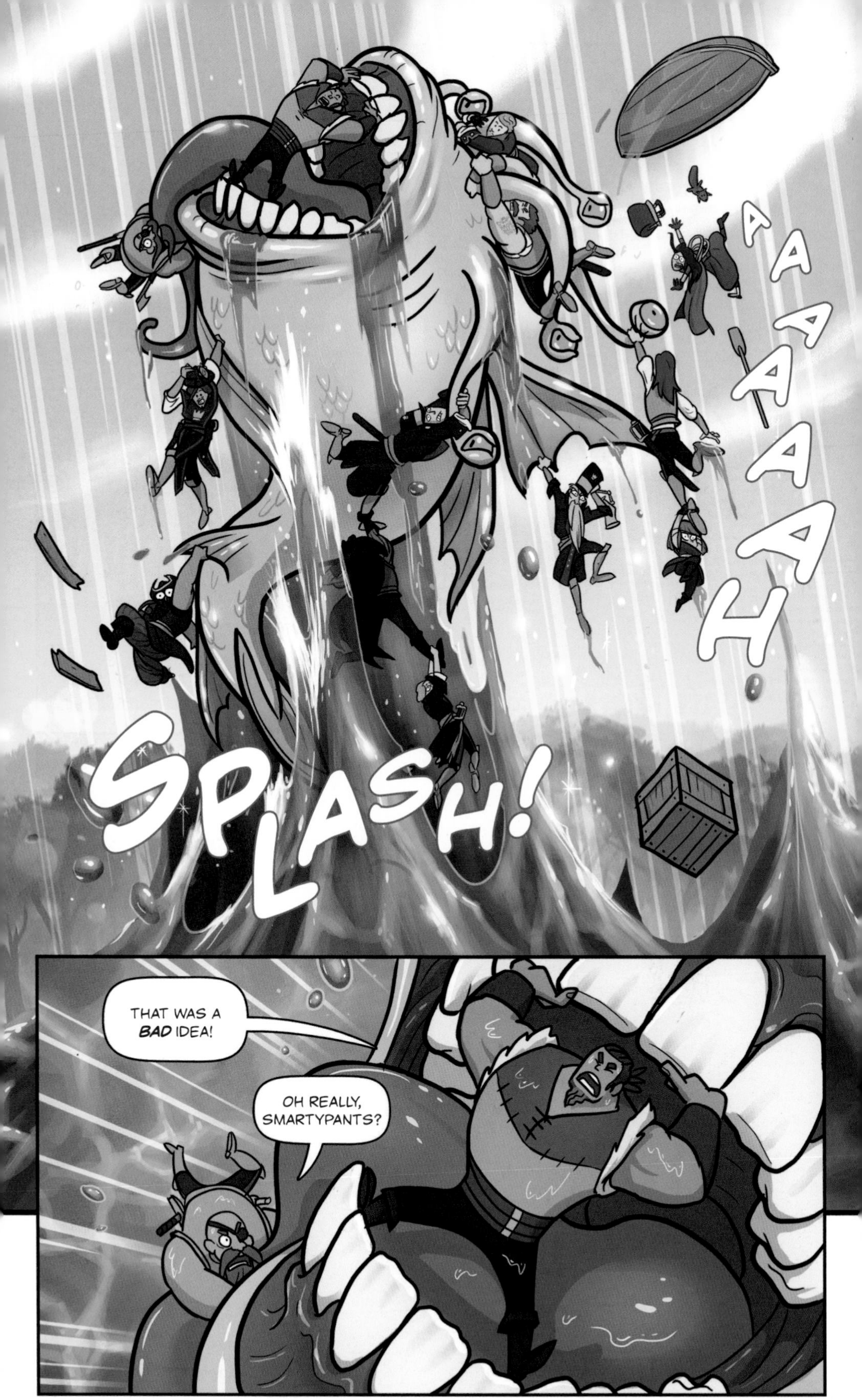
AAAAAAH
SPLASH!
THAT WAS A BAD IDEA!
OH REALLY, SMARTYPANTS?

ABOUT THE AUTHOR

Haiko Hörnig spent his childhood in his parents' comic book store, where he developed a love for sequential art at an early age. In middle school, he quickly became friends with Marius Pawlitza. The two of them first enjoyed role-playing games together and later started to make comics. Since 2013, Haiko has worked as a screenwriter for animated shows and feature films. A House Divided is his first published book series. He is based in Frankfurt, Germany. He's also active on Twitter (@DerGrafX) and Instagram (@ahousedividedcomic).

ABOUT THE ILLUSTRATOR

Marius Pawlitza was born in Poland in 1984 and grew up in Ludwigshafen, Germany. Years later, he studied communication design in the German city of Mainz. It was a good excuse to spend as much time as possible playing video games and making comics with Haiko Hörnig. Since 2011, he has worked as an art director for different agencies and companies in Frankfurt, in addition to creating sequential art. On Twitter, he's @pengboom.